THE ORPHAN ARK

THE ORPHAN ARK

ORDINARY EVERYDAY ISABELLE: BOOK ONE

SCOTT PINKOWSKI

Copyright ©2024 by Scott Pinkowski

This is a work of fiction. Names, characters, businesses, places, events, locales, and incidents are either the products of the author's imagination or used in a fictitious manner. Any resemblance to actual persons, living or dead, or actual events is purely coincidental.

First Printing, 2024
ISBN 979-8-218-36264-5

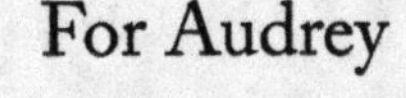

For Audrey

CONTENTS

1 Just Another Morning......................... 1
2 The New Girl 9
3 An Unheeded Warning 16
4 The Creek.. 20
5 Into Darkness................................. 27
6 Not Just Another Morning 34
7 Insult and Injury............................ 39
8 The Mask Slips................................ 47
9 Unexpected Help............................ 54
10 A Special Gift 61
11 The Decision 67
12 The Dream 76
13 Training Day 82
14 Donning the Mask.......................... 90
15 Unusual Suspect............................. 97
16 Total Chaos....................................105
17 Exodus 112
18 The Orphan Ark.............................119
19 Going Viral 124
20 The Hospital Vigilantes.................135
21 The Telltale Phone.........................145
22 Oddgum Raidor 150
23 The Rift..155
24 Rainbow Glitter Pants....................164
25 The Men in Black...........................170
26 The Good Doctor...........................176
27 The Breath Before the Plunge 182
28 The Battle of Beacon Hill...............187
29 The Gumshoe.................................197
30 Ultimatum.....................................206
31 Unexpected Allies 212
32 Into the Lion's Den 221
33 Downfall 230
34 In the Shadow of the Ark...............242
35 The Good Cop 250
36 Restoring Power 256
    Epilogue...264

1
JUST ANOTHER MORNING

Isabelle Cooley scrolled through the eight hundredth line of code. Bathed in the soft glow of the screen, her eyes flicked back and forth. She was looking for perhaps one errant line—one value out of place. Something. Anything that could be causing her robotic personal assistant MechAnna to speak so rudely. Being called a "fatuous ninny" or a "blockheaded lummox" was starting to get old.

Of course, the robot's rude speech was a moot point if it couldn't power up for more than a few seconds without frying its circuit board. That was a more pressing problem, but she'd have to settle for scouring the code for now. It was something she could do in total silence and near darkness without waking her brother.

Orange sunlight had just begun leaking around the edges of the curtains when the shrill cry of her father's alarm clock began echoing in the hall.

Six o'clock. She'd have another half hour of peace before her dad came knocking on the door to rouse them.

The ten-year-old stirred and rose of his own accord. "Good morning, egghead!" he cried, popping out of bed.

"Oh no—"

Mason rushed over and put her in a headlock, ruffling her dishwater blonde hair.

She struggled free. "Get away from me, you towheaded cretin!"

"Dad, Izzy called me a crouton!" He dashed out of the bedroom the two siblings were temporarily sharing.

Through the open doorway, Isabelle could see all the way down the hall as their father leaned out of the bathroom door, holding his toothbrush. He slurred through a mouthful of toothpaste, "Isabelle, don't caw yo brudder uh cwootawn."

She straightened her glasses. No point in correcting them; she probably ran less risk of getting in trouble for calling her brother a small cube of toasted bread.

The chaos that was their temporary living arrangement came into focus in the growing morning light. Mason's clutter was everywhere. His dirty laundry was already strewn all over the carpet and there was a paper plate encrusted with some unidentifiable remnant of food, just visible under his bed. Her lip curled as she slowly shook her head.

"Dad!" Isabelle yelled toward the open door. "When are all the renovations going to be complete?"

After a few moments, her father appeared at the threshold, buttoning his light blue oxford shirt. "What's wrong, Izzy?"

"As if moving our rooms isn't bad enough. Do we *really* have to *share* this room?" She crossed her arms and jerked her head toward the paper plate.

The corner of his mouth twitched. "I'll say something to him," he said. "Try to be patient. I know this is difficult, but you and your brother will both be better off moving out of those tiny basement bedrooms. A few more weeks and Mason can move upstairs to the attic and you can have all *this* space to yourself."

Isabelle's blue eyes widened. "A few more *weeks?*" *Totally unacceptable.*

"Well, this is the way things are going to be," he said with an air of finality. He straightened his collar and headed back down the hallway.

How will I get anything done? She sighed and rose from her seat to start getting ready for school, but her gaze gravitated back toward her workbench and the photograph of her mother taped to the desk lamp. *Has it been two years already?* In the photograph, a red-haired woman clutched younger versions of Mason and Isabelle, her glowing face forever frozen, mid-laugh, at some long-forgotten joke. The image was burned into Isabelle's mind, yet she struggled to remember the sound of her mother's laughter.

She shook her head and redirected her thoughts to work.

Despite being hastily relocated there the day before, her workbench was tidy and neat except for the remains of a disassembled smartphone that lay on the desk in several pieces. Sitting off to the side of her laptop was the intelligent robotic personal assistant, which she'd named MechAnna.

Isabelle was a ninth-grade student at Cavett Academy, a private secondary school for those who excelled in academics and showed promise in various technological fields. Since she had demonstrated the aptitude, the academy allowed her to enroll in their advanced robotics program a year early. She was the only ninth-grader in Mrs. Stacey's program.

Isabelle had been dismantling and rebuilding household electronics since she was practically in diapers. Endlessly tinkering with some project or another, she devoted all her spare time to her robotic inventions.

She glanced down at one of her old creations, the Shnoob-o-matic-3000, a robotic arm situated next to a small rack of shoes in the corner behind her desk.

"Hey, Shnoobs, black flats, please," she said.

The rickety boom arm whirred to life and its rubber-tipped grasper closed around one black flat and one white canvas shoe. With a grating flutter of clicks, it swung around and presented the mismatched shoes. Gritting her teeth, she wrenched them from the Shnoob-o-matic-3000's death grip before tossing them aside and turning her attention back to her current project.

While MechAnna wasn't much to look at yet, it was to be her *magnum opus*. It sported a blocky, articulated head perched atop a tracked chassis along with two manipulator arms that allowed it to interact with its environment. In addition to its tank-like drive tracks, it had two frontward protruding flipper tracks designed to assist the machine when moving over uneven terrain. It could negotiate stairs or even flip itself upright if it tipped over.

Where Isabelle hoped MechAnna would shine, however, was with its natural voice user interface and advanced AI. Isabelle's lofty goal was to develop an autonomous robot that could assist physically disabled people.

Do I really have time to run a test before school? She rummaged in the plastic bin next to her desk that was filled with ordinary household objects and at last settled on a glass jar.

"The old jar test," she muttered to herself. "Keep it simple."

It was the moment of truth. Maybe the last-minute tweaks from the night before had done the trick. She hastily scooted into her seat, took a deep breath, and placed the jar on the desk before MechAnna.

"Hey, Anna," she said, using the command to bring the robot out of sleep and into ready mode. Two rings of light representing MechAnna's eyes shone, a pale blue.

"What now, imbecile?" came the synthesized voice—sweet, soft, but oddly patched together and jagged at the edges.

"That's no way to greet your creator," Isabelle said as she stared at the status reports flashing across the screen. Although she expected this kind of response by now, it was still off-putting. What she really wanted to know was if the circuit board was going to hold up. "Anna, please open this jar for me." She crossed her fingers on both hands.

"Opening the jar, idiot." The robot's head whirred and locked onto the jar. Its arms unfolded from their resting position and stretched toward the jar. Suddenly, MechAnna froze and the blue rings of light blinked out.

"Not again." Isabelle sighed. "I hope you didn't fry another one."

But the faint burning smell told her otherwise. Deflated, she slumped back into her chair and stared at the photo of her mom.

I promise I won't ALWAYS be a failure.

Mason rushed into the room to grab his house key from a hook on the wall, nearly crashing into Isabelle in the process.

"Almost forgot my key, robo-brain!" He paused, his mouth twisting into a sly smile. "Aren't you going to get ready for school?"

"I *am* getting ready," Isabelle said.

"Looks like you're just playing with your robot." Mason ran his fingers through his wavy blond hair. "You know that thing is a waste of time."

"At least I'm trying to do *something* to help people someday!" she snapped, her round face reddening.

"Whatever."

"Didn't Dad tell you to clean up the mess under your bed? We're going to get ants. . ."

But he was already gone. Turning away from her workbench, Isabelle suddenly realized she was still in her pajamas. She'd have to hurry or she'd be late.

* * *

After negotiating the obstacle course of toolboxes and drywall sheeting left behind by the workmen who were remodeling the basement and attic, Isabelle walked into the kitchen dressed in a printed sundress and black leggings. Mason was already sitting at the table, stuffing his face with spoonful after spoonful of something caked in globs of sugar. Hunched over his bowl, he was reading the back of the cereal box.

It made Isabelle's teeth hurt just watching him. She shuddered and instead poured herself a nice, sensible bowl of shredded wheat before asking him to pass the milk.

"Mmff," he mumbled as he slid the jug in her direction.

Their father was stirring a cup of coffee as the morning news blared from the small countertop television. Tall, round-shouldered, and bearded, he was the graphics department manager at The Valley Journal, a local newspaper.

"And now a very odd story," said the television anchor. "A burglary last night in Rose Valley's Tech Basin. Surveillance cameras at Delphi Dynamics, located at the fourteen hundred block of Blackburn Avenue, have captured images of what appear to be *robots* making off with undisclosed technological components . . ."

Isabelle snapped to attention as her dad leaned over to watch the report.

"Rose Valley Police responding to the silent alarm say they witnessed two robots fleeing the scene by taking flight."

Her father's brow furrowed as video footage of the crime scene cut away to a graphic rendering of the robots. The four-legged machines sprouted an array of helicopter-like rotors from their bodies.

"Just like drones," said Isabelle, wide-eyed. The rendering of the robots, bristling with a variety of tools and appendages, gave her the impression of a pair of walking Swiss Army knives.

"Alright. Mason? Izzy? I want you both to come straight home from school, okay?" said their dad, continuing to frown at the television.

"Mmmff urm," Mason said, still stuffing his face with sugary cereal.

Isabelle tore her attention away from the screen. "But Maddy and I were going to go to Jasmine's to do homework."

"Izzy, please."

"But, Dad, I can't get anything done here with Mason constantly bugging me! Do you think I'm going to get kidnapped by robots or what?"

"Izzy, it's not up for discussion." He wagged a finger in her direction, and his tone shifted to one of authority.

"Fine!" She knew better than to press her luck any further.

The siblings helped their dad tidy up the kitchen before heading out the front door on their way to school.

It was a beautiful April day in Rose Valley, Virginia. The air was cool and the sun was just breaking over the treetops as they stepped onto the porch. Birdsong created a harmonious cacophony all around them. A few other kids were walking to school past the neatly trimmed lawns along Mine Street. A young woman jogged by with her dog on a leash. Neighbors nodded or grunted good-mornings to one another as they got into their cars.

"It's not fair," said Isabelle as they descended the front porch steps. "That tech burglary has *nothing* to do with me going over to my friend's house to do homework."

"So, you'll have to do your nerd lessons at home. Big deal." Mason's sharp face twisted into a weasely smile.

"Why do you always have to be so churlish?" she asked, knowing she wouldn't get a real answer.

"Why do *you* always have to use words no one understands?" He turned and headed down the sidewalk toward James Monroe Elementary School. "See you after school, Doo-Doo-Head McFarts-A-Lot." Even for Mason, it was a pretty pathetic attempt at name-calling.

"You're incorrigible!" she yelled after him.

"Thank you," he chirped. He passed two girls on the sidewalk, walking the opposite direction. "Here comes the Charge of the Nerd Brigade!"

The ninth-grade girls paid him no notice. They slowed to a stop at Isabelle's front sidewalk.

"Did you see the news?" Isabelle asked.

"I did," said Jasmine Hubbard, a slender girl with two frizzy buns atop her head. "It's crazy. We have burglar bots right here in Rose Valley." Half a head taller than the other two, Jasmine's black and pink track suit zipped and zopped whenever she moved.

Isabelle frowned and shook her head. "These things are going to give robotics a bad name. I've been working so hard to develop robotics to *help* people, and now all anybody's going to talk about are robot criminals."

The mousy, ponytailed girl accompanying Jasmine shuffled her feet and lifted her gaze, her cheeks a rosy pink from the crisp morning air.

"Negative news sells more than positive," said Maddy McCarthy. A wisp of brown hair fell across her face and she awkwardly swept it aside with the back of her hand.

"Exactly!" Isabelle said.

"It won't always be like this," said Jasmine. "You're going to have your big breakthrough—maybe you'll work out a few bugs—then all the world will recognize the good you're trying to do."

"You've got to hand it to them, though," said Maddy, grinning, "quadcopter blades . . ."

"I know, right?" Isabelle was unable to suppress her own grin. She allowed herself a twinge of admiration for the thief's ingenuity. Although she couldn't condone what the shadowy figure behind the mysterious robots was doing, she had to admit that the robots themselves were pretty cool. "Anyway, my dad's all worried, so he wants me to come straight home after school."

"Aw, so no homework at my house tonight?" Jasmine said.

"Apparently not for me." Isabelle sighed, her thoughts returning to her robotics project. *It would be enough to know I helped just one person. I'm tired of being ordinary everyday Isabelle.*

2
THE NEW GIRL

"WELL, IT SOUNDS LIKE you've really struck a brick wall," said Isabelle's robotics instructor Tamara Stacey. Isabelle had caught her before class to ask about MechAnna's circuit board problem. "I'm sorry, Isabelle, I don't have an answer for you right now. If I think of anything, or I find someone to help you, I'll let you know." Mrs. Stacey's eyes twinkled over the top of her eyeglasses and she smiled at her youngest robotics student. "Go ahead and take your seat. I'm getting ready to start class in a moment."

Isabelle's shoulders slumped as she turned to walk back to her table.

"Isabelle," said Mrs. Stacey in her gentle voice.

She turned around, hopeful that Mrs. Stacey had thought of something already.

"Brick walls are not there to keep us out. They're there to let us prove how badly we want to succeed."

Isabelle fought back the urge to roll her eyes. *No, brick walls are there to smash our failing projects against.* She respected Mrs. Stacey, but she was in no mood for her inspirational adages today.

She hated the idea of having to run to her for help in the first place, but she was simply out of options.

She'd thought advanced robotics at Cavett Academy was going to be fun, but as the school year wore on, she began to dread the two-hour sessions. MechAnna's progress was at a standstill, and that was after running into problem after problem. She'd been working on MechAnna for the whole school year and knew the project would account for a large percentage of her final grade.

She sat down at the table she shared with Jayden Romano, a tenth-grade boy who always seemed to be wearing headphones on his buzzed head. She watched Jayden's fingers as they flitted over the keys of his laptop. His expression was stony as the keys clacked. Somehow noticing that she was looking at him, he paused only long enough to pull off his headphones, letting them rest around his neck.

"What?" He went back to typing without looking up.

Isabelle glanced up to Mrs. Stacey who was still organizing papers on her desk as she prepared for class. Jayden was the closest thing Isabelle had to a friend within her robotics class. As the youngest member of the class, she didn't often talk with anyone. Sharing a table with Jayden, however, had allowed her to slowly become acquainted with him and come out of her shell.

"How goes your project?" she asked as she awkwardly adjusted her hair.

Without looking up, he shrugged. "Done. Well, almost. Just a bit more debugging."

The fact that Jayden was all but done with his project didn't help her feel any better about her own lack of progress. She knew Jayden had been working on a robot that could pick up and sort various objects by size. Another student, Meghan, created a robot that used a ballpoint pen to draw any photographic image you presented to it. Many others were in the final stages of their projects, and some had already finished.

"Where's your bot?" asked Jayden, looking up at Isabelle.

"MechAnna is at home," she said, folding her hands in front of her on the table. She was resolved to not let her distress show. "Everything's under control."

Jayden raised a single inquisitive eyebrow. "That bad, huh?"

Her resolve crumbled. "Okay, I'm stuck. The circuit board keeps self-destructing whenever a motor or servo actuates. I don't suppose you—"

"Your bot is a little too advanced for me," said Jayden as he turned back to his laptop.

Isabelle nursed her shame. "Yeah, she's a little too advanced for me as well," she muttered under her breath.

Jayden's eyes darted back to Isabelle as his fingers continued to clack. "I guess it's too late to start over with a less ambitious project?"

No answer came to her lips, but indignation bubbled beneath the surface. Being left behind while her classmates thrived was one thing, but to admit defeat by scrapping MechAnna and beginning a new, less challenging project would be unbearable. She'd be letting herself down, she'd be letting her dad down, she'd be letting MechAnna down . . . and she'd be letting the memory of her mother down. Somehow, worst of all, she'd be proving Mason right—that her robot really was a waste of time.

When Isabelle signed up last spring, her academic adviser had warned her that Mrs. Stacey's program was advanced, but she wouldn't be dissuaded. Although the class was normally reserved for tenth-graders and above, Cavett Academy wasn't about to hold back one of its youngest and brightest, and Isabelle wasn't about to back down from the challenge.

Now, though . . . she was doubting that decision. *Will I get kicked out of the academy if I fail?*

Every time her thoughts went down this dark path, she invariably gave herself the same pep talk. *No, I am not going to fail robotics. I'm going to stick with it and figure this out. I am going to succeed!*

Even when the raging waters of failure threatened to swallow her and pull her into the abyss, she repeated the words to herself.

"Time to get started," said Mrs. Stacey, standing up. "But first, I'd like to introduce you to a new tenth-grade student we have joining us today."

Isabelle straightened up in her seat.

"This is Crystal Skorch, who's moved here all the way from Fairfax." Mrs. Stacey stretched an open palmed hand toward a girl sitting at a table at the back of the room. "Let's give Crystal a nice Rose Valley welcome." The class mumbled a discordant greeting as the girl at the back table looked up from the notebook she was doodling in. "Crystal, would you like to tell us a little about yourself?"

The girl's narrow face immediately reminded Isabelle of a timber wolf—calm and confident. Her gray eyes were fierce and sunken into her pale face. She was tall and wiry and looked a little older than the typical tenth-grader. But perhaps the most striking feature of Crystal was her short and spiky hair. The top was dyed a bright blue while the sides and back remained their natural color of straw. A digital camo army jacket that looked to be a couple sizes too big for her hung on the back of her chair.

"Well, there's not much to tell," Crystal said in a smooth voice. The corners of her mouth twitched into something close to a smile. "I actually moved here last year; I've just been homeschooled until now. I really like it here in Rose Valley. We didn't have anything like this academy back in Fairfax, so I had to learn all about robotics on my own." Crystal's eyes scanned the room, focusing in turn on each student as she continued talking. When her wolf eyes fell upon Isabelle, an icy jolt spread out from the back of her neck. Why was she feeling so creeped out by this new girl?

"... It's always been my dream to come to Cavett Academy. Now that the dream is a reality, I'm really looking forward to working alongside you all." Crystal paused, seemingly having run out of things to say. "Thanks for welcoming me, Mrs. Stacey." The amicable expression dropped from her face and she slumped back into her seat.

Isabelle stole a glance at the newcomer. "That was kind of generic," she whispered to Jayden. His eyes met hers, but he said nothing.

"Thank you, Crystal," said Mrs. Stacey. "Mr. Lim, would you please go ahead and give Crystal a quick tour of the robotics lab?"

Daniel Chang-yong Lim was Mrs. Stacey's assistant from the college. College students could get volunteer credits for assisting with the STEM programs at the academy, and Daniel was one of a handful of regulars that rotated in and out on different days. He'd been standing by at the side of the room with his hands in the pockets of his khaki pants. He had an unruly head of black hair and metal-rimmed glasses along with an orange checkered shirt. Mrs. Stacey stubbornly referred to him as Mr. Lim, but he always insisted that the students call him Daniel.

He nodded and walked to the back of the classroom, motioning for Crystal to follow along. Through the large glass panels that made up the back wall of the classroom, Isabelle could see Daniel showing Crystal around the lab.

"The Tech Fair due date has been moved up to the First of May," said Mrs. Stacey to the class. There was a sudden outburst of stifled groans and excited whispers. "I know, I know," she continued. "It can't be helped. There's been a scheduling conflict at the Shenandoah Rose Convention Center and they have to set up earlier than expected."

The air left Isabelle's chest as if she'd been struck by a wrecking ball. Although it was only a few days, a few days could make all the difference with MechAnna. Isabelle began her worrying process all over again, hoping the inevitable pep talk she was going to give herself would be one for the ages.

Mrs. Stacey searched the faces of her students as she paced down the aisle between the rows of tables with her hands linked behind her back.

"I expect each and every one of you to be ready to go on time this year." Reaching the end of the aisle, she paused and turned to face the class. "Today is going to be a free work day. Those of you who are still finishing up your projects are going to need to put your time to good use."

Isabelle didn't know if it was her imagination or if Mrs. Stacey's eyes really did linger on her a moment longer than everyone else. A cold bead of sweat formed on her forehead.

Daniel and Crystal returned from the lab and Crystal took her seat. Most of the students immediately entered the lab, but a few remained at their tables working on their laptops. Daniel checked in with each of the students, offering help wherever it was needed.

Since Isabelle knew she couldn't progress any further with MechAnna's development until she solved its circuit board problem, she decided her time would be best spent poring through MechAnna's thousands of lines of code. She pulled her laptop from her backpack and placed it in front of her, relieved to see that Jayden was staying behind. He clacked away with his headphones still hanging around his neck.

As she waited for her laptop to boot up, she could hear Mrs. Stacey talking to Crystal at the back table. Crystal was telling her about a project she'd been doing back in Fairfax. Isabelle thought it sounded like she was talking about using a bot equipped with ultrasound to detect clogs in pipelines or something.

Isabelle stifled a grin as she wondered if there could be a more boring application of robotics. The new student seemed like a perfectly normal girl, although she couldn't explain the visceral reaction she had when Crystal looked at her. She decided all that nonsense about first impressions being all-important was just that: nonsense.

"I guess she seems okay," she said to Jayden in a low voice.

His key clacking suddenly ceased and he glanced at Isabelle out of the corners of his eyes. "I wouldn't be so sure."

Isabelle cocked her head, curiously. "Why?"

"She lives right down the street from me. She's bad news—I'm telling you."

Isabelle was startled; she'd never heard Jayden say a word about *anyone*.

"Don't be so mean," she whispered. "Shouldn't you give her a chance?"

"I don't want to get into details, but I'm warning you. You'd better steer clear."

"Don't be ridiculous."

3

AN UNHEEDED WARNING

ISABELLE LEANED AGAINST A LIGHT POST near the academy's rear lot as she idly kicked a yellow parking block. It was the end of another uneventful school day, and another opportunity to be productive had slipped through her fingers. Except for a little bit of coding during robotics class, no progress was made on MechAnna. She was busy imagining how foolish she'd look at the Tech Fair when Jasmine and Maddy walked up.

"You guys want to walk with me 'til my house?" she mumbled, barely raising her eyes from the concrete.

"Of course." Jasmine playfully dragged Isabelle along by her arm. "Come on."

Isabelle knew they had to walk past her house to get to Jasmine's anyway, but her low spirits had her convinced she was a third wheel. They cut across the soccer field and walked along the border of school property, where a creek was hidden from view behind the thick wall of trees. The flowing water had carved a deep gully over the years.

The girls walked along the tree line and talked about their plans for the evening. As Maddy chattered on about the big pre-engineering final exam that was coming up, Isabelle had been keeping an eye on a lone figure in the distance sauntering toward them. The afternoon sunlight glinted on the tell-tale blue and yellow hair of Crystal Skorch.

What's she doing out here?

Crystal was holding some sort of electronic device about the size of a small television remote control. She slowly swiped it in an arc toward the trees, then held it up to her face. When she noticed them watching her, she hastily tucked the device into her back pocket and approached. The oversized digital camo jacket hung off her shoulders making her look even more rawboned than she had in the classroom.

"That's a new student from my robotics class," said Isabelle to her friends as Crystal drew nearer. "I guess I'll introduce myself." Before she could greet the newcomer, she was cut off.

Crystal scowled and spoke in a cold, mocking tone. "Well, hello, nerds! What are you doing over here? You need to clear this area." She stole a furtive glance behind her before stabbing her finger toward the school.

Jasmine's lip curled and she put her hands on her hips. Maddy tried to ignore the confrontation and was about to walk around, but Crystal took a sidestep to her left and blocked her from passing. Maddy quickly stepped backward and averted her gaze.

"You heard me, losers," Crystal said. "This part of the field belongs to me when school is over and you nerds need to be gone."

Jasmine's amber eyes flashed with anger. "This is *school* property."

Isabelle chuckled nervously. "Come on, Jasmine, there's no need to press the issue." Annoyance at being hassled and a desire to avoid confrontation collided just under the surface of Isabelle's calm exterior, leaving her jittery.

Maybe Jayden was right.

Crystal scanned up and down the tree line. "Why are you still here?" Her tone was now dangerous. "I told you to clear out." Her steel-gray eyes were locked on Jasmine.

Jasmine planted her feet and folded her arms across her chest.

"This is the path we take every day to get home. You can't tell us what to do!"

Isabelle had been friends with Jasmine since kindergarten and had learned that she could sometimes have more bravery than common sense. She worried this was shaping up to be another one of those times. She ignored the nervous twinge in her stomach and placed a hand on Jasmine's shoulder.

"Don't mind us," she said. "We're just passing through and then we'll be out of your—um—hair."

Crystal's blue hackles were already raised before, but now her eyes went hard and her brows dropped into a menacing scowl.

"Sounds like you nerdlets are looking for a good butt kicking." Then she shoved Maddy's shoulder, causing her to stumble backward.

All hopes of avoiding confrontation were cast aside as a white-hot rage flared in Isabelle's chest and coursed through her shaking limbs.

"Don't you try to—"

But Crystal pounced with a speed and dexterity that belied her gauntness. Before she could react, Crystal had snatched Isabelle's backpack off her shoulder and held it just out of her reach.

Isabelle's cheeks burned scarlet as her good sense finally caught up to her impetuous emotions.

"What were you saying, nerd?" sneered Crystal.

Isabelle grabbed for the backpack, but Crystal evaded every lunge like a smirking bullfighter. "What's your problem?" she said, voice quivering with anger. "Why don't you leave us alone?"

"It's simple," said Crystal as she glanced up and down the tree line once again. "I don't want you here! You need to be gone."

Isabelle made another attempt at her bag, but Crystal shoved her down with an outstretched arm. Isabelle hit the ground hard, her palms and backside stinging. As adrenaline dumped into her system, her mind stuttered between fight and flight and her heart pattered into overdrive. She was still in shock. She was no stranger to bullies, but usually when she confronted them, they'd back down.

"Whoa! Not cool!" Jasmine rushed forward, but she, too, was easily shoved to the ground.

Maddy bent down to help her friends. "Give it back!"

Crystal shrugged as if she suddenly lost all interest in the confrontation.

"I don't have time for this," she said. "Go *get* it!"

She hurled the backpack into the brush and down the creek's embankment. A snapping of twigs and a leafy thud told Isabelle that somehow her bag had avoided the water.

Crystal, meanwhile, stepped past them and stalked away along the tree line without so much as another word or a backward glance, pulling the electronic device out of her pocket as she strode away.

4

THE CREEK

"**W**HAT AN INSUFFERABLE JERK!**"** Jasmine brushed herself off, glaring in the direction Crystal had gone.

Isabelle stared blankly at the wall of trees in front of her and shook her head. "Jayden warned me to steer clear of her but he wouldn't say why . . ."

"He was embarrassed," said a watery-eyed Maddy as she readjusted her ponytail. "I'd wager he had a confrontation with her and it didn't turn out well for him. No boy is going to want to admit to being beaten by a girl." Maddy crossed her arms and sighed heavily.

"Are you going to be okay?" asked Isabelle.

Maddy lowered her gaze. "I'm fine. What about your backpack?" Jasmine and Isabelle turned back toward the thick tangle of branches that ran along the creek. "Maybe we should tell somebody," Maddy said.

"About Crystal? What good would that do?" Isabelle's eyes narrowed. The school liked to make a big deal about zero tolerance for bullying, but they seemed to tolerate a lot more than zero. For as long as Isabelle had been in school she'd had to deal with bullies. Adults had always stressed how important it was to report bullying so something could be done about it. In the real world, however, Isabelle found that doing so seldom had satisfying results.

She drew a long breath. A knot was forming in the pit of her stomach as she imagined having to explain to her dad why he needed to buy her a new laptop. "Well, I guess I'm going down. I'm obviously not going home without my backpack. Are you going to wait for me here?"

"Silly," said Jasmine, "we're going in with you."

Maddy's eyes widened. "We are?"

"Of course we are."

The sides of the embankment were steep, but Isabelle was able to wedge her feet against trunks and roots while she steadied herself by grabbing branches overhead. Branch by branch and root by root, she carefully climbed down toward the creek bed with her friends following close behind.

The vice around her chest loosened when she caught a glimpse of her backpack hung up on some vines near the bottom.

"I found it!" she called to her friends, although she couldn't see them through the thick brush.

Jasmine's voice came from the tangle of foliage to her left. "I think we're close to the bottom. Keep going down. It looks clear down there!"

Isabelle glanced up at the looming embankment, sorry she'd underestimated its treacherousness. "You're right. We'll meet at the bottom and regroup." Slinging her backpack over her shoulders, she tugged on a vine to test its strength before making a final swing toward the creek bed. Eventually, her friends emerged from the brush at the bottom of the embankment into a surprisingly open area.

The creek was low for April—a slow trickle of ankle-deep water at its deepest, and a dry bed of smooth rocks in other parts. The still air smelled of wet sand mixed with the earthy, mulchy aroma of the exposed roots. Isabelle unzipped her backpack and inspected her laptop. It seemed to be in one piece. She let out a long sigh of relief.

"Wow!" Jasmine looked downstream and then upstream. "Who knew it was so pretty down here?"

Isabelle had the impression of being inside a tunnel. The overgrown trees on either side of the creek had woven together overhead, forming an arched canopy, and what little sunlight that could penetrate dappled her surroundings and gave everything a weird greenish tint.

Nearby, Maddy was battling a vine that snagged her arm during the descent. She seemed to be losing.

"We're not going to be able to get back up *that* way," said Jasmine.

Finally tossing the vine aside, Maddy scanned for an exit, twitching like a timid rabbit. "Are you saying we're *trapped* down here?"

"Well, we have two choices, as I see it." Isabelle scratched her chin. "We can try to search around for an easier place to climb out, or we can just head downstream."

"What good will that do?" huffed Maddy.

Isabelle pointed. "If we follow the creek, it will take us toward Mine Street."

Jasmine craned her neck to look downstream. "Oh yeah, there's a tunnel under the road."

Isabelle smiled. "That's right. If we enter that tunnel, I bet we'll come out on the other side—in Hilltop Park." The creek bent to the south where it then ran parallel with Mine Street, and there was a big culvert where Mine Street and Mechanic Street intersected. She'd seen it in the winter when the trees were bare.

Jasmine's mouth pulled into a thin smile as she watched her friend squirm. "Look on the bright side, Maddy. We get to explore."

"Oh, goody," Maddy said in a deadpan voice. "If we're going to do it, we'd better get going. Isabelle's supposed to be going straight home."

They walked in single file, trying not to get their shoes wet. The dry areas of the creek bed were mostly flat, but from time to time they had to hop on stepping stones to navigate the deeper parts. Isabelle realized she was actually enjoying this sidetrack adventure from their normal walk home.

Maddy, on the other hand, seemed to be keeping a constant watch for an easier way to climb out, but the steep angle of the banks never lessened.

The creek soon curved to the left (as Isabelle expected), and after a short distance, they reached the end of the line. The girls stood at the gaping maw of a five-foot-tall corrugated metal culvert. It was flanked by two sloping concrete wing walls which directed water flow when the creek was higher. Above the culvert was a concrete barrier topped with chain link fence. Motor traffic zipped by on the street above the culvert.

"Just through there." Jasmine pointed into the darkness. "I'm pretty sure we can make it all the way through. We should have no problem climbing out. The creek's not much more than a ditch over there."

Maddy looked around once more to make absolutely sure there was no alternative. Seeming to resign herself to her fate, she reached into her backpack and pulled out her smartphone. Smiling, she activated her flashlight app and turned to her friends.

"I don't know what you girls would do without me." But her jaw dropped when she saw the yellow and black industrial sized flashlight that Jasmine had just produced from her backpack. Maddy scoffed. "Who carries a flashlight like *that* everywhere they go? Seriously."

"What can I say?" Jasmine grinned as she clunked the switch and it burned with the intensity of a hundred suns. "I like to go on adventures."

Shaking her head, Maddy returned her phone to her backpack and peered into the tunnel.

With flashlight in hand, Jasmine led them into the culvert. The pipe ran for a good fifty feet before connecting to a rectangular concrete drain tunnel. Stepping inside, the girls now had to stoop down to move through. The inside surface of the concrete tunnel was smooth and level on all four sides. Every so often they passed a drain inlet that also let in some light. They almost didn't need the flashlight after all. Occasionally, the muffled moan of a car passing overhead echoed eerily through the passageway.

Isabelle relished the tingle on the back of her neck. The damp tunnel was somehow a welcome change from the safe glow of her computer monitor.

As they cleared a bend in the tunnel, Isabelle could see broken concrete and debris piled on the ground just ahead.

"What's this?" There was a large, jagged opening in the concrete wall to their right. Just inside the opening was a white plastic bucket, a toolbox, boards, and a hard hat.

"It looks like someone's in the middle of repairing this." Maddy lowered her voice to a whisper. "We'll get in trouble if they catch us in here." Her eyes darted back and forth.

Jasmine brought the beam of her flashlight into the opening, revealing rough, rocky walls. "This doesn't look right. We're only a few feet underground, and here's a cave. It *must* have been here when they built the street and this drain tunnel. Why would they build on top of a cave?"

Isabelle peered inside. "Maybe it's not a cave. Maybe they're just adding on to the tunnel."

"Adding on to a drain tunnel?" Jasmine shook her head. "I don't think so, but I *do* know there's no way they'd build here if they *knew* there was a cave. Is the ground stable here?"

"There *were* coal mines under this town, you know," said Maddy. "You live on *Mine Street*, remember?" She leaned over to peek into the opening, all the while clutching onto the sidewall for dear life. "The mines are all abandoned now, of course."

"Could this be a mine?" Isabelle said.

"Only one way to find out." Jasmine stepped inside the jagged opening.

"Whoa, whoa, whoa! If you think I'm going to let you go in there, you're nuts!" Maddy grabbed Jasmine by the sleeve of her tracksuit.

"Where's your sense of adventure, girl?"

"Adventure? Are you kidding? It's bad enough we're traipsing through a giant storm drain, but now you want us to go, sight unseen, into a—into a cave? Or a mine? A mine-cave?" Maddy pulled Jasmine back into the concrete tunnel by her sleeve. "Don't you know how dangerous mines can be? Especially mines that have been abandoned for eighty years?"

As Jasmine and Maddy bickered, Isabelle's curiosity began to grow. She decided there was no harm in taking a peek.

"Let me see that light."

"Sure," said Jasmine, handing the flashlight to Isabelle and turning her attention back to Maddy. "It *won't* cave in!"

"How can you know that?"

"Look, the walls are rock solid . . ."

Isabelle took one step into the opening, shining the light all around to inspect the surface of the walls, floor, and ceiling. It looked solid enough. Maybe Jasmine was right. She took another step in, and another, unnoticed by her friends. The passageway slanted downwards and there was a remarkable temperature drop. It became cooler and cooler with each step.

Another few steps, and Isabelle heard the hollow sound her feet made on the floor. She was standing on ancient planks of gray, dusty wood. She directed the flashlight beam upward. Massive timbers reinforced the ceiling.

"It *is* a mine!" she whispered to herself. There was a gap between the scaffolding she was standing on and the wall to her right. She inched sideways and aimed the beam of the flashlight straight down into the gap, but there was nothing but blackness for as far as the beam could reach.

I must be standing over a mine shaft!

The instant Isabelle decided that standing there was not a good idea, the century-old wood let out a moaning, echoing creak. A rush of panic spilled over her like a bucket of icy water. She froze in place and held her breath. A cold sweat beaded on her forehead and the hairs bristled on the back of her neck.

How could I let myself do something so reckless?

Carefully, heart pounding in her chest, she took a step backwards. Again, the wood moaned and shuddered under her weight. She slowly looked down and saw she was still standing on wood, and through the gaps between the planks was darkness. The echoes of her friends' arguments wafted in from the other end of the passage.

One more step. She shifted her weight to make the final backward step onto the safety of solid rock.

A thunderous crack echoed through the cavern, and Isabelle tumbled into darkness.

5

INTO DARKNESS

THERE WAS A BRIEF MOMENT of sickening weightlessness, then splinters of wood were raining down around her. It had all happened so fast; she didn't even have time to register the terror. She was already sprawled on a pile of sand before her mind could grasp what had happened. The hammering in her chest raged, unabated, as she struggled to catch her next breath.

"Isabelle!"

"What happened!?"

"I told you so!"

"Isabelle!"

Jasmine's and Maddy's voices were echoing into the darkness after her. At last, she found her voice.

"I'm okay!" she called back up, spitting out sand. She groped around, feeling for her glasses. She could just make out the shapes of her friends peering down at her through the opening she created in the scaffolding.

"Oh, thank goodness!" cried Maddy. "I'll run and get help!"

Alarmed, Isabelle called up. "Hold on, Maddy. Let's assess the situation." She was not eager to explain to adults how she ended up in an abandoned underground mine.

Looking around, she considered just how lucky she was that the sand pile was there, and even luckier that she managed to miss the bottomless pit of the mine shaft just a few feet away. She put her glasses back on, brushed herself off, and walked over to get the flashlight she dropped during the fall. Crazy shadows streaked across the cavern wall as she picked it up.

Panning the light around, she noted she was in a cavern about fifty feet across with steep walls of unhewn granite. One end of the cavern had a large opening that led to the mine shaft (which she narrowly missed).

With a wave of relief, she noticed a wooden ladder leaning against the wall near the broken scaffolding. It might be tricky to navigate the messy, broken scaffolding, but she was certain she had found her way out.

"We're coming down to get you!" came Jasmine's voice from above.

"What? No! Do *not* do that!" called back Isabelle. "There's a mine shaft!"

Too late. One after another, the girls landed on the sand pile. Looking up again, Isabelle realized she hadn't fallen that far, perhaps ten feet onto the shelf of rock. "Why didn't you listen to me?" She hoped nothing would go wrong with the ladder now that all three of them were in the same predicament.

On one hand, Isabelle was glad her friends stuck their necks out to rescue her, but on the other, she thought they could have planned her rescue a little better. She pointed.

"Be careful, there's a mine shaft over there and it goes straight down. I don't know how far."

Her friends stood up and brushed themselves off, backing away from the edge. Jasmine picked up a stone and tossed it into the shaft. The girls listened. It seemed like an eternity before they heard the distant, echoing *sploosh* as the rock hit water in the sump at the bottom of the shaft.

Maddy turned away from the pit. "Well, we'd better focus on getting out of here."

"We have a ladder," said Isabelle. "And it's a good thing too, since you guys dove in so recklessly."

"We could have climbed back out." Jasmine pointed to the remains of the wooden scaffolding.

Isabelle crossed her arms. "Maybe, but if not, we'd all be stuck down here forever."

"Not forever. Well, at least until those workmen come back." Jasmine smirked.

"What if they close off the wall while we're still down here?" asked Maddy as she fidgeted.

"Nobody's getting walled up," said Jasmine, rolling her eyes in the darkness. "And I didn't hear *you* offer a better plan!"

"I offered to run and get help, remember? I don't know why I followed you down here. I guess it was temporary insanity in the heat of the moment!" shot back Maddy.

Isabelle groaned. Every second they argued was another they weren't climbing back out. "Enough, guys."

Jasmine turned on the spot, looking all around her. "Let's have a look around before we head back out. When will we ever have an opportunity to see something like this again?"

Isabelle sheepishly remembered that it was her own curiosity that got her here in the first place. Still, Jasmine had a point.

Maddy wrung her hands. "We'll get in so much trouble if they catch us down here."

Isabelle aimed the light all around, illuminating a stack of sandbags near the broken scaffolding.

"What are they working on down here that they need sand for?" asked Jasmine as she stepped gingerly across the cavern floor. They crept around the perimeter of the cavern, with Isabelle aiming the flashlight as they went.

"Beats me." Isabelle stopped when she came to a roughly triangular opening in the wall she hadn't noticed before. A faint light seemed to be coming from the passage beyond. "I bet this is a way out." Isabelle hunched over and aimed the light inside. Jasmine and Maddy peeked over her shoulder. "I don't know what the city planners were thinking when they built that storm drain. Did they not have maps showing where all the mine shafts were? They built right on top of it."

"I don't think this part was built by the miners," said Maddy. "I mean, up there where you fell obviously was, but not down here." Maddy had a point. Down here there were no more planks or timbers, or any sign that human hands had used the cavern except as a base to build the scaffolding.

"Well, let's see where this comes out, shall we?" Isabelle turned to enter the triangular opening, but she stopped short when she realized it was a dead end.

"What about the light?" asked Maddy, whose view was blocked by Isabelle.

Ahead, there was nothing but stone where the passage abruptly stopped. Isabelle was confused; there *was* a light. *Where was it coming from?* Then she saw it.

"Here," she said, squatting down.

Sitting on a pile of sand on the floor was a blue, spherical object about the size of a bowling ball. Its perfect, smooth surface was emitting an eerie blue light. Isabelle became aware of a faint ringing, not unlike the sound of a tuning fork. An odd, pulsating sensation vibrated her hair and skin as she looked on in wonder. Grains of sand around the base of the object jumped and danced in weird concentric ripples. Isabelle instantly knew she was looking at something extremely out of the ordinary.

"What is it?" asked Jasmine, her face bathed in dull, blue light.

Isabelle was speechless.

Jasmine extended a finger to touch the sphere.

"Don't!" cried Maddy. "We have no idea what that is."

Jasmine froze and glanced at Maddy before pulling back her hand.

Isabelle considered all the data. She ran possibilities of what this object could be through her head, but nothing seemed to fit. *It's clearly not a natural mineral. It looks manufactured, but what material glows like this? It doesn't look mechanical, but what about this sound? It's not extra-terrestrial, is it? Is it?*

"I have no idea either," she said at last. She put her hand out to see if she could feel any heat coming off of it. Maddy gasped, but Isabelle shot her a reassuring look. "No heat, so it's not—"

Zap!

The passageway filled with a flash of blinding, electric-blue light as miniature branches of lightning arced from the sphere to Isabelle's outstretched hand. All three girls shrieked, as two more times in quick succession, the sphere flashed.

Zap! Zap!

It was as if a photographer was in the cavern snapping photos with a blue atomic flashbulb.

"I'm blind!" cried Maddy as she recoiled away from the sphere. Jasmine was rubbing her eyes and blinking.

Panic stabbed at Isabelle's chest. Her hand was numb and tingling. Whatever she'd expected, this was not it. *Why did I get so close to it? Why did I let myself fall down into this cavern? Why did I climb down into the creek?* She closed her eyes and the shape of the sphere swam before her in the darkness. Stunned, she blinked a few more times, and her vision began to return, although the searing blue spot remained.

"That's it!" cried Maddy. "I am *so* out of here!"

"What *is* that thing?" yelled Jasmine, rubbing her eyes hard with the heels of her hands.

"We need to get out of here!" Maddy's voice was shrill and breathless.

"I think you're right, Maddy." For once, Jasmine seemed to have had her fill of adventure. "Let's go."

As they left the passageway, Isabelle glanced back and noticed that the soft blue glow had extinguished. The sphere lay quiet, a dull, bluish silver.

The girls hurried back through the circular cavern and positioned the ladder against the remains of the scaffolding. With a little effort they climbed out of the pit and back into the concrete tunnel.

Sweet relief washed over Isabelle. With any luck, her dad hadn't called home yet from work to check on her and Mason. If he had . . . she'd need to make up a good story that had nothing to do with subterranean exploration or mysterious flashing spheres.

With hardly a word between them, they hurried down the rest of the length of the tunnel, following the daylight to another corrugated culvert at the opposite end from where they first entered. They stepped into the blazing daylight, squinting, and climbed out of the shallow creek bed and onto a sloped mowed section of lawn in the aptly named Hilltop Park. They were at the lower edge of the beautiful park near two red brick columns which marked the entrance. The walkway in front of them wound upward toward Beacon Hill, which lay at the center of the park and overlooked the neighborhood of Old Town. Perched atop the hill stood the statue of Rose Valley's most famous citizen, Percival Cavett, the 18th century inventor and philanthropist, holding his lantern high to illuminate the way.

Isabelle savored another surge of relief that she was again in the sunshine and open air. She looked back at the culvert. The memory of the glowing sphere haunted her. She had the overwhelming feeling she had witnessed something she wasn't supposed to. *What in the world was it? Why was it glowing? Why did it flash? Why did it STOP?*

"I've got to run," said Isabelle, fully aware she was likely to get in trouble for not coming straight home. "Let's not mention this to anyone, okay?" She handed the flashlight back to Jasmine.

"I don't think anyone would believe us anyway," Jasmine mumbled as the girls trudged up the slope toward the sidewalk.

"But—" started Maddy.

"Promise."

Maddy's face was pale as chalk. "That thing is *not* normal—"

"Promise me, Maddy!" Isabelle said. "I have to get home. We can discuss this later."

"Fine."

Isabelle started down the sidewalk as Jasmine and Maddy stood, talking in hushed voices. She passed a silver pickup truck parked alongside the road with its hood raised. A gout of white steam sizzled from the radiator. A man in a bright yellow reflective vest was standing in the truck bed, rummaging in the toolbox. He paused and looked directly at Isabelle, then back towards her friends. Isabelle thought his slicked back hair and waxed mustache looked old-fashioned and strangely out of place for a city workman, but what unsettled her even more was the black patch that covered his right eye.

She wondered if he saw them come out of the culvert and if they had left behind any sign of their trespass. Her stomach lurched when she remembered the broken scaffolding.

She put her head down and ran.

As she hustled down the sidewalk along Mine Street, she wondered when the blue ghost of the sphere that was burned into her retinas would fade. When she arrived home, Mason was sitting on the front porch steps playing a game on his tablet.

"Where have *you* been, dingleberry?"

"None of your business." She picked a long cobweb off her sleeve as she stomped up the steps past her brother.

"Dad called. I told him you were in the bathroom."

Isabelle wrestled with a twinge of gratitude. She said nothing, but he must have guessed what she was thinking.

"Think nothing of it, booger breath."

6
NOT JUST ANOTHER MORNING

The shrill cry of the alarm clock shattered the morning silence.

Isabelle awoke, too groggy to fully open her eyes. She reached for the snooze button but it was not there. She wondered if she'd knocked it off her bedside table in her sleep. She groped at air. No table.

"What the . . ."

She opened her eyes and found the ceiling was six inches from her face.

"Ahhhh!"

To her horror, Isabelle was levitating five feet above her bed.

Panic and confusion clashed as she flailed. Footsteps hurried down the hallway—her dad must have heard the scream.

Instinctively, she grabbed the edge of the sheet draped over her and pulled; the other end was tucked between her box spring and mattress. She descended, but felt a gentle, constant pulling sensation as her body began to rise again. The feeling made her think of a cork being held underwater. She grasped the sides of her mattress to keep from rising off the bed again just as her father burst into the room.

"What is it, sweetie?"

Thinking quickly, Isabelle said the first thing that came to her mind. "Um, I just had a bad dream—that I got an F on my robotics project."

Her father smiled. "We both know that will never happen. Are you going to get that?" he asked, motioning to her shrieking alarm clock.

"Right," she said, chuckling nervously as she clutched the mattress on either side of her with a death grip.

Her dad turned to head back to the bathroom, leaving her door open just a crack.

She let go of the mattress and scrambled for the clock, knocking it from her table and unplugging it in the process. Thankfully, the shrieking ceased, but she started to rise again. She grabbed her mattress and pulled herself back down into a sitting position on the bed.

What is happening?

As she sat on the edge of the bed, she bobbed up and down like a helium balloon on a string. Her heart thumped so hard she thought it might burst, but at the same time her mind was searching for an explanation. *Am I dreaming? Is something wrong with Earth's gravity? No! It's just me!* Mason's bed was empty. *How did my brother get up and leave the room without noticing me floating above my bed?*

She let go of the mattress and allowed herself to rise once more, experiencing the weird sensation of weightlessness. As she hovered in the air, she could lean this way or that and slowly drift through the air, but she seemed to have no control over her rise or descent. She closed her eyes and fought back a wave of nausea.

She heard steps and saw her brother pause at the cracked doorway; thankfully he turned at the last second to answer his dad who was calling down the hallway, asking if he'd brushed his teeth.

Isabelle's panic had reached a fever pitch. She did *not* want her brother to see her floating in the middle of their room.

She had to feign normalcy until she could figure out what was happening. She flailed her arms in a swimming motion, hoping she'd descend, but it had no effect.

"Don't come in here!"

"Why not, poindexter?" he said as he started to open the door.

She went for the big guns. "I'm naked!"

"Ew!" Mason slammed the door shut. "Dad, Izzy's parading around the room naked and I need to get my key!" She heard her brother's complaining recede as he walked down the hallway.

Fighting back her panic, she did the only thing left she could think of. She closed her eyes and concentrated.

Down.

She was picturing herself moving downward. Pushing all other thoughts and feelings aside, she imagined herself standing in normal gravity. When she opened her eyes a moment later, she was standing in the middle of her bedroom floor with a trickle of sweat on her forehead.

Okay, now I know I'm going crazy. Did that really just happen?

The pounding at her door brought her back to her senses. "Are you getting ready for school, or what?" came her father's muffled voice.

"Yeah, Dad. Just a minute," she said as she swiped her glasses off of her bedside table and crammed them onto her face. Quickly and shakily, she changed into her school clothes and let her brother into the room. He nearly bowled her over to grab his keys.

Maybe this is just my imagination. Aside from her weird floating experience, everything else seemed perfectly normal. *Or a dream. Nothing but a harmless little dream that spilled over into my waking life. Yep, a dream!*

By the time she got to the kitchen Mason was already done with breakfast and out the front door while her dad was drinking his second cup of coffee. "Better hurry, sweetie." Isabelle's stomach was in knots, so she just poured herself a glass of orange juice and sat down at the table.

"Did you get some sun yesterday, or what?" he said. "You look a little sunburned." Isabelle reached up and touched her cheek, which felt warm. She shrugged. She didn't remember getting an unusual amount of sun the previous day.

"Another tech break-in," said her dad, nodding to the television.

"Uh huh." *Maybe these hallucinations are stress related. I'm stressing myself out over too many things—yes, that's it.*

The news anchor was explaining that for the second night in a row, a team of robots had broken into a high technology company headquarters located in Rose Valley's Tech Basin and made off with advanced and valuable hardware. This time, the security cameras at Meridian Robotics had been disabled. Police were theorizing that some kind of ultrasonic weapon might have been used.

As Isabelle was listening, she noticed she was hovering six inches above her seat. She grabbed each side of her chair and pulled herself down just as her dad turned around after rinsing out his coffee cup at the sink.

He must have noticed the strange look on her face. "What's wrong?"

"Nothing!" she said a little too loudly. *Down,* she thought. *Down.*

"I'm starting to worry about you, Izzy. You've been acting a little . . . off today. Are you sure there's nothing bothering you? You know you can talk to me, right? About anything." Isabelle noted an awkward sincerity on his face.

"No, I'm peachy," she said, flashing the best fake smile she could muster.

"Alright." His eyes narrowed. "Better get going or you'll be late for school. Oh, and come straight home from—"

"—school again today." Isabelle parroted the end of his sentence in perfect unison. "Can I still stay at Maddy's tonight?"

"We'll see. We can talk about it tonight when I get home. For now, you'd better get going. You're going to be late."

"Yup!" Isabelle sat staring at her dad.

"Well?" he said.

Ever so carefully, she shifted to the side of her chair and put a single foot on the kitchen floor. Normal gravity.

"Thank goodness," she muttered to herself.

"What was that, Izzy?"

"Nothing, Dad. Bye! Love you!"

"See you after school, sweetie."

Isabelle walked down the front porch steps, concentrating the whole time on maintaining normal gravity. *This isn't a dream. What am I going to do? Should I have told Dad? Is this my life now?*

Well … at least she wasn't ordinary everyday Isabelle any more.

Off in the distance, Mason disappeared around the corner on his way to school. Maddy was waiting at the front sidewalk, standing stock-still and wide-eyed. Isabelle, concentrating on keeping herself literally grounded, hardly noticed Maddy's odd expression.

"Hey, Maddy, where's Jasmine?" But her friend continued to stare straight ahead, looking as rigid as a wooden plank. "Maddy?"

"Running late," said Maddy, stiffly.

"Something weird is going on." Isabelle's brow furrowed. "I think I'm going crazy."

Maddy's head snapped around.

"What? What's going on? What's weird?" Maddy said, breathlessly.

Isabelle was so taken aback she didn't notice Jasmine, who marched right up to them, beaming.

"Hey guys, you'll never guess what happened to me." said Jasmine. "I've got superpowers!"

Isabelle's and Maddy's mouths dropped wide open.

7
INSULT AND INJURY

The usual Friday morning buzz of Mine Street seemed to dissolve all around Isabelle as everyone started quickly talking over one other. After a moment of confusion, Jasmine and Maddy allowed Isabelle to recount the morning's events.

"You didn't tell your dad?" asked Maddy.

"No." Tears welled in Isabelle's eyes. "I don't know why, but I didn't want Dad or Mason to see me like that. I felt so helpless. I felt like a freak."

Jasmine raised a finger. "It was that sphere we found yesterday. It did this to us. That has to be it!"

Isabelle's chest throbbed. Like a bolt of blue lightning, comprehension struck.

"I think whatever power that was inside that sphere somehow—somehow transferred to us," Jasmine said. "Remember how it flashed when you got too close? Then afterward it wasn't glowing anymore?"

Isabelle sighed. "We don't know the first thing about what's happening to us. Assume it *was* that sphere. Do you know where it came from?"

"No . . ." Jasmine said.

Isabelle drew a deep breath before continuing. "We don't know why or how it transferred this—power—to us. If that's what we should call it. Who made it? How long it's been down there? If it can hurt us? I can't believe I'm saying this, but we don't even know if it's of this world." Isabelle remembered the comment her dad made earlier about how she looked sunburned. "Or if we're all going to die of cancer, or radiation sickness, or whatever!"

"Okay," said Maddy, uneasily, "we're not going to figure this all out right now. We'd better get going. We're going to be late."

They hurried down the sidewalk. After a few moments, Jasmine broke the silence.

"My morning was insane."

"What happened to you?" asked Isabelle.

"While looking for my shoes, I accidentally lifted my desk with one hand." Jasmine seemed unable to suppress her grin.

Isabelle and Maddy offered blank stares.

"It's super strength!" said Jasmine, flexing her biceps. "Not only strength but speed too! I've been testing it out all morning."

Isabelle's forehead crinkled up. "Wait. You didn't show anyone, did you?"

"I think Samantha and Aniyah might have seen me lift the sofa over my head."

"Showing off for the twins? Really?" Isabelle's face flushed.

"They're two," said Jasmine. "Who are they going to tell?" She turned to Maddy. "What about you?"

"Me?" Maddy's mouth hung open for a moment. "When I woke up this morning . . ." she trailed off, flustered.

"It's okay, Maddy," said Jasmine. "Go on."

Maddy sighed and closed her eyes. "When I woke up this morning, my old teddy bear was moving around the bedroom on its own."

"What?" The blood drained from Isabelle's face.

Jasmine's mouth dropped open. "Get out of town!"

Maddy swallowed. "It was horrifying! You have no idea! After a minute, I started to suspect I was doing it myself. So, I tested it and I found out it really was me."

"No flipping way," said Jasmine, wide-eyed.

"I can't tell you how relieved I was to learn that Mr. Fuzzfuzz wasn't possessed."

"Mr. Fuzzfuzz?" Jasmine exchanged looks with Isabelle.

"Don't judge me!"

Isabelle found herself chuckling at the absurdity of it all.

Maddy took a deep breath. "Seriously, I was starting to question my own sanity. The real problem was that things near me were moving around at random. You should see my room. It's a total wreck."

The girls made way on the sidewalk for a boy who was walking past them to the junior high school. Maddy clutched the straps of her backpack, waiting until she was certain he was out of earshot.

"It's taking complete concentration to not cause chaos everywhere I go," she said. "By the time I got here, I was able to at least keep random objects from jumping around. Did you notice how spacey I was this morning, Isabelle? That's why. Total concentration. It's telekinesis. This is so—weird. I don't know how to describe these feelings. I'm using my mind in ways I never knew were possible." Maddy looked pleadingly at Isabelle and then at Jasmine. "Moving objects with my mind isn't like I'm reaching out with my hand and moving them. It's like I am the object." Maddy exhaled uneasily. "I must sound crazy."

Isabelle grinned. "You're saying that to the girl who was floating around her room this morning. I thought I was crazy too." Her mind raced with wild thoughts, each more far-fetched than the last. "That level of concentration you're talking about—that sounds similar to what I was experiencing. It's taken complete concentration to keep from floating off the ground," she added.

Maddy clutched at Isabelle's arm as they hurried across a crosswalk. "We need to tell someone!"

"No way!" Isabelle squirmed.

"Why not?" asked Jasmine, as if this was the most ridiculous thing she had ever heard.

"Think about it," Isabelle said. "Do you want to be poked and prodded by scientists and doctors? Do you want to be taken away from your family? You'll be a specimen. A test subject. Whatever this is, it's not natural, and the authorities will do everything they can to turn you into a lab rat. Or try to tap into these abilities for profit, or lock you away. Or worse."

"Maybe you have a point," Maddy said.

Jasmine bristled. "Just think what I could accomplish. I could be a rich and famous athlete. I could do anything. The Olympics, professional soccer, tennis, golf, basketball—you name it! If I could learn to control it like you guys—"

"Control it?" hissed Isabelle. "I'm not controlling anything. I could barely keep it together this morning! There's no way to know if any of us could learn to control it."

"Maybe we could tell my dad," Maddy said. "He's a doctor. He can tell us what's happening. He won't let anything bad happen to us."

"I don't know, Maddy," said Isabelle. "How many of your dad's patients are complaining about symptoms of uncontrollable flying or telekinesis? I don't feel like we should tell anybody. Not yet."

Maddy frowned and crossed her arms.

Jasmine stopped in the middle of the sidewalk and bounced on the balls of her feet.

"I'm telling you; we have these powers for a reason," she said. "We're meant to use them."

Maddy continued down the sidewalk, beckoning Jasmine to follow. "We should all decide together what to do. Promise you won't use these powers until then."

"Power?" Isabelle said. "More like a curse. I agree. We should not do or say anything."

"Not even a little during P.E.?" Jasmine said.

"Absolutely not!" said Isabelle. "We need to discuss this whole situation."

"But, my dad—"

"This is probably beyond your dad's ability to help us," Isabelle said.

The girls left the neighborhood of Arcadia and were passing through Old Town on their way to Cavett, the neighborhood which shared its name with Cavett Academy.

They walked in the cool shade along the right side of the old thoroughfare, the morning sunlight striking the red brick facades of the buildings across the street as they hurried on their way. Isabelle had always joked that the neighborhood of Old Town should be renamed Ghost Town, but this morning there were signs of life: the coffee shop had a few customers sipping coffee at bistro tables set out on the sidewalk. A green-aproned barista smiled and said good morning as the girls passed.

Isabelle couldn't help but relish the earthy aroma of the coffee. Something about the smell of this particular shop awakened old childhood memories of her mother getting ready for work in the early hours of the morning. She shook the memories aside and continued to turn over, again and again, the same thoughts and worries.

A nagging question lingered. "Maddy, did you say you *could* control it?"

Maddy seemed to snap out of her own introspection and glanced over at Isabelle. Her ponytail bounced and bobbed with each step.

"Not at first. After the initial shock, when I calmed down— then I could move some things at will." Maddy looked around to make sure no one else was within earshot. "I made Mr. Fuzzfuzz walk around and do a dance."

Jasmine burst into laughter.

Isabelle smiled. "It sounds like you were controlling it quite well. What about you, Jasmine?"

"For me, it's just natural. I don't have to think about being super-strong or super-fast. I keep breaking things, though. I don't know my own strength."

"That sounds a little dangerous," said Isabelle.

"And flying around and moving things with your mind isn't?"

Isabelle frowned. "So, we've got strength," she said, extending a hand to Jasmine, "telekinesis," motioning to Maddy, "and flight," she said. "I can't begin to imagine what all this means. We can discuss it tonight at Maddy's, if I can talk Dad into letting me stay. I don't know if we should risk trying to talk about this at school, either. Nobody but us three can know about this." Isabelle looked gravely at Maddy, who lowered her eyes to the ground as she walked along the sidewalk. "Not even your dad."

"Okay, Isabelle. I promise."

Isabelle realized they were at the intersection of Mine and Mechanic Streets. She stared at the darkness beyond the chain link barrier. On the other side and down the embankment was the entrance to the underground drain tunnel where, just yesterday, her life took a drastic turn. Goosebumps rose on her arms as they crossed the street toward Cavett Academy's campus. Somewhere below them was the mysterious object that seemed to be the cause of all this weirdness.

Isabelle continued to stare over at the darkness beyond the trees. "I wonder what that . . ." She stopped mid-sentence as the ground shook beneath her feet.

All three girls froze in their tracks. Again, the earth moved and the resonating thud made Isabelle's knees wobble.

When they reached the sidewalk, Isabelle scanned the length of the tree line, looking for the source of all the noise. After another rumbling thud, Maddy had her hands over her ears while Jasmine was pointing at a column of gray smoke billowing from behind the brush. Isabelle thought she heard a man's voice coming from behind the trees.

"What's going on?" asked Maddy with an ashen face. Instinctively, the girls ducked behind a silver pickup truck that was pulled up on the grass next to the sidewalk.

A moment later there was a commotion at the tree line as a man staggered out from the brush and fell to his hands and knees. He must have just clambered up the steep embankment. He hauled himself to his feet, frantically looking over his shoulder as he ran. His mop of disheveled brown hair looked as if it would have been immaculately slicked back under normal circumstances. As he sprinted toward them, Isabelle could make out the unmistakable eyepatch and waxed mustache: it was the man who was watching them as they came out of the tunnel the day before.

What's he doing—

Just then, a four-legged machine about the size of a German Shepherd emerged from the trees and stumbled after the man. With uncanny agility, the robot gathered its rubber-tipped legs beneath it and it regained its balance.

Maddy's iron grip dug into Isabelle's shoulder.

"It's one of those robots from the tech burglary!" Jasmine said.

The memory of yesterday morning's news came flooding back. The metallic beast matched the rendered image in the newscast perfectly. The machine whirred and clacked as it stepped toward the man with an unsettling grace.

As Isabelle marveled at its flawless engineering, another nearly identical robot burst out from the brush. She let out a gasp and ducked back behind the truck. This one was suspended in the air, driven by its four helicopterlike rotors. Its four legs slowly folded underneath its body as it gained height. Dangling beneath the flying robot was a net pouch which contained—

"It has the sphere!" hissed Jasmine. "From yesterday!"

The robot lilted and swung a metallic appendage toward the man. A resonating thud emitted from the machine. The grass around his feet rippled in the shockwave as he dove and rolled out of harm's way. The truck lurched in the wake of the attack and several car alarms shrieked across the street.

"What the hell was that?" wailed Jasmine, holding her ears.

Isabelle's eardrums ached and her guts heaved from the force. She couldn't fathom the power this weapon must possess. *And it wasn't even aimed at us,* she thought.

Maddy sat against the truck's rear tire, clutching her head. "Some kind of sonic cannon?"

Meanwhile, the robot on the ground moved with the fluidity of a living animal as it loped across the mowed grass. What Isabelle assumed was the machine's sensor array was positioned on a stalk that extended from its blocky body. She watched as it scanned around and took in its surroundings, all the while tracking its target.

A variety of other appendages protruded from its body at odd angles, all moving independently of each other. It leveled its weapon at the man who was running toward the truck. A tracking red laser beam streamed across the ground until it found its mark. There was a sharp crack and a forked stream of blue plasma spat from the robot's weapon. In the next instant the man was clutching at his shoulder and tugging at his yellow vest. He struggled to pull off the smoldering garment and slung it to the ground just as he dove behind the truck for cover.

Another attack came from the hovering robot and Isabelle cringed behind the truck, covering her ears. The pressure wave washed over them, this time shattering the driver's side window.

A jolt of horror stabbed at her as she realized that the robots' target was now right beside her.

She craned her neck around the side of the truck to see in which direction would be best to flee. Thankfully, the robots were retreating. She watched as four rotor masts sprouted from the back of the machine. Telescoping blades snapped into place and whirred to life. With a high-pitched whine, the robot lifted off the ground to join its twin. Together, the two robots swayed in the air and disappeared over the tops of the trees and out of sight, the sphere still dangling in the net beneath one of them.

The man, out of breath, at last paused to stare at the three girls hiding behind his truck.

"You!"

8

THE MASK SLIPS

The man picked himself up off the ground and peered over the hood of the truck.

He held up a cautioning hand, his eye glued to the treetops where the robots had disappeared. "Wait here," he said.

Trembling, Isabelle quickly stood up and brushed herself off. She beckoned to her friends to follow. It was all she could do to keep from fleeing in terror.

When it became apparent that the robots were gone for good, the man clenched his fists and muttered under his breath, seemingly cursing his own failure.

"We need to get going," Isabelle said.

"I saw you three yesterday over at Hilltop Park."

Isabelle wasn't expecting a British accent: it was as out of place in Rose Valley as his quirky appearance. She took a step backward and glanced around.

A small group of people had gathered across the street. Apparently drawn by the noise, they now pointed at the trees where the robots had disappeared and talked in hushed voices. One was talking on their phone.

"That wasn't us," Isabelle said. "You—you must have us confused with someone else." Her heart raced as she tried to calm her voice. "We don't know what's going on here, and we want no part of it."

She took a step to leave, but didn't move.

With a sickening pang of horror, she realized she was hovering six inches off the ground. Her breath escaped as if she'd been punched in the gut. She tried to speak but a stifled yelp was all she could manage. Jasmine and Maddy quickly pulled her down, each grabbing an arm. Isabelle closed her eyes, exasperated with herself for so blatantly blowing her cover. Jasmine and Maddy exchanged a worried look.

The man's eyebrows rose and he smirked. "Not you, eh? There's no mistake; it was you. And I need to talk to you—I mean, Dr. Anton is going to want to talk to you."

"Dr. who?" asked Jasmine.

"Dr. Stephanie Anton. It's about the . . ." He paused and manically pointed in the direction the robots flew. 'It's about the—*thing*. It's very important that she see you." He glanced again at the treetops. "We have a dire situation here. Did you not *see?*"

Maddy stepped forward. "What do you and this Dr. Anton have to do with that thing?"

Isabelle's mouth dropped open. "Maddy!"

The man drew a long breath and attempted to smooth his disheveled hair. His one, green eye moved between Isabelle and her friends.

"Yesterday, I was transporting it, but I was being followed by a couple of chaps in a black SUV. To cut a long story short, I scarpered and the chase went off-road. They got stuck and I was able to get away, but I damaged my radiator. Near that tunnel was as far as I got, so I hid it there—underground. I thought the good doctor was going to murder me when she heard, but what else could I do?"

"Who are they?" Maddy pressed. "Who was chasing you?"

"I'd better not say." He shook his head. "I covered it in sand; I thought it would be insulated from tracking. Things cooled down today, so I came back for it, but now these drones beat me to it. Out of the frying pan and *straight* into the fire!"

"Whose robots are they?" asked Maddy.

"I can't tell you that, either."

Isabelle watched every move the stranger made. His arm twitched irregularly where the robot had shot him.

"As for you." His eye locked onto Isabelle. "I know you're involved. I saw the sphere lost its phosphorescence and now I know why. You're going to have to explain yourselves. What did you do? Did you touch it?"

Near panic, she decided that denial would be the safest route.

"We don't know what you're talking about. We don't know anything. And if you'll excuse us, we're going to be late for school."

Isabelle marched past the man and started cutting across the soccer field toward Cavett Academy's rear parking lot. With a last backward glance, Jasmine and Maddy fell into step alongside her.

"Wait!" he called. "The good doctor is probably going to murder me for this, but you should know. That thing is *not from here*. You really need to understand what's going on—"

"Sorry," Isabelle said as she walked away. "I think you've got the wrong girls."

She glanced over her shoulder. He thumped the hood of the truck with an open palm in frustration but made no move to follow them.

Maddy leaned toward her friends as she walked. "Did you hear what he said? The thing isn't from here. It must be from outer space!"

Isabelle could only shake her head in stubborn disbelief. "How can it be?"

Maddy scoffed. "After all we've experienced, that thing coming from outer space is your sticking point?"

"What is going on? asked Jasmine, wide-eyed. "First superpowers and now all this? Those robots were actually shooting at that guy!"

"Why do those robots even exist?" said Isabelle. "And who made them?" Just yesterday morning she learned of the robots and the tech burglaries. She never would have dreamed she'd find herself dropped into the middle of all the intrigue.

"And who is this Dr. Anton?" added Maddy.

Isabelle shook her head in disgust. "I can't believe I slipped up! I can't believe I let him see me floating." She covered her face with her hand, wondering how long it would be before she'd be a test subject.

Jasmine nudged her. "You were barely off the ground." Her eyes darted sideways.

"I recognize him," Isabelle said in a low voice. "He was there yesterday when we left the tunnel. We must have gone in right after he hid the thing. I walked right past him yesterday."

Jasmine stole a glance over her shoulder. "So, what's the deal? Is he a construction guy working for the city or what?"

Isabelle scoffed. "No, he doesn't work for the city."

Maddy scratched her chin thoughtfully. "Maybe we should have asked more about that Dr. Anton. Maybe she knows something about what happened to us."

Isabelle shook her head. "No. How do we know we can trust this guy? And whatever happened to not talking to anyone about anything?" She shot a stern look toward Maddy. "We don't know what we'd be getting into. It's not safe."

"What if they can tell us something about what it was?" asked Maddy.

"Whatever it was, it would probably be best if we didn't get involved."

"We're already involved, aren't we? We have freaking superpowers!"

***

Isabelle, Jasmine, and Maddy got to their first classes just in time to avoid getting a tardy slip. The rest of their morning was, for the most part, surprisingly normal. Jasmine accidentally ripped the lid off of a desk but was able to play it off like it was a faulty hinge. Her teacher had a maintenance worker bring in a new desk. She was sullen all morning, but kept her promise during P.E., although a basketball did inexplicably deflate in her hands.

While Jasmine struggled, Isabelle and Maddy found it progressively easier to hold their bizarre new abilities at bay. Maddy seemed perfectly fine, and Isabelle was able to quickly regain control at the slightest feeling of weightlessness.

Maddy had convinced the other two they should at least look up Dr. Anton's name on the internet, and Isabelle suggested they could make good use of the daily twenty-five-minute break before STEM classes.

Although the library was deserted, they situated themselves at the rearmost computer cubicle. Isabelle opened her backpack and retrieved a slip of paper she had written Dr. Anton's name on.

Maddy glanced over. "I don't think she's a local physician. I would have heard her name before."

"I don't think she's a physician, either," said Isabelle as she pulled up a browser tab with a search engine and keyed in the doctor's name. "Doctor . . . Steph . . . anie . . . Anton." Isabelle scanned the search results and clicked on a likely looking web link. "Here we go," she said. "Why does this not surprise me? This is some sort of directory of contributors and writers for extraterrestrial life *studies*." She couldn't help a bit of sarcastic emphasis on the last word. She scrolled down the list, which included a photo, credentials, and lists of published works for each contributor.

"Look at *that* guy!" said Jasmine, pointing. "I've seen him on TV, on the History Network." Jasmine gestured with her hands out in front of her. "I'm not saying it was aliens . . . but it was aliens," she said, mimicking the outdated meme which featured this particular, wild-haired and charismatic contributor.

Maddy giggled.

Isabelle scoffed. "Interesting company our new friend is keeping." She mentally compiled what little she knew about the popular TV show: mostly, that it was built around far-fetched assumptions and pseudoscience about how ancient extraterrestrial visitors had a hand in shaping Earth's civilizations. She feared she'd kill a substantial amount of brain cells if she actually sat down and watched an episode.

She took a deep breath and tried to open her mind. As she continued scrolling through the contributors' names, another thought intruded into her mind; the mere fact that she and her friends had superpowers could not be ignored. She didn't know why she was being so snobby about paranormal science. She had to admit to herself that something genuinely paranormal had already entered her life.

Isabelle at last found Dr. Anton's entry and clicked. An expanded view of her biography appeared on the screen. The square photo showed a smiling, olive skinned woman with curly, shoulder length hair framing her sharp features. "Let's see. Harvard PhD. Astrophysicist. It says she's done a lot of important work with exoplanets. Detecting exoplanet atmospheres. It lists all her books and published works."

Isabelle hit the back button and returned to the search results and clicked on a few other links. As she expected, she thought many of the sites looked less than reputable. "Hmm. This blogger says Anton is insanely wealthy. It says she started her career as a well-respected scientist. Then her work took a turn for the bizarre. Now she hosts a podcast, a MoovTube channel, and stays on the fringes of what would be considered respectable science."

"Wait," said Isabelle. "This next one is *her* actual blog." She clicked on the link and read aloud the article topics. "Let's see. 'Panspermia and the Fermi Paradox'; 'The extraterrestrial origins of intelligence'; 'E.T. may not be like anything we expect.' She just goes on and on. There are a lot of articles here. It's easy to see why she lost her credibility," said Isabelle as she clicked the back button on the browser and the screen returned to her search list.

Maddy looked up. "I don't see what the big deal is. These seem like valid scientific topics to me. What good is science if you don't have an open mind toward all the possibilities?"

Isabelle ignored her and continued scrolling. The next link showed a thumbnail of a video. She clicked and the screen switched to the popular video-sharing website, MoovToob.com.

It was an episode from the History Network show that Jasmine mentioned, about how aliens influenced ancient civilizations on planet Earth. Isabelle scanned fast-forward. She stopped as the scene switched to a head and shoulders shot of the woman. Printed across the bottom of the screen was, "Dr. Stephanie Anton, astrophysicist."

Jasmine pointed. "Oh wow! So, I guess Dr. Anton was on the History Network too."

On screen, Dr. Anton was talking about extraterrestrial life in a smooth voice. ". . . When talking about life in the universe, one must always add the tag, 'as we know it.'" Dr. Anton's on-screen image made air quotes with her fingers. "Out there, in the universe, life may exist that looks and behaves like nothing we expect it to. Life may have happened using building blocks and elements that could never have assembled themselves here on Earth, in environments that Earth life could never exist in." The scene cut away to a computer graphics model of a chain of carbon atoms with other atoms attaching to it, as the narrator's voiceover began again.

"I guess it's safe to say the cheese has slid off her cracker?" Jasmine said.

"A few days ago, I'd have agreed without a doubt," said Isabelle, "but today, I'm not so sure."

9
UNEXPECTED HELP

THIRD AND FOURTH PERIODS WERE SET ASIDE for STEM classes and it was the time of day that Isabelle had been dreading. She was not looking forward to facing Crystal again.

While Jasmine spent her two hours of STEM classes at the Malisia Science Hall for biology, Isabelle and Maddy took theirs in the Cavett Tech Center.

They entered through the wide, automatic doors of the south concourse. The sprawling complex was the crown jewel of Cavett Academy. Students came to Cavett from all corners of the state to take advantage of its award-winning STEM programs. Isabelle, Jasmine, and Maddy were three of just a handful of local students.

The cavernous south concourse had a high, slanting glass roof with a framework of steel girders. Sunlight flooded the airy lobby and the shadows of the steel beams crisscrossed the floor.

As the laughter of students walking to their classrooms echoed, Isabelle and Maddy stopped at the far end of the lobby. This was where they usually parted ways. Today, Isabelle paused and took a quick look around to make sure no one was within listening distance.

"Don't suppose anyone was talking about the disturbance we witnessed this morning with the robots?"

Maddy shook her head. "Not a single mention."

"That's weird. It happened in broad daylight. They were shooting sonic cannons and plasma guns! There's no news crews or gossip or anything?"

Maddy again shook her head. "You'd think everyone would be on high alert with all the burglaries." She shrugged. "I'd better get going."

"See you after class." Isabelle turned to walk down the concourse on her way to robotics. Maddy hurried toward the entrance of the main building where pre-engineering classes were held.

When Isabelle arrived at the robotics classroom there were about twenty students already there, getting a head start on their work or talking among themselves in small groups. She went straight to her table, which happened to be nearest the entrance, and settled in.

As she sat there, thoughts of the robotic tech burglars lurched into her mind. As if a string of robotic burglaries cropping up in Rose Valley wasn't bizarre enough on its own, now she had to face the fact that these robots were somehow involved with the mysterious glowing sphere that granted her gravity-defying powers.

How could Rose Valley be the epicenter of such an inconceivable turn of events? Even more, how could Isabelle and her friends find themselves mixed up in the middle of it? And could that man be trusted when he implied that the sphere came from outer space?

She marveled at the robot team's grim efficiency, their sleek economy of design. Even though she knew burglary was wrong, she couldn't help but admire the robots themselves. *They* didn't know their actions were wrong. Her thoughts strayed to the real culprit. Perhaps a solitary robotics genius, working feverishly in the shadows. She shuddered.

The clacking of nearby keys brought her back to the real world.

Jayden, with his nose buried in his laptop and his ever-present headphones on, hardly noticed that she'd joined him. Isabelle pretended to look out the window, but she was really trying to determine through her peripheral vision if Crystal was there. Sure enough, sitting at a table at the back of the room was a completely benign-looking Crystal Skorch.

Maddy had suspected Jayden was embarrassed by some earlier confrontation with Crystal; maybe it was better not to ask. But Isabelle knew that her unquenchable curiosity would win out over her desire for discretion.

"So, what happened with you and Crystal?" she asked in a low voice.

Jayden continued to clack on his laptop keys. *Of course, those infernal headphones.* She tapped his shoulder. Jayden pulled the earpiece off of his nearest ear and she repeated her question.

"You warned me to steer clear yesterday, remember?" she added. "Why? What happened?"

Jayden seemed to shrink behind his laptop. "I promised someone I wouldn't tell."

Isabelle dismissed the statement with a wave of her hand and a shake of her head. "Come on. You know you can trust me."

Jayden leaned closer to whisper. So much for his promises. "Last Sunday, I was skating with Benji Ross at the Hill and we saw . . . *her.*" Jayden's eyes flicked sideways to Crystal's table. "Benji asked me to dare him to go talk to her. You know. *Talk* to her. So, I dared him."

Isabelle risked a glance to the table at the back of the room. Crystal was wearing a red plaid vest over a long-sleeved undershirt that seemed to clash with her electric blue hair. Pale as ever, she looked as if she barely had the strength to hold her head upright as she jotted notes in her tablet, but Isabelle knew, all too well, how looks could be deceiving. She could swear she saw Crystal's eyes dart upward for a fraction of a second, but quickly turned her attention back to Jayden.

"That girl is like a kung fu master or something," Jayden said. "Benji didn't even have a chance."

Isabelle leaned closer, wondering what horrors must have befallen Benji Ross.

Jayden paused, directing a solemn stare at his new confidante. "Atomic wedgie. Right there in broad daylight. It was horrible." Jayden wore the shell-shocked look of a battle-weary soldier.

Isabelle wished she had learned these details a little earlier. It would have been useful to know the new girl had a penchant for violence and a hair trigger. However, Benji Ross had always been sort of creepy and was always pestering girls. It was a comforting thought that he finally got a little of what was coming to him, even if it was at the hands of Crystal Skorch.

Mrs. Stacey walked into the classroom and those who had been chatting quieted down immediately. Jayden leveled a final, grim look at Isabelle, and it was understood that the information that he had just shared was in confidence. Isabelle dipped her head in a subtle nod.

"Hello," said Mrs. Stacey in a singsong voice. Her jet-black hair was pulled back into a loose bun, and her entire face seemed radiant as she smiled at her students. "Today's going to be another free work day. You're going to continue work on your final projects. The Tech Fair will be here before you know it. Miss Schaal or I will be available to answer any questions you have. Get to it!" She clapped her hands.

Standing off to the side of the room was a blonde, pony-tailed young woman who had raised her hand in acknowledgment and smiled when Mrs. Stacey mentioned her name. Suddenly, it seemed, most of the boys had questions and were waiting in line to talk to Miss Schaal.

How typical, thought Isabelle. Of all the assistants, Isabelle preferred Daniel. Not only did he seem to be the most knowledgeable and the most helpful, but he seemed to truly enjoy working with the students.

Jayden remained at their table, though. With his headphones on and his face in his laptop, he had already shifted his full attention to whatever task was at hand. Although he barely noticed her, she was relieved that he'd be keeping her company. She was starting to get the feeling that today would be another unproductive day.

Isabelle watched as Mrs. Stacey walked to the back of the classroom and spoke to Crystal, who didn't look very happy. Isabelle's heart leaped with joy as Crystal closed her tablet and got up out of her seat. Had her bullying ways finally caught up to her? Was she getting kicked out of robotics class?

Isabelle's fluttering heart dropped into the pit of her stomach when instead of exiting the classroom, Crystal pulled out a chair across from Isabelle and plopped down into it.

Isabelle slowly hovered out of her seat. The weird sensation of weightlessness filled her stomach with a squirming ball of eels. *Not now. Down!* She hooked her feet around the legs of her chair. Crystal must have noticed the look of horror on Isabelle's face because she just rolled her eyes. The touch of a hand to Isabelle's shoulder made her jump. Mrs. Stacey's soft voice was at her side.

"Crystal is going to be working with you today. I think she might be able to help you with that circuit board problem you were telling me about yesterday." Isabelle could only watch helplessly as Mrs. Stacey sent a wide-eyed Jayden to an unoccupied table to work on his scripting before heading over to chase away some of the rabble that had gathered around Miss Schaal.

Mrs. Stacey was always mixing and matching partners according to what she thought were her students' strengths and weaknesses. She seemed to love the idea of her students collaborating. Bouncing ideas off your colleagues was sometimes useful, but Isabelle didn't know if that was the case if you were paired with a sociopath.

"Okay, nerd. Let's not make this any harder than it has to be," said Crystal in a low enough voice that Mrs. Stacey would not hear her. "Draw your circuit."

Isabelle sat motionless and furrowed her brow. *What is she up to?*

"Your circuit," Crystal said. "Give me a schematic."

Isabelle stared and blinked.

"I don't have all day!" snapped Crystal.

Mrs. Stacey was at Meghan's table answering a question and looked over to make sure everything was alright. Crystal put on a greasy, fake smile and Mrs. Stacey turned back to Meghan, apparently satisfied that all was well.

Isabelle took out a piece of paper from her backpack along with a purple gel pen.

"Nice backpack," said Crystal with the faintest hint of a smile.

Isabelle was *not* amused. She began neatly drawing out a schematic which represented MechAnna's circuit. She drew the symbol representing the battery with a fuse and the on / off switch, all neatly labeled. She included the placements of her switching regulator and linear regulator, along with labels showing the voltage needs of her motors, servos and the microcontroller. Lastly, she drew in the placements of the capacitors along with their ratings.

When her schematic diagram of MechAnna's circuit was complete, Isabelle slid it across the table in front of Crystal who glanced at it momentarily.

"Microcontroller resetting?"

Isabelle nodded, trying not to look impressed that Crystal was able to determine that from one quick glance. *Is my error that obvious?*

"You need a separate power supply for the micro and the motors," said Crystal. "Put a couple of capacitors on your micro power supply: 100 microfarad filter and one nanofarad decoupling. Your motors are drawing a lot of current and when they switch directions it's causing a dead short. That's sucking your current like crazy.

"It's either *that* voltage drop or the resulting EMI noise on the power supply line that's causing your micro to reset. Either way, a separate power supply will fix it." Crystal paused, then slyly smiled. "Fried some boards, have we?"

Poker faced, Isabelle mentally ran through Crystal's suggestion and analyzed it. *She must be trying to trick me.* But after careful consideration, she concluded that the solution seemed feasible. In fact, it made perfect sense. *But why is she helping me?*

Isabelle's heart fluttered at the thought she might finally be able to progress further on her project. Suddenly, she couldn't wait to get home to put this new plan into action. She reached out and slid the diagram back toward herself and hesitated, unsure if her mouth could form the words she needed to say. She placed her purple gel pen neatly on the table and folded her hands in front of her.

"Thank you," she said at last.

"You're welcome, nerd." Crystal stood up and walked back toward the robotics lab.

10

A SPECIAL GIFT

IT TOOK A BIT OF PERSUASION, but Isabelle was able to convince her dad that staying at Maddy's house would be just as safe as her own, although he did make her promise they wouldn't go anywhere.

Since Isabelle got to spend the night at her friend's house, Mason insisted on being allowed to spend the night at his friend Gavin's house, no doubt for an all-night sugar-fueled video gaming session.

While Isabelle was waiting for Maddy's dad to pick her up, she sat at her workbench with MechAnna's disassembled parts spread out before her. On the other side of the room, her dad struggled with repairing the sliding closet door that had come off its tracks. She didn't mind the company. He'd been working a lot of hours lately and she hadn't seen much of him this week.

He looked around at all the clutter. "I hope the upstairs renovations aren't going to drag on. We need to get your brother out of here and into his own room. It's like *The Odd Couple* in here." When Isabelle gave him a blank stare, he shook his head. "Never mind."

"He's not a very good roommate," she said. "Boys can be so gross."

He nodded. "Remember, it's only temporary. I don't imagine it's fun staying in the same room, but he's your brother and he loves you very much; he just has unusual ways of showing it."

"I guess so," said Isabelle as she removed MechAnna's circuit board from its chassis.

"Isn't that your grandma's phone?" asked her dad as he rummaged in his toolbox for a different size screwdriver.

Isabelle glanced at the disassembled parts of the smartphone that were cluttering the workbench. "Her old one," she said as she applied a bead of solder to MechAnna's circuit board. "She gave this one to me when she got her new one."

"Did she know you were going to destroy it?" he asked with a smile.

"I didn't destroy it, Dad, I'm scavenging certain components."

"Of course."

A moment of silence passed as Isabelle examined the circuit board, then pushed her glasses back up after they slid halfway down her nose.

"Listen, Isabelle," said her dad. "I want you to know that I'm so very proud of you. You'll never know how much I admire you—how brilliant and resourceful you are. I can't even begin to comprehend all these things you excel at."

"Aw, Dad," she said glibly without looking up.

"Making sure you had an opportunity to get into the academy was one of the best decisions your mother and I made." He paused and looked back down into the toolbox. "I know you're going to go far in life. You've got such a bright future ahead of you." Her father's tired, blue eyes glistened. "You guys are both growing up so fast. I'm sorry if it seems like I'm never here for you. Things haven't exactly turned out like your mother and I planned."

Isabelle looked up from her work and saw the sadness in his eyes. She felt a renewed wave of appreciation for her father, along with a fresh sting at the loss of her mother.

"I miss her too."

He nodded.

She regretted that she didn't remember much about her mother before she got sick. Only bits and pieces. She'd never forget the decline, though—the spiraling descent. Every agonizing day would be forever etched into her soul.

What she did remember made her proud. Her mom spent her whole life helping other people before herself. Her children. Her family. Her patients—they were always first for her.

At this moment, more than ever, Isabelle saw similarities within herself. Her mother's strong desire to help people must have rubbed off on her. Maybe it was the underlying purpose of building MechAnna all along.

Isabelle put down the circuit board and turned toward her dad.

"Nothing I ever do will mean anything if I can't help people. Just like Mom did. Any gifts I've been given," she paused and looked at the remains of the phone, "will be put to that use. If I can."

But those words had a second meaning. She wondered if the mysterious gifts given to her and her friends could be put to use to help people as well. *How could I not realize this possibility before?*

A muffled drone and the crunching of gravel coming through the bedroom window told Isabelle that Maddy's dad had just pulled into the driveway.

"My ride's here." She unplugged her soldering iron and returned it to its rack before taking one last look at MechAnna who was spread out on her workbench in several pieces. She hoped she'd have time to finish up her modifications before the weekend was over.

"You have fun at Maddy's tonight," said her dad as he wrestled with the sliding closet door. Isabelle ran up for a hug and he disentangled himself from the door enough to plant a kiss on top of her head. "Have Dr. Matt text me when you're ready and I'll come get you tomorrow." He turned back to his work. "Oh, yeah! I almost forgot. Mason is already over at Gavin's and he forgot his toothbrush. Since you're going that way, can you have Dr. Matt stop so you can drop it off?"

Her brother's travel toothbrush kit sat on his unmade bed.

"Sure, no problem," she said as she picked it up, but under her breath she was cursing Mason's irresponsibility. "Alright. Love you, Dad. Enjoy your quiet evening!" Isabelle grabbed her sleeping bag and backpack and headed for the front door. Parked outside was Dr. McCarthy's white SUV. Isabelle climbed in to find that Jasmine was already inside with Maddy.

"Hey, girls! Hey, Dr. McCarthy!"

"Hello, Isabelle. You *know* you can call me Matt," he said.

"Okay, Dr. Matt."

He chuckled.

Dr. Matthew McCarthy, along with a handful of other family physicians and specialists, were employed by Bear Run Family Medicine in Rose Valley. Isabelle had been friends with Maddy for so long that Dr. Matt was like a second father.

"You girls have any big plans for tonight?"

"Just going to watch movies, Dad. Can we order pizza?"

"I don't see why not, love."

"Dr. Matt," said Isabelle. "Could you please stop by the Barnards' house? Mason is spending the night there and he forgot his toothbrush. Again." She held up the travel toothbrush kit as she rolled her eyes.

"No problem, Isabelle. Just a little detour."

After a few minutes, Dr. McCarthy turned onto a side street in the neighborhood of Taylor and stopped in front of a Victorian home with a large front porch.

"Glad *you're* going in and not me," whispered Jasmine.

Isabelle glared at Jasmine and Maddy who giggled, and climbed out with toothbrush in hand.

"This will only take a second." She trudged up the front walkway, and bounded up the steps to ring the bell. A moment later the door opened and Isabelle had to take a step backward in surprise. For a terrifying moment she thought she was being confronted by a ghost, but it turned out to be Gavin's mother who was covered from head to toe in a white powder and holding a wooden spoon and a large mixing bowl.

Isabelle quickly recovered. "Oh, hey, Heather," she said smiling.

"Hello, Isabelle. Is everything alright?" asked Heather Barnard as she churned what appeared to be chocolate cake batter in the mixing bowl. "I'm making a cake!" she said, as if her appearance was perfectly normal for such an endeavor.

Isabelle took a deep breath in an attempt to avoid laughing. "My brother forgot his toothbrush. I was just dropping it off."

"Alright, honey," said Heather as she stowed the bowl under one arm and then the other, trying to find a way to take the toothbrush kit without smearing it with her chocolate cake battered hands.

"Your hands are full," said Isabelle. "I can just run it in to him."

"Right," said Heather with a grin. "Gavin's room is at the end of the hall." She pointed to the left and dripped brown batter on the foyer floor.

"Thanks," said Isabelle as she crossed the open concept living room and entered the hallway. At the end of the hall, she found the door halfway open so she stepped inside. "I brought your toothbr . . ." She stopped dead.

Sitting on the edge of the bed was Gavin Barnard who was holding a plastic toy pony with a lustrous, multicolored mane in one hand. In the other hand was a small plastic hairbrush. His eyes bulged and his chubby face flushed red. He quickly stashed the pony and hairbrush out of sight and flicked back his mop of curly hair.

Isabelle decided not to say anything. If Gavin wanted to admire Pony Pals, that was his business. She could tell by his reaction though that he'd probably rather not talk about it. She wondered if this is what they usually did when Mason came over or if Gavin was just passing the time until Mason got out of the bathroom.

"Where's my brother?" she asked, glancing around at the cluttered ten-year-old's room.

"He's making use of the facilities, m'lady," said Gavin, nodding toward the hallway.

Isabelle cringed. "Well, can you tell him I was here and dropped off his toothbrush?" She stepped into the room and plopped the toothbrush kit on top of Mason's duffle bag which she found lying next to Gavin's bed. Without waiting for a response, she turned to head back down the hallway.

"Fare thee well and tempt not the fates . . . m'lady," his voice receded as she headed toward the front door. After saying good evening to Gavin's mom, who had somehow managed to fill the kitchen with smoke, Isabelle excused herself and hurried back out to Dr. McCarthy's SUV.

As she went down the front walkway, she found herself keeping watch for the silver pickup truck. Thankfully, it did not appear.

11

THE DECISION

MADDY AND HER FATHER LIVED in a modest split-level house on the western edge of Greenview, which bordered Isabelle's neighborhood of Arcadia. Greenview was a large neighborhood that contained the country club, golf course, and Lake Argyle which was created in the 1960s to generate hydroelectric power. Maddy's mother was a pediatrician who lived and practiced in Roanoke. Isabelle always assumed Maddy stayed in Rose Valley with her dad to make attending Cavett Academy a lot easier.

Sleepovers at Maddy's were always the best because of the elaborate home theater her dad had built in a lower-level room. To say that Dr. McCarthy was a movie enthusiast would be an understatement. There was even a popcorn maker and a glass candy counter installed along the rear wall near the projector booth. The soundproofed walls near the entrance were adorned with framed classic movie posters, which he switched out and rotated from time to time.

The girls changed into their pajamas before the pizza arrived and set up camp in the theater room. They sat on the floor near the sofa in the front row, munching on candy from the snack counter.

"I still wonder if we should say something to my dad about what happened to us yesterday," said Maddy as she selected an orange gummy bear from her bag.

Alarmed, Isabelle swatted at the floor in front of her. "*Shh!* He might hear you."

"*I* still think I could be rich and famous with my super strength and speed," said Jasmine as she separated two red licorice strips that were stuck together.

"That's all well and good for you," said Maddy, pretending not to hear Isabelle, "but how would you propose I could turn *my* telekinesis into wealth and fame?" She nibbled the head off her gummy bear.

"*Shhh!*" Although their talk might sound like nonsense to an outsider, Isabelle still worried. "Do either of you not have an *ounce* of concern that the sphere could have come from outer space?"

"That's a good question," said Jasmine, ignoring Isabelle. "You could become a secret telekinetic basketball star. No matter how bad you were, you'd never miss a basket."

Maddy looked thoughtful for a moment. "I suppose I'd give myself away when I inevitably shot the ball to the wrong hoop, realized it at the last moment, and made the ball fly all the way back across the court."

Jasmine snorted laughter and Isabelle let out an exasperated sigh.

"We could rob a bank," Jasmine said, with a quick sideways glance in Isabelle's direction.

"Jasmine!" Isabelle's mouth dropped open.

"We could!" said Maddy, feeding off of Isabelle's reaction.

"I can't believe you guys are actually discussing this!" Isabelle looked at one friend in disbelief and then the other, and back again. Although she knew they were kidding, she didn't approve of the lack of reverence they had for their new abilities.

Maddy rocked backwards and forwards on the floor with laughter. "That would make us rich and famous in all the *wrong* ways!"

The three girls were curled up with blankets and pillows on the sofa, whispering and laughing when Dr. McCarthy came in with a pizza box.

"Girls, I just got a call from the hospital and I'm going to have to go in. I trust you're going to be fine watching movies here alone for a while," he said as he handed the pizza box to Maddy.

"Not a problem, Dad. We're not little kids anymore."

"One of my patients is in the emergency room and is asking for me, specifically," explained Dr. McCarthy. "I just hate to invite you girls over and then leave you all alone . . ."

"It's okay, Dad. We got it."

The girls sat on the floor around the pizza box and each grabbed a slice as they waited for Dr. McCarthy to leave.

At long last, Maddy was the one to break the ice. "Dad's gone. We can talk seriously now." There was an uneasy silence.

"Well, there's no use denying it," said Jasmine at long last. "We have superpowers."

Isabelle internally cringed every time the word 'superpowers' was mentioned. She thought it sounded trite—almost ridiculous. If only it wasn't such an apt description.

She drew a deep sigh. "So, it's obvious that the blue sphere transferred some sort of energy to us." Although she could pin down this incredible fact, a thousand other questions still swirled within her mind.

"What about the robots? And that man they were shooting at?" asked Maddy.

"What about them?" Jasmine said.

"Aren't you guys curious to see what this Dr. Stephanie Anton might have to say?"

"Not enough to risk exposing ourselves," said Jasmine. "They don't need to know anything about us. We didn't take their *thing*. We didn't even touch it."

Isabelle picked uncomfortably at her pizza. "But those robots took it. That can't be a good thing. Didn't he say he hid it there? He went to retrieve it, but the robots got there first?"

Maddy nodded. "So, it would seem two factions are after this object. And it's the one that burglarizes tech companies that won out."

Isabelle's jaw tensed up. "I'm as curious as anyone to find out about the source of these powers, but I'm terrified." She looked up at Maddy. "What if this energy hurts us? What if *they* try to hurt us? What if they try to exploit us? What if they try to take us away from our homes?"

Maddy hesitated. "But we're still in over our heads. If we talk to someone—"

"I don't think so." Jasmine shook her head. "This is *our* secret. Us three."

Despite the paralyzing fears, Isabelle sensed the energy coursing through her and prodding her to a greater purpose. So many doubts lingered in the fringes of her heart and soul, but one urge rose above them all. As plain as knowing the reflection in a mirror was hers, she knew these invisible powers were now a part of her. They called to her. It seemed like it was the only thing that could penetrate her fears and summon her to rise to a new purpose.

Isabelle cleared her throat. "I have something to say."

Maddy muted the sound to the samurai movie that had been running in the background as Isabelle got up to her feet.

"For as long as I can remember, I've been working very hard to try to make the most out of my strengths and to use them to help people. I work hard at robotics so I can try to make the world a better place. Take MechAnna, for instance. My goal is for her to assist people."

Isabelle clenched her fists as she spoke. "I bring that up because yesterday something changed for me. I might now have a *new* strength. You're my two best friends; I think you'll believe me when I say I'm *not* going to act like a normal girl."

Jasmine and Maddy grinned and nodded in agreement.

"You know I'm not going to be selfish or foolish. I'm not perfect. I struggle with doing the right thing sometimes. But you *know* me! You know I'll say, 'What good is having an ability if I haven't made a difference in the world?'"

Jasmine grinned. "Right on!"

Isabelle paced back and forth in front of the movie screen as her friends watched her every move. Behind her on the screen, two samurai dueled on a desolate beach. "You have new strengths too." She waved a hand in their direction. "I'd like to call them 'gifts.' We don't fully understand these gifts. Or why they came to us. But I *do* know we can't ignore who we are."

Isabelle paused and watched her friends' reactions. Jasmine was silently nodding while Maddy's face betrayed no emotion whatsoever.

Isabelle drew a long breath and plowed forward.

"Now, we can let someone take these gifts away. Or we can use them for evil and selfish reasons. Or . . . we can use them to do some good." Goosebumps rose on her arms.

Slowly, at first, her voice started to rise. "I'll go so far as to say it's our *responsibility* to use these gifts to help people. If you had the power to save someone, wouldn't you?"

She stood silhouetted against the movie screen and extended her arms at her sides as swords clashed silently behind her. *Up!* Isabelle told herself. For the first time ever, she voluntarily and purposefully harnessed her gift. She rose three feet off the floor and hovered there, slightly bobbing up and down. The queasy feeling in her stomach was gone. Now she experienced a pulsing change in the air pressure all around her and an inexplicable inner urge to unleash herself—to explode into flight. She took a deep breath and suppressed the urge. *Now is not the time.* Still, it took discipline to ignore the needling sensation between her shoulder blades that was spurring her to soar forward. Even her hair seemed to break free of gravity's hold as it swayed in slow motion as if underwater.

Maddy's jaw dropped. "Whoa!"

"That's what I'm talking about!" Jasmine said, clearly fired up.

Isabelle's normally soft voice rang out with authority. "We should learn to *control* these gifts. We should *hone* these gifts. We have to *protect* these gifts." She lowered her voice. "That means it stays a secret. That's the only way we'll be able to help people," she paused, "and not hurt ourselves or our families in the process." Suddenly finding herself at a loss for words, she shrugged. "That's how I feel. I want to know how you feel."

A moment of silence passed that seemed a lot longer than it actually was. Maddy spoke up.

"You're basically talking about us becoming superheroes."

Isabelle settled back down to the floor, knitting her brow. "When you put it that way, Maddy, it sounds dumb."

"You *know* I'm on board," said Jasmine hopping up and giving Isabelle a hug.

Maddy got to her feet and put her hand out, palm down. She looked at Jasmine and then at Isabelle. "Don't leave me hanging, now," she said. "Team on three."

Isabelle and Jasmine looked at each other, confused, then it dawned on them.

They put their hands in with Maddy. "One, two, three. Team!"

* * *

The girls stayed up late into the night, talking about what had happened to them. Eventually, the topic came up of how they planned to hide their true identities. Jasmine assumed they'd have their own unique outfits, like comic book superheroes. Maddy suggested they should all match, since they were a team.

The idea of costumes really captured Isabelle's imagination. Maddy brought in her sketch pad and colored pencils. They all sat on the theater floor coming up with ideas and jotting down the pros and cons of each design.

At around half past midnight, Dr. McCarthy came home from the hospital and walked into the theater room to check on the girls. Isabelle and Jasmine hastily covered their drawings with blank sheets of paper. The end credits of one of their favorite animated movies was scrolling on the screen behind them. Maddy stood up to greet her dad.

"You girls are really burning the midnight oil, eh?" The paper in Maddy's hand caught her father's attention. "What's this, love?"

He took the drawing and studied the green and black spandex costume. Maddy's ears turned red.

"Are you girls planning on becoming superheroes?" he asked with a grin.

Maddy's face turned ashen and she stuttered and struggled to speak.

Jasmine leaped to her feet and spoke up. "That's a character for the comic book I'm planning to write. We were working on character design together," she said with a sweet smile. "That's, um, Broccoli Girl."

"Well, it's very good, Madeline," said her father. "I'm sure Broccoli Girl has her hands full trying to get little kids everywhere to eat their vegetables." He smiled at the drawing. "You take after your mother. I can't even draw a straight line."

"Thanks, Dad," she said, snatching the paper back.

"Well, I'm off to bed. You girls should probably do the same."

"Good night, Dad. Love you."

"Good night, Dr. McCarthy."

"You can call me Matt."

"Good night, Dr. Matt," Isabelle said.

Dr. McCarthy chuckled as he exited the theater and was off to bed.

Maddy exhaled. "Thanks, Jasmine. That was some quick thinking. He really caught me off guard there."

"You need to get ahold of yourself, girl," Jasmine said. "It wasn't like he *actually* suspected you of being a superhero."

Maddy huffed in frustration. "I know. I just panicked."

"That just goes to show you how easy it could be to accidentally give away the secret," Isabelle said. "One slip-up and the cat's out of the bag."

Jasmine scratched her chin, thoughtfully. "Well, superheroes aren't supposed to exist. We could go around and tell everyone and they'd just think we're crazy."

"You've got a point," Isabelle said, "but, it's best not to say anything to anyone. Just in case. Sooner or later, someone will see something. What if they saw our drawing, and then saw our costumes, and put two and two together?"

The girls were mulling that over when Maddy broke the silence.

"Broccoli Girl?"

They all burst into laughter.

They cleaned up their mess in the theater room and got ready to retire to Maddy's bedroom for the night. Maddy offered to join her friends on the floor with their sleeping bags, but Isabelle and Jasmine insisted, as they always did, that she could sleep in the comfort of her own bed. After they were settled in, they lay awake talking for a while longer in the darkness.

Isabelle soon found her thoughts straying to the mysterious robotic burglars. Everything about them captivated her—the way they moved, their versatility, even the apparent formidability of their advanced weapons. During a lull in the conversation, she rolled onto her side and asked, "Who do you think is behind those robotic burglars we saw?"

"Hm?" Came Maddy's voice from the darkness. "The tech burglaries? I don't know. I haven't heard anything new."

Jasmine's voice came from the nearby sleeping bag. "Robotics is your thing, Isabelle. What's your take on it?"

Isabelle drew a deep breath. "They're clearly a genius. They have access to ridiculous amounts of money and resources. Undoubtably a sociopath."

"Sounds like a recipe for disaster," Jasmine said.

Isabelle wondered if she and her friends would someday come face to face with the figure behind the burglaries. She wondered if their combined powers would be equal to the criminal's resourcefulness. She wondered if the robots were truly as dangerous as they seemed.

Isabelle was pulled out of her musings by Jasmine. "How will we get costumes?"

Maddy peered over the edge of her bed. "Order them online? Or maybe we could have them made somewhere."

"That could be traced back to us," Isabelle said.

"Right," Maddy said. "We'll have to come up with *something* short term. Let's all see what we can come up with to hide our faces. It's important our identities are protected."

"So, it's agreed," Jasmine said. "Our training begins tomorrow, but where will we do it?"

"I've been racking my brain on that one," said Maddy, "It's got to be somewhere secluded, yet somewhere we can still reach on our bikes."

"What about Granger Park?" Jasmine said. "I bet I can get Dad to load up our bikes in the truck and drop us off up there if I tell him we're biking the trails."

Isabelle frowned in the darkness. "I don't know if we can get away with practicing up there."

"The area I had in mind is pretty remote," Jasmine said. "The chances of someone stumbling across us up there is pretty slim."

Isabelle could barely make out Maddy's whisper in the darkness: "Yes, but someone *could.*"

"We'll figure it out," said Jasmine. "Don't you worry."

Before long, Maddy and Jasmine had both fallen asleep, leaving Isabelle alone with her thoughts. She stared up at the stripes of light on the ceiling that angled in through the window from the streetlamp outside. Being alone in the darkness put things in a new perspective. It felt different when her friends weren't there to reassure her at every step. For about the one hundredth time, Isabelle wondered if she was doing the right thing.

Up. She rose off the floor inside her sleeping bag. She relished the pulsing thrill that surrounded her skin, pulling on her from all sides. *Down.* She practiced fine tuning her flight control in the darkness as her friends slept.

12
THE DREAM

I**SABELLE AWOKE TO FIND HERSELF** staring at wisps of yellowish clouds in a darkening sky. Warm sand clung to her arms like a powder as she sat up. She couldn't remember why she'd been sleeping on this stretch of beach, but her body was calm. It was only her mind that kept grasping for something flitting just outside her reach.

Water surged and ebbed on the white sand in front of her. A cliff of gray rock loomed behind her and tapered toward the sea to her left and right until the jutting crags disappeared beneath the calm waters of the cove. She'd never seen the ocean before. She couldn't fathom what she was doing there now—or how she got there. One thing was sure, the sea was every bit as beautiful as she dreamed it would be.

Am I dreaming?

A twinge of disappointment mingled with her will to not wake up and break the spell. Out across the water, a thin band of land twinkled with pinpoints of light. The spires of some distant city faded into the haze as the suns hung low over the horizon.

Suns?

Isabelle blinked. Now she knew she was dreaming. She marveled at how vivid a picture her subconscious mind could paint of this alien world. The breeze was warm and salty and even the twinkles of light reflected on the water were rendered with photorealistic precision.

Her eyes landed on a lone figure, sitting on a rock facing the sea. He cast two shadows on the sand as he silently stared at the city across the water.

She didn't want to disturb his introspection but the lucidity of this dream intrigued her. How could she pass up this opportunity to converse with the stranger she'd conjured up in her subconscious mind? The warm sand bit at the soles of her feet as she approached him.

As she drew nearer, she was puzzled by the boy's familiarity. His light brown skin and buzzed head reminded her of Jayden Romano from her robotics class. Her stomach lurched.

He was even dressed as Jayden might be on any given day—in a button-up baseball jersey, jeans and high-tops. Before she could stop herself, she heard herself ask, "What are *you* doing here?"

Without turning his attention from the scenery, he answered. "This was my home."

"What?"

"Well, not mine." His voice was solemn and steady. "But it was home for others like me. It was all gone long before I came to be."

"You're not Jayden?"

The boy glanced over and shook his head.

Isabelle stared across the water to the shimmering lights on the horizon before settling down to sit in the sand next to him. She decided to play along.

"Who are you?"

The boy turned. His deep brown eyes and soft features almost glowed in the dying light of the suns.

"I guess I'm a figment of your imagination." He grinned and looked down at his own hands, as if noticing them for the first time.

"Are you referring to the fact that this is obviously a dream?" asked Isabelle, motioning to the world around her.

The boy's attention drifted back to the horizon. "Dreams are true while they last. Do we not live in dreams?"

Isabelle's mind raced to stitch together the meager tidbits he offered. Half annoyed, half amused, she tilted her head and smirked. "So, if this world *was* your home, that clearly makes you an alien." She nodded toward the sinking binary suns.

"In this dream, it would seem that *you're* the alien," said the boy, raising his eyebrows and returning the smirk.

"Touché," said Isabelle, rolling her eyes. "How can you speak my language?"

He chuckled. "I'm not. I'm a figment of your imagination, remember?" He smiled and met Isabelle's eyes. "It's *your* mind that's translating what I am, making me into what you see— turning me into something you can understand. Something familiar. Perhaps something you even admire?"

Isabelle's cheeks flushed pink in the fading light.

"In truth, I am something—if you'll excuse the expression— so *alien* that we would not be able to communicate under normal circumstances. You wouldn't look upon me as an equal. You wouldn't even be able to look upon me at all. Although, long ago . . ." He nodded toward the city on the horizon. "Long ago, the others like me—they were not very unlike you. We even had many of the same flaws. We certainly shared your arrogance and ignorance."

With each passing moment, the boy seemed less and less Jayden like. Her confusion mounted. "There are others like you?"

"Oh, yes," he said. "There are others like me, just as there are others like you." He gazed down at the sand around his shoes. "Except you're different. You see, not everyone can do what you're doing right now."

An uneasy feeling crept through Isabelle's gut. There was something too real about this dream. Something too lucid. "Is that why you're talking to me right now?"

"Ah. Getting down to brass tacks." His brown eyes again rose to meet Isabelle's. She couldn't look away, although she wanted to shrink and hide.

"We need your help," he said.

"How can I help you?" she said. "You're just a figment of my imagination!"

"You have something that belongs to us," he said.

"I don't know what you're talking about."

"You do know." He extended his empty palm and the familiar glowing blue sphere materialized and hovered there.

Isabelle opened her mouth to speak but found no words.

"You've stolen the very essence of our lives. Without it, we will perish. We must find a way to put things right before it's too late. For a millennium we've been hunted. Now, you will be."

She awoke.

*   *   *

Isabelle stared at the unfamiliar ceiling for a long moment as she tried to remember where she was. *I'm at Maddy's,* she thought with relief. Reality began to sink in, but she refused to let the bizarre dream fade. She replayed the details in her mind, hoping to prevent their evaporation.

Jasmine was stirring in the sleeping bag next to her. Maddy was perched on the edge of her bed. Isabelle sat up, still dazed.

Jasmine stretched. "I just had the weirdest dream," she said, shaking her head and staring into space.

"Dreams are true while they last," muttered Maddy from the edge of her bed.

Isabelle's ears throbbed in shock and her mind raced for the solution. How could Maddy have plucked the very words from her own dream?

Jasmine's mouth hung open as she stared at Maddy in bewilderment.

"Do we not live in dreams?" Jasmine and Isabelle said in perfect unison.

Maddy flung herself from the bed onto her knees, clutching the sleeve of Isabelle's pajamas in one hand and grabbing Jasmine's shoulder with the other. "Did we all just have the same dream?" she asked, looking back and forth between her friends.

There must be a logical explanation. Maybe one of them was talking in their sleep, sowing the seeds of suggestion in the others' sleeping and susceptible minds.

Jasmine seemed lost in thought for a moment. "Did you see the two suns?" she asked. "And the city across the water?"

"Yes!" Maddy said.

Isabelle's heart thumped harder.

Jasmine seemed to be straining to pull the details of her dream back into focus. "And Morgan Freeman was there on the beach and—"

"Morgan Freeman?" Maddy's face scrunched in confusion.

"You heard me! Morgan Freeman was telling me he was a figment of my imagination," said Jasmine.

"Wait a minute," said Maddy, shaking her head. "You mean Nikola Tesla wasn't in your dream?"

"Nikola Who-now?" asked Jasmine.

"Nikola Tesla!" Maddy motioned to Isabelle as if this was all just a normal misunderstanding that Isabelle would help clear up. "He was sitting on the beach looking at the city across the bay."

Jasmine frowned. "Just what have you got against Morgan Freeman anyway?"

"Nothing, of course," said Maddy. "You know we can't control who shows up in our dreams."

Isabelle inhaled sharply. "Maybe we can in a roundabout way."

Jasmine looked to Isabelle. "Who'd you get?"

Isabelle quickly ran through a mental list of engineers and scientists that could fill in. Somehow this seemed too important to lie about. "It was Jayden."

Jasmine and Maddy exchanged a knowing look.

"That doesn't make sense," said Maddy. "Why such a broad range of characters?"

Isabelle bristled. "Look, our dream had nothing to do with Jayden. Or Nikola Tesla or Morgan Freeman. That was just our own minds filling in the blanks. The—*person*—in our dream was someone who has something to do with the blue sphere and it sounds like they're in trouble because of us."

Jasmine seemed lost in thought for a long moment before speaking up. "When he accused us of stealing his life's essence, he showed me the sphere. How can one small thing be that important?"

"But look what it's done to us," said Isabelle. "These powers are no small thing."

Maddy's eyes bulged. "What if it's some kind of trap?"

"It could be, for all we know," Isabelle said. "But we can't ignore the fact that we all had the same dream."

"Maybe this dream connection is a side effect of—you know—what happened to us," Jasmine said. "Not necessarily an outside force reaching out to us?"

"Is there any reason to believe that someone is really in danger?" Maddy said. "Or that any of this is true?"

"Technically, no," Isabelle said. "When he said he was a figment of my imagination, I thought he was referring to his form. Maybe he meant the whole dream?"

"So, we're still going to Granger today?" asked Maddy.

Isabelle shrugged. As the minutes ticked by, the dream seemed more and more distant and easier to dismiss. "I don't see why not."

13

TRAINING DAY

GRANGER STATE PARK WAS A SPRAWLING TRACT of wilderness situated around Lake Granger. It was a wildlife preserve and featured picnic areas, several hiking trails, and a scenic bike trail that twisted through the woods. Isabelle had almost forgotten how beautiful it was. She had fond but hazy memories of family picnics there, before her mom's health started to decline.

Isabelle and Maddy sat on a table in a picnic area that was in front of a stand of pine trees. They'd sent Jasmine ahead to scout for a good spot to practice: they all agreed she'd be able to cover more ground with her powers. The bike ride from the parking lot where Jasmine's dad had dropped them off was modest, but Isabelle's legs were still burning as she took in her surroundings.

The ground was blanketed with an ochre mat of needles and the trees murmured in the breeze. Isabelle savored the woody-sweet smell of the pines behind her, and the magnificent view of the city nestled in the valley below. Woodlands sloped downwards and away from them and the hazy Blue Ridge Mountains stretched off in the distance from horizon to horizon. Isabelle marveled at how the roads and neighborhoods of Rose Valley seemed to bend around the contours of the twisting James River and the smaller, jutting ridges that covered the valley floor.

"What made you change your mind?" Isabelle said.

"What do you mean?"

"About us trying to hone these powers and put them to use. At first you were all about telling your dad, but later you were right on board."

Maddy drew a long breath. "It's hard to explain. At first, I was scared. But as time goes on, I feel more and more in control." Her brown eyes bored into Isabelle. "You won't believe how these powers of mine have grown—how in tune I feel with everything around me. I can move light objects, heavy objects, it doesn't matter. Multiple objects. Things with complex moving parts. Like I said, it's hard to explain. I feel confidence. I feel peace. I almost want to say I feel *powerful.*" Maddy grinned.

Isabelle could hardly believe her ears. *Is this the same Maddy I've known since we were five years old?*

Isabelle gave her friend a grave look. Maddy dropped her gaze to her shoes.

"Yes, I'm aware of how dangerous that feeling of power could be," she said.

"I'm feeling some of those things too," Isabelle said, "but there's always that nagging question of—"

"If we're doing the right thing?" Maddy said.

"Precisely," said Isabelle, smiling.

Maddy shrugged. "I guess what I'm trying to say is, using these powers for good is the only way I can live with what's happened to me, and for me to still be 'me.' Does that make any sense?"

Isabelle smiled. "Yes, I think it does." *I could get used to this new, more confident Maddy.*

Just then, Jasmine came effortlessly pedaling up the trail behind them. "I think I found a good spot," she called from her bike.

Maddy and Isabelle mounted their bikes and followed.

Jasmine took them down the scenic bike trail that ran right alongside the western shore of Lake Granger. Keeping up was no easy task as they had to constantly remind her to slow down. They pedaled along the rising and falling trail with the lake to their right. When they reached a large, towering rock formation just off the trail to their left, Jasmine stopped and told them they had to go on foot from here. They dismounted and walked their bikes off the trail, following Jasmine's lead.

When they reached the far side of the rock formation, Jasmine told them to leave their bikes there, making sure that they couldn't be seen from the trail. She pointed to the grassy, flat hollow below them.

"It's perfect!" said Isabelle.

Maddy put her hands on her hips and stared down into the hollow. "I can't believe we're really doing this."

Isabelle took a deep breath as she scanned the natural beauty all around her. "This is just the first step."

The hollow was hidden from all sides unless someone walked right up to the ridge the girls were standing on. The rock formation towered over the hollow to the east. Time and the elements had caused limestone boulders of all shapes and sizes to crumble off and tumble down the slope. A ridge ran along the south side of the hollow, where they stood, and gently bent north in a curve, forming the west side. To Isabelle, it almost looked like they were standing on the lip of a massive bowl. To the north was miles of thick forest—a mix of oak and pine trees. The ground below was mostly flat, but had a gentle rise toward the forest and was covered in prairie grass.

After making their way into the hollow, Isabelle called her friends to her side. "So, we're all in agreement that the first order of business is to make sure we all have total control over our abilities?"

Jasmine and Maddy nodded.

Since yesterday morning, neither Isabelle nor Maddy had lost control of their abilities. There had been no unwanted outbursts.

With time, the suppression of their powers seemed to become second nature. Although they found they really had to focus their will for the powers to manifest, they both agreed they still needed to hone their skills.

Jasmine, on the other hand, had problems. Keeping her speed, strength and agility suppressed was easier said than done, and Maddy hypothesized that since Jasmine's powers were physical, they must be more difficult to control.

Jasmine agreed to try meditation exercises with Maddy, although she was skeptical.

"This probably is not going to work," she kept repeating as Maddy brought her to the east end of the hollow. The two girls sat cross legged facing each other next to a large boulder. After Maddy talked Jasmine through different meditation techniques, she asked Jasmine to push on the boulder to test her strength. Each time, the boulder moved as if it were papier-mâché.

"We didn't come all the way out here to *not* use our powers," said Jasmine, impatiently.

"Control is essential. Before you run, you must walk." said Maddy, sitting in a lotus position. "Try again, Grasshopper."

"Who are you calling 'Grasshopper . . .'" muttered Jasmine under her breath.

Nearby, Isabelle was testing in-flight steering techniques. So far, she'd been able to rise and descend at will, but horizontal control was sketchy, at best. She knew that any motions she made with her arms and legs only had minimal effect. Despite this, it was a great relief to let loose and attempt to fly without restraint.

She thought back to how she grounded herself to prevent being seen by her father on the morning she discovered her powers. On that morning, she closed her eyes and visualized herself descending. *Maybe it works both ways.*

Hovering five feet above the ground, she closed her eyes and pushed all other thoughts and doubts out of her mind. She visualized herself flying forward. *Forward.* She inched ahead. *Yes! Forward!*

She jolted forward and stopped abruptly. "Whoa!" Isabelle began to sense that itching tingle between her shoulder blades again—a calling urge to soar. She took a deep breath and regained her composure. *Baby steps.*

When she was satisfied she'd mastered control of small horizontal movements, she started more complex movements. She moved diagonally, then in arcs, then changed directions, each time increasing the distance she moved.

"Any change at all?" asked Maddy as Jasmine reached out and shoved the boulder with a single hand. Again, the heavy boulder tottered in place.

"No, I just don't know my own strength," said Jasmine.

"I'm confident that mind will prevail over matter," said Maddy. "Try again."

Jasmine groaned.

"If you keep thinking it won't work, then it won't," Maddy said. "We can't have you going around breaking things. You might accidentally hurt someone. Clear your mind of all doubts. Clear your mind of all ambitions. Humble yourself before the universe."

Jasmine shook her head in disbelief. "Give me a break! Do you hear yourself right now, Maddy?"

"Do it!"

Jasmine closed her eyes and exhaled. She sat in silence for a moment . . . then reached out and pushed the boulder.

It didn't budge. She pushed again and the boulder remained resolute. She had somehow managed to switch her power off at will.

Maddy smiled. "You have learned well, Grasshopper. Let's try it again."

Jasmine's mood improved after she began to have success in suppressing her abilities. After a few minutes, Jasmine could turn her strength on and off like a switch. After mastering the boulder-push, Maddy and Jasmine decided it was time to move on to new lessons. They invented a drill where they stood facing each other about fifty feet apart near the massive rock formation. At their feet were rocks and boulders of all shapes and sizes. Maddy lifted soccer ball sized stones with her telekinetic power and propelled them directly at Jasmine. Jasmine either dodged or ducked them, letting them impact the formation behind her.

Rock after rock exploded into dust behind her. The thwacks of the stones pelting the wall echoed through the hollow. Occasionally, Jasmine would extend her arm and let a rock break against her palm. After a few minutes, bits of broken rock piled at Jasmine's feet and her hair was dusted with a fine powder.

As they became more proficient at it, Maddy ramped up the speed and fury with which she hurled the rocks. Maddy found that using hand gestures helped her focus her powers. Gestures that mimicked lifting helped her more easily move the rocks off the ground and caused them to hover. Forceful pushing or punching motions sent them streaking toward her friend.

Jasmine ducked, jumped, flipped, and spun as she avoided every missile. Maddy widened her stance, scowled with concentration, and lifted two rocks at once, sending them both toward Jasmine in a blur. Jasmine turned sideways as the rocks passed harmlessly on either side of her, shattering into a shower of dust and shards behind her.

"You've got to be faster than that, girl!" Jasmine yelled, laughing. She laughed a little too long and almost caught a rock in the face, deflecting it with her forearm and tumbling to the side.

"Ha ha!" cried Maddy.

Jasmine kicked a nearby rock toward Maddy's head, but another rock leaped up from the ground, deflecting it. A volley of rocks came forth and Jasmine deflected or dodged every single one.

Isabelle hovered ten feet off the ground and watched from a safe distance as her friends dueled. She was amazed at their skill, but especially shocked at Maddy's aggressiveness.

"These girls are going to be unstoppable," she said to herself as she grinned down at them.

Feeling euphoric, Isabelle closed her eyes. *Fly*, she thought.

She surged forward, certain she'd left her stomach somewhere behind her. Her hair whipped her face and tears streaked from the corners of her eyes as she rushed forth through the air. Her body flattened into a horizontal position as she intuitively zoomed around the hollow with pinpoint precision. Her heart screamed that she was always meant to fly: her whole life had been leading her to this. She finally and totally gave in to the nagging urge. It was exhilarating.

She darted along the ridge and careened around the rock formation. Twisting in the air, she banked between two tall pine trees . . . but something was in the way.

She flared to a stop and found herself hovering face to face with a boy.

The blood drained from Isabelle's face as she realized she was staring at the chubby face of Gavin Barnard. Apparently, he'd climbed a tree on the ridge to spy on them.

Isabelle suppressed the jolts of panic that were surging through her body and lowered herself to solid ground. Gavin stared down at her, horror-struck. His cheeks were a splotchy red and his eyes were wide.

In her state of shock, she was unsure if she could speak in a convincing manner, but she tried: "Where's my brother?"

Gavin's mouth hung open for a moment, then he stuttered, "He went home already."

"Does he know?"

"No, m'lady."

Isabelle gritted her teeth. "You're alone?"

Gavin nodded.

"How much have you seen?"

Gavin gulped. "I haven't seen anything."

Isabelle frowned. A moment ago, she was face to face with him while hovering twenty feet off the ground. She glanced to her left. From his vantage point in the tree, he could probably see Jasmine and Maddy playing their rock game right now. She could hear the thwacks of Maddy's rocks echoing through the hollow below. Gavin was a crummy liar.

Although her heart fluttered with horror, she forced herself to glare at him.

"You'll leave *now* and you'll tell *no one* what you've seen today." She hoped her bluff would resonate. "Ever."

Again, he nodded, his curly hair bouncing.

Isabelle doubted she could utter another word without her voice cracking, so she simply raised a single finger to her lips. "Shhh."

Turning on the spot, she walked away, looking for a path back down into the hollow.

14
DONNING THE MASK

ISABELLE AWOKE ON SUNDAY MORNING sore from the previous day's bike ride. She shuffled to the kitchen and found Mason sitting at the table eating a bowl of cereal.

"Well, if it isn't the cootie queen!"

Isabelle ignored the obligatory insult and grabbed a bowl from the cabinet.

Mason watched carefully as Isabelle poured herself a bowl of cereal and closed the box.

"We're out of milk."

Isabelle clenched her jaw and glared at her brother who was happily munching away at his own cereal. "You could have told me before . . . Never mind." She reopened the box, awkwardly poured the cereal back in, resealed the bag and re-closed the box lid. After putting away the cereal, she went to the refrigerator and pulled out a package of bagels and a tub of cream cheese.

"You're not going to ruin *this* for me, are you?" She glared at her brother, but he seemed to be in his own little world as he poked away at his tablet.

She bit her lip and resisted the impulse to ask him if Gavin had mentioned seeing anything out of the ordinary. She'd been on edge ever since he cut their training session short yesterday, but Jasmine and Maddy had repeatedly assured her there was nothing to worry about.

After enjoying her bagel on the back-porch swing, Isabelle retreated to her room to work on MechAnna. Pouring all her attention into her creation seemed to be the only way for her to calm her mind.

On Friday afternoon she'd started implementing Crystal's suggestions for fixing MechAnna's circuit board, but she'd left for Maddy's sleepover before she could complete them. She'd rerouted the first power source and installed the second, but that was as far as she got. Reorienting herself with where she was with the project, she remembered she only had the capacitors to add.

She rummaged through the drawers of her crafter's box and quickly found the two capacitors she needed before plugging in her soldering iron. After a few minutes, the capacitors were soldered securely to the board and MechAnna was reassembled. Isabelle ran a few tests, then powered her up.

"Hey, Anna."

"What is it, meat bag?" said the synthesized voice. MechAnna's blocky head swiveled around.

"Meat bag. That's a new one," Isabelle said, unfazed. "Anna, run proprioceptive acuity test." She unplugged her soldering iron and replaced it on its rack before shifting in her seat and bringing her laptop out of sleep mode.

She held her breath as MechAnna's limbs whirred to life and ran through their range of motion. She pumped her fists with joy as MechAnna's arms folded back into their idle position with not a hint of smoke.

Just then, Isabelle's dad passed by the open door, tousle headed and holding a cup of coffee.

"Who are you talking to in here, sweetie?"

Servos and gears whirred as MechAnna's head swiveled around and looked directly at Isabelle's father.

"Dad, meet MechAnna," she said, beaming with pride. "Anna, this is Dad."

"Greetings, human filth," said MechAnna in its amicable synthesized female voice.

"Oh, wow. I didn't know she could do *that*. Hello." He raised a hand and wiggled his fingers. "That's pretty neat."

She blinked at her father. He was saying 'hello' to an intelligent robotic personal assistant that his daughter created from scratch and all he could come up with was, 'That's pretty neat?'

"Well, I'm glad you're so excited. I'll leave you to it then." He turned to leave. "Beep boop, human filth," he chimed in a robotic voice as he disappeared into the hallway.

"Anna, go to sleep."

"Affirmative, maggot." The robot went still and its eyes dimmed.

Isabelle stared at her creation. One of her major problems seemed to be solved . . . so why wasn't she feeling more relieved? She frowned as her mind raced for the solution. MechAnna sat silent and still—raw and unhoned.

Just like me.

She thought back to the conversation with her father on Friday night and how she then knew that her supernatural ability would be put to good use. Secret, but used to its fullest potential. Why should MechAnna be any different?

Again, the robotic burglars intruded into her thoughts. The fact that she had the misfortune to bump into them on Friday morning still seemed like some surreal dream. What if MechAnna possessed something that could help combat them?

As Isabelle stared at MechAnna, deep in thought, a new worry came crashing down onto her already burdened conscience. Her family—her father, her brother. Would they be safe if she really followed through with fighting crime? Would some criminal look to hurt one of them to manipulate her? What about Maddy's mother and father? What about Jasmine's parents and her baby sisters? In all the commotion and confusion of what was happening to her in the past 72 hours, she hadn't given thought to how her decisions might affect the people she loved. A thousand irksome worries began to gnaw at her.

She longed for the refuge of her friends' support. She gritted her teeth at her laptop as she launched her video conferencing program, VidHype, and checked to see if her friends were online. A quick glance showed that Jasmine was. She double-clicked on her screen name.

A few moments later a window popped up with her friend's smiling face.

"Hey, girl!" Jasmine's voice came from the laptop, small and tinny.

"Hey. Do you know where Maddy is?"

"Yeah. Actually, I'm playing a game with her right now."

"Tell her to launch VidHype." Isabelle pushed her eyeglasses back up into place with a single finger. "I want to talk to you guys together."

Jasmine's key clacking came through the speakers of her laptop as she relayed the message to Maddy. A moment later, Maddy's screen name jumped up to the list of online friends. She double-clicked on it. Another window popped up.

"What's up, Isabelle?" asked on-screen Maddy.

"Just wanted to talk to you guys."

"Everything okay?" asked Jasmine.

"Yeah, I'm fine." Isabelle leaned back in her seat. "I've fixed MechAnna's circuit board."

"Finally!" came Maddy's voice from the laptop.

"Congratulations," said Jasmine. "See? I told you you'd work out the bugs."

"And," said Isabelle as she glanced over at the robot, "I've been doing a lot of thinking. Maybe Anna could—you know—help us utilize these abilities of ours."

Jasmine smiled. "A smart-mouthed robotic sidekick! I like it!"

Isabelle winced at how trite it all sounded.

Maddy exhaled. "I don't know, Isabelle," she said. "Let's face it. Anna is not in the same league as those burglar robots. They'd eat her alive."

Maddy's words stung, but Isabelle knew she was right. She'd been thinking about the criminal robots' sensor arrays. The robots seemed to function at a high level when it came to interacting with their surroundings, and she knew there had to be some kind of optics. "I was thinking more along the lines of countermeasures. What do you think, Maddy? What are those robots using to see?"

Maddy seemed lost in thought for a moment. "I'd say they both have FLIR cameras."

"You're the engineer. How could we counter that? Could we jam it?"

Maddy frowned. "We'd have to know a lot more about the cameras and how they're broadcasting data."

"What about a laser pointer?" asked Jasmine.

"No," said Maddy. "It would have to stay aimed directly at the device's sensor at all times. But you've got the right idea. You'd need some kind of IR emitter."

"Anna already has one," said Isabelle. "She's equipped with a built-in remote control for a variety of electronic household devices."

Maddy nodded. "Okay, but that would be way too weak. You'd really have to amplify it. Maybe you could increase the number of emitters. Or utilize different lenses."

Isabelle slowly nodded. At last, she knew what she had to do. "Thank you so much for helping me brainstorm," she said. "I've been doing nothing but stressing. As if dealing with Anna isn't enough, that dream, and now Gavin—"

Jasmine snorted. "That curly-headed little troglodyte? Let him tell someone! They'll think he's even more crazy than usual."

"Maybe I've been overthinking things again," said Isabelle.

"Alright, Isabelle," said Jasmine. "Let's hear more about this breakthrough you've had with Anna!"

Isabelle could tell Jasmine was trying to help take her mind off things. Her friends had watched MechAnna rise from her humble beginnings over the months, but had never seen her fully functional. A smile spread across Isabelle's face. "Want to say hello?"

"Of course!"

"Sure!"

Isabelle twisted in her chair to retrieve her robot. "Hey Anna."

The light blue discs blinked to life and the gray plastic head swiveled to look for its creator. "What is it, dirt bag?"

"Whoa, you got roasted!" howled Jasmine.

Maddy lifted a finger to offer her sage advice. "Right. That attitude might undermine your robot's helpful purpose."

"Yeah," said Isabelle. "It's a bug I need to work out before the Tech Fair. For the life of me, I can't find the code that's causing it. The good news is I've solved the circuit board. With no other distractions, I should be able to track down this bug. It's probably just one little line of code." She pushed aside the nagging thought that it was only with Crystal's help that any progress was made at all.

Jasmine raised an eyebrow. "You need to take a break, girl. You're overworking yourself. We're getting ready to play another round of *Divide and Conquer.* Do you want to join?"

"Maybe I *should* take a break," said Isabelle.

"One more thing before we sign off," said Maddy. "You two still haven't told me what you came up with to hide your identities. Like masks or something. Bring it with you tomorrow to school, but keep them hidden in your backpacks, okay?"

"Oh! You're going to love mine!" said Jasmine.

Isabelle had forgotten. "Alright. I'll come up with something before tomorrow."

"See you guys in the game." Jasmine prepared to log off.

"Give me a couple of minutes and I'll be there," Isabelle said.

They all signed off from their video conference and Isabelle put MechAnna back to sleep. She got up and walked to the doorway of her room and peeked down the hallway. She could partially see into the living room and determined that her dad was on the couch watching a baseball game.

Stealthily, she padded down the hallway and entered her dad's bedroom.

Creeping up to the bedside table, she quickly opened the drawer and rummaged around inside. At last, she found what she was looking for. Her heart raced as she stared down at the purple sequined sleep mask that had once belonged to her mother. She stuffed it into the pocket of her pajama bottoms and tiptoed out of the room.

15

UNUSUAL SUSPECT

Isabelle and her friends chatted and laughed as they walked past the brick storefronts of Old Town on their way to school on Monday morning.

Things were looking up for Isabelle. Not only had she broken out of her slump with MechAnna, but she'd put all the anxiety and fear about their new abilities behind her. Gavin was nothing to worry about. The future was rife with opportunity and untapped potential.

Jasmine couldn't seem to stop smiling. "That training session was awesome."

"I know," said Maddy. "You really made great strides in getting your strength under control.

"It's hard to believe it's just been a few days when I look at how your power has grown, Maddy," said Jasmine. "You don't even need to practice. You're *that* good."

"Oh yeah," Maddy said. "About those robots we saw. They tried to rob *another* tech company, but they were thwarted by the police!"

Jasmine raised an eyebrow. "Did they catch them?"

"Did they find out who's behind it all?" asked Isabelle.

"Nope," said Maddy. "The police were staking out the Tech Basin where they thought they might strike next and they were right. They stopped the heist, but they couldn't keep the robots from slipping away."

Jasmine smiled. "At least they prevented another robbery."

"A small victory," Isabelle said. Again, she wondered what kind of person had the technological talent and the sheer gall to attempt such brazen crimes.

Maddy's face suddenly lit up with recollection. "Remember we were supposed to come up with a way to hide our identities? Did you all come up with something?"

"Totally," Jasmine said.

"Such as it is." Isabelle sighed.

"I have a little surprise for you," said Maddy. "A little extra touch to complete the . . ."

Isabelle looked up to see what was wrong.

Maddy stared at the chain link barrier to their right. Isabelle realized they were near the intersection of Mine and Mechanic Streets. All three girls stopped in their tracks. A yellow school bus trundled by in front of them and two high school girls strode by on the opposite side of the road, but all Isabelle saw was the tree line and the mysterious darkness that lay beyond.

Hidden behind the thick growth of trees and below the chain link barrier was the opening to the tunnel. A casual passerby could be forgiven for not knowing there was a creek or a tunnel there at all. Isabelle was sure that all three of them were wondering the same thing. *Where did that sphere come from and what has it done to us?*

Isabelle's skin began to crawl. Anxiety swept over her and the squirming mass of eels returned to her stomach, but there was more. There was an overwhelming feeling that they were not alone—that they were being watched. Her friends seemed to be sensing it too.

As soon as she saw the black SUV parked across the street, her heart skipped a beat. Gathering herself, she nudged Maddy's arm and they continued moving down the sidewalk.

"I see them too," said Jasmine out of the corner of her mouth. Maddy kept walking with her head rigidly forward.

Isabelle dared another look at the black SUV. Seated in the front were two figures wearing black neckties and suit jackets. The driver was wearing a brimmed felt hat and his partner wore sunglasses. The driver's arm rested along the open window and his hand clutched the door. Oddly, he was wearing gray suede gloves.

Fearing she'd been staring too long, she forced herself to turn her head.

There had been an ice-cold detachment to the driver's stare. Isabelle was sure he was looking right at her, but there was no flare of recognition. He seemed to stare right *through* her. *Usually when you catch someone staring at you, they look away.*

Isabelle couldn't resist the urge to look again. She marshaled her courage and turned her head.

The men's faces were almost porcelain white and had a high sheen to them, like they'd rubbed petroleum jelly all over their skin. Their lips looked unnaturally red. *Are they wearing lipstick?* Their features looked identical—they could be twins. And they didn't converse with each other, or move at all.

They just sat and stared.

* * *

Isabelle arrived outside Mrs. Stacey's robotics classroom with the two strange men in the SUV weighing heavily on her mind. Jasmine was creeped out but said there was no need to worry. Maddy wouldn't stop talking about secret government agencies, conspiracies, and cover-ups. Unsure *what* to think, Isabelle decided to push the thought of them aside for the moment.

When she arrived, the door to the robotics classroom was closed and most of the students were gathered outside in the concourse. There was an unusual amount of whispering this morning and she couldn't help but think something was wrong.

She scanned the scene for Jayden and wrestled with an odd twinge of relief when she found him leaning against a pillar with his headphones on. She walked up and tapped his shoulder. He took off his headphones and let them hang around his neck.

"What's going on?" she said. She nudged aside the memories of her recent dream. How mortifying would it be if Jayden knew his visage had played a starring role?

Jayden blinked and raised an eyebrow. "What rock have *you* been under? Haven't you heard what happened this weekend? Police are in there with Mrs. Marshall—"

Isabelle shook her head. "What's the principal doing in there? Where's Mrs. Stacey?"

"Mrs. Stacey is a suspect in the tech burglaries. She's on a leave of absence."

Isabelle's first reaction was to laugh, but Jayden's expression was like stone.

"You're serious?" Her hand shot up to stifle a yelp. A thousand questions surged into her mind, but all she could ask was, "Why?"

"The police have some evidence—"

"That's ridiculous!"

"Listen, Isabelle," said Jayden, calmly. "The FBI questioned her this weekend. Forensics found some component that had broken off one of the robots at the scene of the latest break-in attempt. They traced its serial number to a batch that was sold to the academy."

"This is crazy. Mrs. Stacey is no evil mastermind!"

"There's always the possibility it was one of us." Jayden gestured to the throng of students scattered around near the classroom entrance, talking in hushed voices.

Isabelle opened her mouth to speak, ready to declare that notion ludicrous, but stopped short. *Could the evil mastermind really be one of us?*

Jayden crossed his arms. "What I can't figure out is what *these* guys are doing here." He inclined his head toward the closed door. "They're not FBI, they're local detectives." When he noticed the confused look on Isabelle's face, he explained. "Usually, federal law enforcement would run the investigation when there's a high-profile industrial espionage outbreak like this. Not local police." He shrugged. "Maybe this case is different because robots were involved." He frowned and shook his head. "Or maybe it's something else entirely."

Isabelle couldn't understand how Jayden could remain so calm and analytical with their teacher under suspicion and a major crime investigation hitting so close to home.

The door opened and a man's deep voice came from the classroom, apologizing for cutting into the principal's time. The students waiting in the concourse parted and let two men pass through on their way to the exit.

First came a mustached, middle-aged man in a brown suit jacket who smiled and said good morning to the students as he passed. His dark head of hair was dusted with gray at the temples and his face was rough but friendly—almost grandfatherly. His young partner, wearing a slim-fitting dark suit and a close-cropped beard, followed, silent and wooden.

Mrs. Marshall stood inside the doorway and motioned for the students to enter. Silently, they filed in and took their seats.

Tall and regal, even under these stressful circumstances, Mrs. Marshall stood in front of Mrs. Stacey's desk in a gray tweed skirt suit. Normally wearing a warm smile, today her face was solemn and she looked as if she might not have slept the night before.

"Good morning." A long, agonizing moment passed as she looked around at the roomful of students. "As I'm sure all of you have heard, an incident possibly involving your teacher, Mrs. Stacey, has occurred outside the academy and has impacted the Rose Valley Community. I've sent emails to your parents, along with a follow-up letter to update your families on the support plan we have in place."

Isabelle had been holding on to the slimmest of hopes that this was all some misunderstanding. She was still struggling to believe what she was hearing. How could federal and local law enforcement get it so wrong?

"I want to reassure you and your families that Cavett Academy is a safe place and we have staff to talk to. If any of you need to speak to someone, you should let a teacher know or visit our guidance counselor's office. As always, our goal is to work together, support each other, and to be productive."

Mrs. Marshall paused. "For the time being, Mr. Lim will be filling in." She beckoned to Daniel who was at his usual station at the side of the classroom.

His eyebrows rose and he pointed to himself. "Me?" he mouthed before making his way to the front of the room.

Nodding, Mrs. Marshall continued addressing the class. "It's my understanding that you're all preparing your final projects for the Tech Fair coming up at the end of this month. So, you're going to have a free work day today to do that."

Isabelle watched as Daniel arrived at Mrs. Marshall's side.

"Go ahead and begin," she said. "Mr. Lim—"

"Just Daniel."

"Yes, Daniel will be able to answer any questions you might have and help you." The room erupted into a hissing swell of whispers. Isabelle watched as Mrs. Marshall spoke to Daniel in a low voice and ticked off her fingers, one by one.

Jayden nodded toward them. "I bet she's telling him what he can and can't say about Mrs. Stacey. She knows we're going to ask."

Isabelle grunted. Jayden was usually right about these sorts of things.

The classroom door opened and Crystal Skorch started to slink toward the back of the room, but an eagle-eyed Mrs. Marshall intercepted her. Crystal's face was shining with sweat and her lips had a blue tinge.

Is she sick?

Isabelle pretended to get out her notebook and review some notes, but from her vantage point near the front of the room she could make out almost every word of their conversation.

"No, I'm fine. It was just a little food poisoning."

"I really think you should see the nurse. I won't give you a tardy, but you need to go now."

"No, I'm feeling fine now," said Crystal, rubbing her stomach with both hands.

"I need for you to see the nurse. That is not a request."

"Alright," said Crystal, her entire demeanor darkening. She skulked out of the room and class resumed.

Isabelle was wondering what was going on with Crystal's health when Daniel came over to her table. She nearly jumped out of her skin when he spoke.

"How's MechAnna coming along?" he asked.

For just a moment, all the intrigue melted away and Isabelle smiled.

"Great! I finally got past the circuit board problem. The microcontroller was resetting because my motors were causing a dead short when they switched directions. I added a separate power supply for the microcontroller to get around it." Isabelle felt a pang of guilt for not revealing that it was Crystal's idea.

He considered her solution for a moment. "I like it," he said, stroking his chin. "Sometimes there's nothing wrong with a little over-engineering. It can give you some extra versatility in the end. Keep up the good work." Daniel flashed an encouraging thumbs-up and started to turn toward Jayden.

Isabelle knew Daniel wouldn't be allowed to say anything, but she plowed forward anyway. She had always had an excellent rapport with Daniel; maybe that would make a difference.

"About Mrs. Stacey," she said in a low voice, "do you know anything? There's no chance that she did something illegal, is there?"

Daniel's breath caught, and he sighed. Isabelle saw a shimmer of something in his eyes; it might have been pity. He stole a quick, sideways look at Mrs. Marshall as she observed the class from Mrs. Stacey's desk, looking as out-of-place as a tree on the lunar surface.

"You know I'm not supposed to talk about it," he said, sympathetically. "But it's just a precaution. They can't very well have her here during an ongoing investigation. I'm sure once they've eliminated her from their list of suspects, she'll be right back."

Isabelle opened her mouth, but Daniel cut her off. "Please don't ask any more. I'm really not supposed to say anything." He turned back to Jayden who was typing with his headphones on.

"How's that debugging coming along?"

16
TOTAL CHAOS

AFTER SCHOOL, THE GIRLS TOOK THEIR USUAL ROUTE home. They turned south on Mine Street, chatting as they went. As they neared the intersection of Mine and Mechanic Streets, Isabelle was reminded of the two strange men they saw that morning in the black SUV. She took a quick look around but they were nowhere to be seen.

"Do you think those weird guys we saw this morning have something to do with what's been going on?" she asked in a hushed voice. "Remember our dream? We were told that someone would be hunting us."

Jasmine shuddered. "Those were a couple of weird-looking dudes, but they didn't seem to be hunting us. They were just sitting there."

"Right," said Maddy. "Maybe they weren't there for us. They were there for surveillance. I bet they're here because of all the activity that's been happening around Rose Valley. It's government agents and—"

"Not there for us?" Isabelle scoffed. "We're neck deep in all the 'activity' that's been happening around Rose Valley. When three people all have the same dream, I think it's worth taking note of the message in that dream!"

"Fair enough," said Maddy.

Isabelle tried to calm her flaring temper. She had the distinct feeling her friends weren't taking things seriously.

They entered Old Town, the historic downtown quarter of Rose Valley. Old brick shops, relics of a bygone era, lined each side of the street. Back in the coal mining and railroad days of Rose Valley, Mine Street was a major thoroughfare, but today hardly a soul was in sight.

"Have you guys seen that girl that was picking on us last week?" asked Maddy, breaking the long silence.

"You mean Crystal?" said Isabelle.

"I guess so. She looks horrible. What's going on with her, anyway?"

Before Isabelle could respond, a clanging noise startled them all. Across the street in an alley between two old brick shops, a man in a black hooded sweatshirt had dropped a prybar and furtively looked around as he picked it back up. He went back to prying at the window of a car parked in the alleyway.

The girls ducked behind a van parked on their side of the street. Isabelle's heart thumped double-time. Several emotions fluttered through her all at once: outrage that he would do this in broad daylight, fear they'd be spotted and harmed. Not to mention, confusion about how she and her friends should react. "Did he see us?" she whispered.

Jasmine peeked around the rear of the van. "No, I don't think so."

Maddy opened her backpack and was looking inside. "This is our chance!" she whispered. "This is what we trained for!"

"We trained for like a *day!*" Isabelle shook her head. "We don't have a plan."

Jasmine bounced on the balls of her feet and clenched her fists. "We don't *need* a plan! We go over there and kick his butt!"

Maddy was still gazing into her open backpack as the man across the street continued to pry at the window. A look of resolve suddenly washed over her face.

"Put on your disguises," she said, quietly.

"Our what?" whispered Isabelle.

"Your mask! Your disguise! To hide your identity." Maddy reached into her bag.

Jasmine seemed giddy with excitement. "It's showtime!" She reached into her backpack and pulled out an elaborate, plumed Mardi Gras masquerade mask.

Isabelle and Maddy stared.

"What?" she said when she saw the stunned look she got from her friends. "My mom collects these! Isn't it awesome?"

Isabelle hesitated, then opened her backpack and took out the purple, sequined sleep mask. She had roughly cut two irregular eye holes large enough to accommodate her glasses. She slipped the mask over her eyes.

Jasmine shook her head in disappointment.

Maddy took out a light blue surgeon's mask and scrub cap that she had taken from her dad's supply. "I almost forgot," she said, rummaging in her bag. "Put these on." She threw them each a hospital gown, a scrub cap, and a set of vinyl gloves. "I was going to tell you about these this morning, but we got sidetracked by those guys in the SUV."

Jasmine looked down at the bundle in her hands, almost at a loss for words. "What are *these* for?"

"You don't want anyone to recognize your clothes!" hissed Maddy. "Put them on!"

Isabelle wondered if she was in some bizarre but lucid dream. "You're kidding, right?"

"No. These are just temporary. Come on. Hurry!"

The girls did as they were told. When they were done, they paused and looked at each other—three figures in hospital gowns, scrub caps, vinyl gloves, and each in her distinctive mask.

"We look ridiculous!" said Isabelle. "We've got a bird of paradise over here," she motioned to Jasmine in her plumed mask; "the Lone Ranger if he danced in a Las Vegas show," referring to her own sparkly mask; "and—well, *your* outfit comes together nicely, Maddy. Good job."

"It doesn't matter how we look," said Maddy. "Are you ready to do this?"

"I mean, if we're going to be taken seriously, we've got to *look* the part. We've got to . . ."

Isabelle realized her friends had already walked out from behind the van and were approaching the man in the alley.

She took a deep breath and tried to swallow the lump in her throat. Adrenaline surged as she stepped out into the open. All the blood drained from her buzzing head and she felt dizzy. It was a short walk across the street, but it seemed like time slowed down with every step she took.

Isabelle finally caught up with her friends and pushed her way in between them, falling into step. The hooded man looked up to see the three masked figures walking toward him. He stopped prying at the window, seemingly not sure if he believed his eyes. His face was half-hidden in shadow, despite the dazzling afternoon sun, but Isabelle could see every line and pockmark in crisp detail. His knuckles blanched as he gripped the prybar.

The girls stopped and stood, three abreast, staring him down while striking their best superhero poses. Isabelle stood in the center with her hands on her hips while Jasmine and Maddy flanked her on either side with crossed arms.

"What is this?" His leathern face seemed to crack as he displayed a mirthless smile.

Isabelle didn't know what the next move was. *What do we say? Do I speak? Wait. Does Jasmine or Maddy say something? Nobody's talking. I'd better say something.*

"Um, stop right there!" said Isabelle in a gruff voice.

"Are you a little girl?" asked the man.

"No! We're—your worst nightmare!" said Jasmine. "No, that sounded stupid," she added under her breath.

The man doubled over in laughter. He pointed the prybar in their direction. "What are you three supposed to be?"

The girls stood their ground.

"Get out of here, kids," he said, dismissing them. "Your mommies and daddies wouldn't want anything bad to happen to you." He slapped the prybar against his open palm in what Isabelle took to be a barely-veiled threat.

For another dozen heartbeats they all stood their ground, neither side backing down. Isabelle was on the verge of panic. *Now what do we do?* Her nerve and sheer bravery had just about reached their limit when Maddy struck.

Like a rattlesnake's strike, Maddy's hand twitched and the prybar flew out of the man's hand, shattering the car window.

Maddy cringed. The thief jumped back, startled by the unseen force that had just ripped the weapon from his grip. He looked down at his empty hand for a moment longer, as if trying to fathom what had just happened. Isabelle froze as terror sunk its claws into her. She couldn't fight; she couldn't flee.

Jasmine rushed forward to grab the man, but he spun out of the way. She stumbled, tripped on the curb, and awkwardly fell into the front of the car: the grill crumpled and the 3,000-pound car tumbled like a toy. With a series of terrible crunches, the car went end over end into the alleyway and came to rest upside down on top of another car. A piercing alarm echoed through the street. Isabelle stared, wide-eyed and stunned. Her nostrils detected the tell-tale fumes of gasoline.

"He's getting away!" shouted Jasmine as the man sprinted down the sidewalk.

Maddy took two steps after him, dropped to one knee, and threw both of her hands toward the yellow newspaper vending machine half a block away. As the man ran past, the newspaper box lifted from its resting place and shot left. Completely missing the thief, it crashed through a store window.

"Not good!" cried Maddy. The crook turned the corner and was out of sight, but Isabelle still stood, her feet encased in invisible concrete.

Jasmine started to run after him but skidded to a halt when she noticed the black smoke drifting from the two cars in the alley. "Aw, man!" she cried, seemingly unsure of which way to run. With a *whoosh*, the cars burst into flames. "No, no, no, no!" she wailed in frustration.

Sirens echoed in the distance. *So soon? Had someone already called 911?*

Abandoning any hope of salvaging the mission, Maddy and Jasmine ran across the street, ripping off their costumes and stuffing them into their backpacks.

"Isabelle, snap out of it! Come on!" yelled Maddy as she backpedaled away.

Finally breaking free from fear's clutches, Isabelle ducked into the alleyway, just as a police cruiser came skidding around the corner two blocks away. *How did they get here so fast?* A small crowd of people had collected around the smashed store window down the street.

Isabelle looked across the street at her friends who had stopped around the corner of a building as they waited for her to follow them. They were wildly beckoning her to run across the street to join them but it was too late. The officers in the cruiser were skidding to a halt right in front of her, flashing red and blue. She was cut off from her friends.

The doors of the cruiser popped open and two officers in black uniforms leaped out, their hands resting on their sidearms. Isabelle looked past the cruiser, but her friends were gone.

With her heart threatening to thump out of her chest, she turned around to look behind her. The alleyway was blocked with the two wrecked cars that were now fully engulfed in flames beneath a billowing tower of black smoke. There was nowhere to run.

In an instant, her choices played out in her mind in agonizing detail. Surrender and she'll take the sole blame for the destroyed cars and the smashed store window. Her dad's heart would be broken and her enrollment at Cavett Academy would be in jeopardy. Fly and maybe she could get away (or maybe she'd be shot at). Either way, she'd be exposing the existence of her power. She'd run the risk of eventually being caught anyway, and become a criminal *and* a scientific test subject.

"Stop right there!" shouted one of the officers. "Turn around and get your hands where I can see them!" Trembling and in a cold sweat, Isabelle raised her hands and turned to face the officers as they closed in on her.

"Lay down on the ground!" bellowed the other officer. She bent her knees as if she was about to go down to the ground. She hesitated. "Lay down on the ground, now!" came his booming voice as he reached for the handcuffs on his belt.

There was only one real choice.

Isabelle swallowed hard and gritted her teeth. She sensed the familiar change in the air pressure all around her and the tugging sensation between her shoulder blades. She rocketed straight up into the air, leaving a swirling whirlwind in the column of black smoke.

She was gone.

The two officers stopped dead in their tracks, looking at each other stupidly as the cars in the alleyway burned in front of them.

17

EXODUS

ISABELLE LOOKED OVER THE LINE OF CODE she was typing. She'd been so intently focused that she'd lost all track of time. Frustration needled at her. Despite devoting her undivided attention to the single line of code she was trying to finish, she seemed to be spinning her wheels. She leaned back and rubbed her watering eyes.

When her vision came back into focus . . . she was no longer in her bedroom.

Her desk seemed to have been transported to a white, featureless room. She blinked as her eyes adjusted to the sterile brightness. Her heart performed a double backflip, every muscle in her body tensed. Slowly, the familiar surreality settled in and she realized she must be dreaming.

She rose from her chair and turned on the spot to examine her surroundings. The wall behind her was dominated by a large, rectangular glass portal. There were several consoles with glowing screens and buttons—the very archetypal image of what she thought the control room of a futuristic spaceship would look like. One of the seats was occupied. She could only make out the silhouette of the boy that was seated there, but she already knew who it was.

As she approached him, the scene outside the portal came into view. The glowing atmosphere of a blue planet curved off into the distance as far as she could see. The unfamiliar shape of an alien continent peered out from behind swirls of white clouds. A sharp line of twilight's shadow bisected the world, separating night from day. It was only when she noticed the clustered lights of a coastal city that the utter darkness of the rest of the continent sunk in. The only sign of civilization was compressed into a relatively small area on the coast. The rest was barren and black.

Isabelle drew a deep breath. "I have a million questions for—"

"They're running the evacuation from there," said the boy. "Difficult times create many heroes, but if you ask me, the real heroes are the ones still down there. Not all of them will make it off." Still dressed in his jeans and baseball jersey, he looked strangely out of place at the helm of the control station. He stared out the portal, his reflection in the glass betraying the sadness in his eyes.

Isabelle's eyes uncomfortably shifted between his reflection and the scene unfolding outside.

"May I?" she asked, nodding toward the empty seat beside him.

"Suit yourself. This is *your* dream, after all."

Isabelle eased into the seat and glanced at the strange controls. They were beyond her comprehension.

She squinted out the window at the dozen or so tiny specks of light rising from the planet's surface in slow motion and imagined each to be a shuttle that was ferrying an untold number of horrified people to the much larger transport ship holding geosynchronous orbit over the city.

"This will be the last time they see their home world," said the boy.

Her heart sank. "So, all this happened before you were . . . Before you came to be?"

"That's right." He turned away from the window and his eyes met hers. Staring into the face of this imaginary kid that looked like Jayden was unsettling, but she couldn't bear to turn away.

"So how can you be showing me all this, if you've never seen it?" She cringed, hoping her question wouldn't somehow offend him.

He smiled. "It's a perfectly valid question." He turned back to the window. "My ancestors' ancestors showed them—they shared their memories. And in turn, my ancestors showed me, as I'm showing you now."

Isabelle pondered what that really meant—to telepathically witness ancient history firsthand across generations. How many foolish religious or political disputes could be settled back on Earth if humans possessed this skill? She shook the stray thought aside.

The control room had gone almost completely dark. When she peered out the portal again, the planet was gone. In its place was a black void. The boy's silhouette stared into the nothingness.

A desperate emptiness gouged at her chest. She knew that practically every single event in human history had one thing in common: it occurred on Earth. Despite mankind's seemingly endless desire to forge ahead to new frontiers, every petty conquest had begun and ended on one single, dusty rock. *But to truly not have a home must be horrible.*

"It's so much more than not having a home," the boy said. "It's to drift aimlessly in an empty void for a lifetime. For a millennium. Entire generations blossoming and wilting without purpose. Trapped in a vessel that's ever decaying, ever shrinking. While we ever decay and ever shrink. Until we are almost nothing. To finally reach the end of the journey and find your entire race is utterly helpless, hunted, and exploited. Powerless to command our own destiny. That is who we are."

Isabelle's eyes strained to pierce the darkness. She wanted to see his face, to tell him she was sorry. She was about to reach for his hand when a light flickered outside the portal.

She yelped. Instead of the boy perched in the seat, the flickering light revealed a smooth, pod-shaped form, colorless and translucent like a grain of rice. Two black specks glared back at her—and blinked.

She awoke.

***

"See you after school, noodlehead." Mason turned and walked away down the sidewalk in front of the Cooley house. As he passed Jasmine and Maddy a few paces down the sidewalk, he started to speak but was cut off.

"Don't even!" Maddy said sharply as they passed.

Isabelle fidgeted with the straps of her backpack. "Thanks for calling to check in on me last night."

Jasmine reached out and gave Isabelle a hug. "We thought the cops had you for sure. We're sorry we bailed on you, but what could we have done?"

Isabelle could hardly blame them. "You're right. There's nothing you could have done. You guys did the right thing to get out of there." She shook her head. "That did *not* go well. How could those officers think *I* did all that damage! What would have happened if I allowed myself to be captured? Could you imagine what my dad would say?"

Isabelle half expected the Rose Valley Police to roll up to the curb at any moment. When her stomach wasn't in knots over the dread of being arrested, her mind kept returning to her latest dream. The boy's plight was palpable and hung over her even after getting ready for her day. Not to mention the glimpse of his alien form she caught in the flickering light. She kept going over the boy's words from her first dream, '. . . *I am something so alien* . . .'

Her skin crawled, even now, just thinking about it. She meant to ask Jasmine and Maddy if they had shared the same dream. Now that they were here, she dreaded broaching the topic, afraid the answer would be yes.

As the trio walked in silence, her mind raced. She wondered about the sphere and the powers it bestowed. She felt guilt for the property damage they caused. Two peoples' cars were totally incinerated. Some poor shop owner had their front window shattered—as if keeping their business afloat in Old Town wasn't difficult enough.

Offsetting these feelings were the sheer exhilaration of flight and the inexplicable feeling that flying was a part of her now—part of her identity. She'd been telling herself that using these supernatural powers to help people was right, but now she questioned if she could truly bear the weight of that responsibility. She wondered if her friends were having the same thoughts.

Isabelle broke the silence. "Dad was really freaking out last night. Big time. He was going on about how all that crazy vandalism happened on the *very* street we walk home on—and in broad daylight. He almost didn't let me walk to school this morning."

Jasmine raised an eyebrow. "Vandalism?"

"That's what the news is calling it," said Maddy.

"Vandalism seems like a funny word for what happened, but whatever," Jasmine said. "What happened to those cars was an accident."

"Two cars destroyed, one of the buildings along the alleyway damaged by the fire, and a store window smashed in. Thank goodness no one was hurt."

A chill crept up Isabelle's back. "I swear those officers were within arm's reach of me when I took off. They were so close I could smell aftershave." She wrinkled her nose. "None of the reports said anything about a flying girl? Or the guy trying to break into the car?"

"Of course not, but get this," said Jasmine. "My dad has a friend who's a police officer and he told Dad that the two officers from yesterday are on administrative leave."

"Does that mean they told people what they saw and no one believes them?" Isabelle said.

Jasmine tilted her head to the side and shrugged. "Maybe. There's no doubt it's related to what happened yesterday. Officers usually go on administrative leave for personal reasons, or if they're under investigation, or for health reasons—"

"*Mental* health if they told anyone the truth!" said Maddy.

"No kidding," said Jasmine.

"But what if someone *else* saw us? If a whole street full of people saw me flying away, it wouldn't take the police long to figure out that something weird was going on," Isabelle said.

"You'd be surprised," Maddy said. "Sometimes UFOs are sighted by dozens of people at once, but the media is happy to write it off as mass hysteria."

Isabelle wondered for a moment if Maddy was about to start peddling her conspiracy theories again.

"In fact," Maddy said, "the authorities would probably make up *anything* to keep people from panicking."

Jasmine frowned and shook her head. "I don't think anyone saw you flying except those two officers."

"You don't think they'd lose their jobs over this, do you?" asked Isabelle, her voice thick with guilt.

"Hopefully they have enough sense to not tell anyone what they really saw," Maddy said.

After a moment of silence, Isabelle plunged forward. "I don't suppose either of you had any dreams lately?" She bit her lip.

Jasmine and Maddy exchanged a knowing look.

"Does that mean yes?" asked Isabelle. The thumping in her chest quickened.

"We didn't want to worry you," Maddy said.

"Yeah, it's no big deal," Jasmine said. "We were talking about it on the way over here."

"No big deal?" shot Isabelle. "Along with everything else that's happened, us having some sort of shared experience dream is *no big deal?*"

Jasmine flinched and Maddy held up a calming hand.

"Maybe that was a poor choice of words," Maddy said. "I'm not saying it's not serious … but I *am* suggesting we don't know if we can trust that what we're dreaming is tied to reality. We think the dreams could be due to all the trauma …"

Isabelle stopped and put her hands on her hips. "Trauma? You don't think this deserves a closer look?"

Maddy stopped and sighed. "Actually, yes. I think Dr. Anton might be able to tell us something about it. Jasmine doesn't quite agree."

Isabelle's jaw worked, but no words formed. *Should we visit this Dr. Anton?* As soon as she finished the thought, the familiar uneasiness set in. *But what am I afraid of?*

Frustrated that she couldn't quite put her finger on it, she crossed her arms and shook her head.

"Never mind," she said at last. "Let's just go to school." Arguing about Dr. Anton wasn't something she wanted to deal with right now. She had far too many other things to worry about.

She barely had time to push that thought aside before she noticed the silver pickup truck from Friday morning was parked at the roadside. She turned; a woman on the boulevard was rapidly approaching them. The eye-patched man remained behind the wheel.

It appeared Dr. Stephanie Anton had decided to press the issue.

Isabelle considered ignoring her or simply running, but as strangely uneasy as the whole situation made her, she had too many questions for this woman. She instinctively put her arms out as if to shield her friends who stood on either side of her.

The tall, olive-skinned woman in a brown leather jacket stopped in the middle of the sidewalk. Isabelle's eyes dropped to the oversized plush bunny slippers peering out from beneath the doctor's black slacks.

Anton spoke in a toneless voice. "You three really are a piece of work. You're not doing a very good job of keeping a low profile, are you?"

18
THE ORPHAN ARK

Sideways glances from Jasmine and Maddy confirmed it, but . . .

"You're Dr. Stephanie Anton, aren't you?" she asked at last.

The woman dipped her head. "And you're Isabelle Cooley, Jasmine Hubbard, and Madeline McCarthy." She nodded to each girl in turn.

Isabelle cringed. *How does she know our names?*

Anton's face twitched as she locked eyes with Isabelle. "I have a problem. I'm not sure how bad it is yet, but I know you're involved. So, it's your problem, too." Her angular features, framed by her curly, shoulder-length hair were ordinary enough, but something about her emanated an off-putting air.

Isabelle took a deep breath. "I don't know what—"

Dr. Anton stamped her foot and clenched her fists. "Oh, come off it! I know what you three have been up to. I know what happened in Old Town yesterday. You girls just couldn't keep a lid on it and now the wrong—people—have found out! Running around, acting like comic book characters? Seriously?"

Maddy shifted her weight from one foot to the other. "Can you tell us about that glowing object?"

Anton's face lit up. "I need you to listen to me and listen well. First of all, the object isn't *just* an object. And it's not the first one that has existed here on Earth. I think you know already it seems to have transferred some sort of energy to you. And you know, of course, that you and your friends can do things. Incredible things." Her eyes bored into each girl, in turn. "Now, think back throughout history—of the stories and legends that have been told through the ages. Gilgamesh. Hercules. Samson."

"Now wait just a minute!" said Isabelle.

Maddy held out a hand to hush her, pleading with her eyes for Anton to continue. Jasmine stood with her hands on her hips, flabbergasted.

Isabelle shook her head. "You're not saying these legends of superhuman powers are true? You're saying the legends could have come about because of . . ." *How can I still doubt it after everything that's happened? I can fly!*

"You'd be surprised at how many of the legends are *exactly* true," said Dr. Anton.

Her words sent a chill down Isabelle's spine. She'd experienced her own superhuman powers firsthand. She couldn't understand why she was having such a hard time believing these types of powers had a historical basis. But a lifetime's worth of healthy skepticism didn't die easily.

She frowned and crossed her arms.

Dr. Anton continued. "When I say the object is more than just an object, I mean to say that it is a vessel."

"A vessel for what?" asked Isabelle.

"Not what. A vessel for *whom*. The sphere is a spaceship. It experienced trouble and ended up on Earth, just like all the others throughout history. There are extraterrestrial beings onboard."

"What?" Jasmine's brows rose and her jaw went slack.

Isabelle's mind raced to the dreams. She strained to remember the boy's story about their exodus and utter loneliness.

"How is that possible?" she asked as she held her hands out in front of her, approximating the size of the sphere. The knot in her stomach twisted a little tighter and another chill trickled down the back of her neck.

"You have to remember, Isabelle," said Dr. Anton, gently, "that when we talk about life, we must always add the tag 'as we know it.' All of Earth's life is carbon based. I'm sure you know this. However unlikely it is that life could develop around another type of atom on different worlds—however unlikely—it *is* possible. Silicon, sulfur, and others. These are theoretically possible. We have yet to determine what the basis of *these* life forms is—we only know they possess intelligence. Against all sane, scientific logic, they exist and they possess intelligence." Anton grimaced. "We can't even determine what the chemical makeup of their vessel is."

Isabelle stammered, her questions tripping over themselves before she could get them out of her mouth.

Anton plowed forward. "We've been unable to establish direct communication with them so far." She nodded toward the truck. "My colleague Roland Gentry has been working on a way. He has a name for the beings—he calls them Orphans." She stepped forward. "Thousands of years ago, these beings lived on a planet, not unlike our own, when—"

"They destroyed their world and had to evacuate," Isabelle said. "They were looking for a new home and instead they found us."

Anton's mouth hung open.

"I—or we—had dreams," Isabelle said.

Jasmine and Maddy nodded as Anton's eyes flitted from girl to girl. Her mouth twitched. "Dreams," she said under her breath. "Of course."

Maddy stared. "Do we know anything else about these—Orphans? What brought them here?"

Anton shook her head. "We don't know much more. As Isabelle said, they never found the home they were searching for. Their spaceships began as massive, city-sized vessels. With no home port and limited resources, their vessels decayed, little by little. These biomechanical ships were rebuilt and recycled uncountable times, each time getting smaller."

Isabelle imagined a millennia long process of generation after generation dwarfing to fit into an ever shrinking and austere environment, endlessly adrift in the vastness of space.

Jasmine's eyes bulged. "No way."

Anton nodded. "Yes way. Thousands of years passed and they adapted. They evolved. They compressed. They shrunk. Now, their corporeal bodies are so infinitesimally small they're almost nothing but consciousness. For being made of almost nothing, their will for survival is remarkable."

Isabelle swallowed.

Anton continued. "Remember when I said there have been other vessels? The Chinese government has a vessel right now, but it's empty. No Orphans left on board. I can't begin to tell you the problems we face in trying to find out the facts. It seems China hoped to monopolize its contact with aliens. Of course, they don't openly claim to have one, but I have sources that say otherwise. They call it *Xinghechuan*."

Jasmine shared a blank look with Maddy, who shrugged.

Anton grinned. "I know. Not a very imaginative lot, are they?"

Isabelle's questions were piling up faster than Anton's answers could quench them.

"What has any of this got to do with what's happened to us?" she said.

Anton drew a deep sigh and lowered her eyes to the sidewalk. "I don't like to speculate. But I think the energy transfer had something to do with how the Orphans interact with their biomechanical vessel. Something happened with you—something went haywire. A mistake."

The sickening knot in Isabelle's stomach turned.

Anton's eyes snapped back up and locked onto Isabelle. "That's why we have a problem. Lives hang in the balance now. We're going to have some important work to do. I understand this may be difficult for you, but from what I've seen, I'm confident you girls will do the right thing." Her gaze jerked skyward as if she was startled by a voice only she could hear. "In the end. I hope." As suddenly as her attention drifted away, it snapped back. "I understand this is a lot to process. I can give you a little time, but things are already critically urgent. The vessel is no longer in our custody, and time is not on the Orphans' side."

"Who took it? What do they want with it?" Maddy said.

Anton ignored her question. "You can find me at 100 Kingfisher Lane. Tell no one else we spoke." The woman's eyes bored through them like lasers. "We will speak again."

Isabelle could only stare, wide-eyed, as Dr. Anton's plush bunny slippers performed an about-face and carried her back to the open door of the truck.

"We need to know more!"

Dr. Anton paused before climbing in. "I'm sorry, but we can't linger here. I know three bright girls like you will be doing your research. Noah Drennan would be a good place to start." She again flinched and stared at empty air as if listening.

Isabelle shared a clueless look with Jasmine and Maddy.

"Find Noah and you'll be on the right track." Without another word, Dr. Anton climbed in and slammed the door shut. In another moment the truck was pulling away, disappearing around a corner.

19
GOING VIRAL

MADDY SHOOK HER HEAD. "Of all the explanations, I never would have dreamed that aliens were living *inside* that sphere."

Jasmine fidgeted with her backpack strap. "So, you believe her?"

"I do," said Maddy. "I always believed extraterrestrial life was an inevitability. I just thought making contact was unlikely. Until now."

Isabelle turned to Jasmine. "You're the biologist. Do you think she's telling the truth?"

Jasmine opened her mouth to speak but stopped short. "Girl, we're studying taxonomy! How am I supposed to know? You're the tech expert. What do *you* think?"

Isabelle drew a long breath. "She said their journey took thousands of years. That could account for the huge distances that must have been traveled. But the decaying and shrinking ships—that part is beyond me."

"Maybe a more important question is do we *trust* her," Jasmine said.

Again, Maddy spoke up. "I do."

Jasmine shrugged. "What does all this have to do with our—abilities?"

Although Isabelle's mind was spinning with thousands of questions, one came to the forefront. "Should we continue to—you know—*use* these abilities?"

Maddy seemed lost in thought for a moment. "She didn't say not to."

"She also seemed to be hearing voices in her head," Jasmine said.

Isabelle put a calming hand on her shoulder. "You're right to be wary. I don't want us to walk into some kind of trap."

"She said lives hang in the balance. Whatever it is she needs help with, it's important. We should go to her place," Maddy said.

"I don't like this," said Jasmine.

Isabelle let out a long sigh. "We're in this together, so we'll decide together. We'll do nothing until we do our research, then we'll talk it through. We'll make an informed decision together."

***

Third period arrived and Isabelle was waiting at her table for Daniel to arrive. She took out her notebook and started jotting down a to-do list of everything she had to accomplish to get MechAnna fully operational in time for the upcoming Tech Fair. At the top of the list was the elusive bug that was causing MechAnna to speak so rudely. Jayden, with his ever-present headphones, was busy clacking on his laptop.

In walked Crystal Skorch, but instead of skulking to the back of the room, she walked up to Isabelle's table, pulled out the empty seat next to Jayden, and plopped down. She sat across from Isabelle with crossed arms. Jayden continued to clack keys.

It seemed Crystal was trying to sear a hole into Isabelle with her cold gray eyes. She wanted to turn away, but didn't want to reveal her intimidation.

Why is she trying to start something now?

Isabelle shrugged. "What?"

Crystal shot a sideways glance to Jayden, before re-skewering Isabelle with her gaze.

"You just think you're hot stuff, don't you?" she said in a low voice.

Her ears burning, Isabelle's eyes darted around the room. No one seemed to have noticed Crystal, not even Jayden. *What is she talking about?*

Determined not to show weakness, she forced her eyes to meet Crystal's. "I'm sure I don't know what you mean."

Crystal slowly uncrossed her arms and leaned in. She looked pale and gaunt as ever.

"You can cut the crap now. I've seen the video."

Isabelle scowled. "What video?"

Crystal rolled her eyes. "Look. I'm going to make this easy." She held her hands out in front of her as if she was holding an invisible volleyball. "A blue-silver sphere, about *this* big. Hidden in the drain tunnel by Hilltop Park last week?"

Isabelle swore she could *feel* the blood drain from her face as a lump formed in her throat.

Crystal leaned closer to whisper: "A *glowing* blue-silver sphere?" She sneered. "Except now it's *not glowing!*"

Isabelle stared as her mind raced. *She's involved! This is all we need!*

"I'm not stupid," Crystal said. "I can put one and one together. I don't know everything that's going on, but I know it's not glowing anymore because of *you*. How much do you know? Tell me!" she said. "What were you doing out there by the creek last week? Did you tell those two dudes in the black suits about me?"

Isabelle could barely find her voice. "So, those two robots are yours?"

"We're risking way too much to have you screw this up. Things are about to get bad if you don't do exactly as I say." Crystal jabbed a bony finger at the wood surface of the table. "Whatever you've taken, you need to give it back." She paused and looked Isabelle up and down. "Whatever you've done to yourself, you need to undo it. And believe me, you'll much rather be dealing with *me* on this!"

Jayden looked up from his laptop and nearly fell out of his chair when he noticed Crystal sitting next to him. The whole room had fallen silent except for a few whispers in the back.

Isabelle's face burned.

Daniel walked in. "Good morning. Take your seats, please."

Isabelle had never been more relieved to see him.

Crystal pried her eyes from Isabelle and glanced up at Daniel. Her mouth twitched into a thin-lipped sneer before she stalked back to her table and sat down.

"What was that all about?" hissed Jayden.

Isabelle shushed him, heart still thumping. Her mind raced. *How did Crystal get involved in all of this? Are those two burglar bots really hers? What does she want with that sphere? Does Anton know?*

Isabelle took a deep breath and resolved to get a grip on herself. If the world around her became a hurricane, she'd have to remain calm in the eye of the storm. She steadied her shaking hands and closed her eyes. *You can only handle one problem at a time, and right now it's robotics. Avoid Crystal. Stick to your tasks and focus. You can do this.*

She opened her eyes and moved to the robotics lab which was situated behind the glass panels at the rear of the classroom. When she started her ninth-grade year last fall, she thought this room would be her sanctuary. Little did she know how much she'd find herself struggling.

She settled in at one of the six free-standing counters furnished with dual computer monitors and a pair of wheeled, high-backed chairs. The Cavett Tech Center robotics lab had everything she and the other students would need to build almost any kind of robot. Some of the students, clad in white lab coats, were assembling components on the tables, while others rummaged through the array of slide-out bins which covered the entire back wall of the lab.

She dared a glance at the glass wall which divided the lab from the classroom. Sure enough, Crystal was seated on the other side, glaring at her.

Isabelle quickly looked away. She knew she had important work to finish. It was now or never. Today would be the last full robotics period before break.

"How are things going with MechAnna?" Daniel asked when he finally made his way over to her counter.

"I'm glad you asked," she said. "I'm going to need an IR illuminator."

"Alright. What kind of wavelength and angle—"

"I need power," she said.

"Okay," said Daniel. "You could use a ZT1. It can deliver 1.15 watts at one amp."

Isabelle frowned. "No. More than that."

Daniel chuckled. "Just what are you planning to—"

"Can we do more, please?"

"We've got the ZT4. It's like the ZT1 but with quad dies, 7-millimeter footprint. It'll get you 4.5 watts at one amp. You'll need a heat sink and you'll want to think about taking some safety precautions. What did you say your application was going to be?"

"More," said Isabelle.

Daniel laughed. "I know I told you over-engineering could be a good thing, but . . ."

"I need six of the ZT4s," Isabelle said.

* * *

"Well, color *me* surprised." Jasmine rolled her eyes.

Isabelle struggled to keep pace with her friends as they hastened through the empty corridors of Cavett Academy's main building.

"You can't pretend like you knew all along!" Isabelle said.

Maddy sighed. "After all that's happened these past few days, I don't know how you'd expect us to react. I don't think I'd be surprised if you told me Percy Cavett was still alive and leading an underground crimefighting syndicate."

"This is serious," said Isabelle as they turned the corner to enter the library.

"I know," said Jasmine. "I'm just saying, all things considered, we should've seen this one coming a mile away! She shows up in your advanced robotics class out of nowhere? During a sudden robotic burglary outbreak? She's obviously a sociopath? Possibly some kind of robotics genius?"

Isabelle's ears burned as she thought back to how Crystal had solved MechAnna's circuit board problem after just a glance at her schematic. *How could I be so blind?*

The library was deserted except for the librarian, Ms. Walz, and two girls huddled together at a computer cubicle. Maddy slapped their pass on the librarian's counter as they walked past.

Ms. Walz didn't even look up from her magazine.

"Well, what are . . . What are we going to do about it?" asked Isabelle as she readjusted her volume to a whisper.

"Nothing," Maddy said.

"You can't be serious."

Maddy stopped dead and drew a deep breath. "I don't mean *literally* nothing. What I *mean* is we stick to our guns and we stay on track. I know finding out about Crystal's involvement is a big deal, but we can't let that knowledge distract us. Anton said we should research, right?"

Isabelle struggled to still her racing thoughts. "She said finding Noah Drennan would be a good place to start."

"That's why we're here."

Maybe Maddy's right. Maybe we need to stay calm and arm ourselves with as much knowledge as we can.

They settled into the rearmost computer cubicle and Isabelle pulled up a search engine tab. She typed the name Noah Drennan and tapped the enter key.

The first few links didn't look promising, but further down there was a black and white photo that caught Isabelle's eye. Her heart skipped a beat as she clicked on the thumbnail.

When the full view of the newspaper clipping came into view, Isabelle studied the picture closely. There was a man who looked exactly like what she thought an old cowboy would look like: masculine features, a tanned and lined face, hard eyes beneath the brim of a cattleman's hat. There was also a younger, baby-faced version of the man, who could only be his son. He had displayed a broad, white smile for the newspaper's cameraman.

But what was sitting between the two men made the hair stand up on the back of her neck.

Although it was a grainy, halftone newspaper photo, she could tell the object was unmistakably similar to the sphere they'd found. It even looked like it was putting off a soft glow. Jasmine and Maddy leaned closer to the screen, peering over Isabelle's shoulder.

The clipping ('Texas Odd-Ball Has a Mind of Its Own') was from a newspaper called the San Brendan Tribune. Isabelle noted the date: August 9, 1984. The clipping was featured on a site about paranormal phenomenon, along with an analysis.

She read aloud. "A mysterious sphere that seems to have a mind of its own has the Raymond Drennan family wondering if it's been visited from outer space. Raymond Drennan of San Brendan, along with his son Noah, were investigating a brush fire at their Arca Varada Ranch when they found a perfect sphere about the size of a bowling ball and weighing 17 pounds. Having dug the ball out of the center of a crater, the Drennans say it appeared to have fallen from the sky. 'At first, we thought it might have come from NASA or the Russians,' says Noah Drennan. After bringing the ball into the house, it began its tale of unpredictability."

"This is crazy," said Jasmine. "When rolled across the kitchen floor of the ranch house, the sphere would stop, change directions, and roll back to the person who rolled it. When rolled across a tabletop, it would stop before it reached the edge, seemingly to prevent itself from falling off. 'Sometimes it will vibrate and make a high frequency sound,' says Noah."

Isabelle recalled the disharmonious drone the sphere made. Glancing over at Jasmine's wide-eyed look, she guessed her friend was thinking the same thing.

Jasmine continued. "After a terrifying weekend when objects allegedly moved around the Drennan house and doors slammed by themselves through all hours of the day and night, they contacted the Air Force, who agreed to send a representative."

Maddy peered over Isabelle's shoulder. "Okay, the author of the website has her analysis here . . . she says the Air Force ran a series of tests on the sphere. According to Noah, they'd agreed to return the object if it was not determined to be radioactive, explosive, or government property. It says the Air Force scientists found it to be none of those things. Yet they were going to renege on their agreement on the grounds of national security. 'This greatly upset Noah, as he had become emotionally attached to the ball,'" she read from the website.

Isabelle blinked. "Emotionally attached?"

Maddy continued. "That would have been the end of it, if not for the unexpected intervention of an Air Force officer. That man was Major Edwin Nowotny, the ranking officer of the detachment in charge of the investigation. What the newspapers won't tell you is that it was said that Major Nowotny was somehow manipulated by the sphere—or by Noah himself. The Air Force's *official* conclusion, and the one repeated by the newspapers at the time, was that the object was found to be a hoax—that it was nothing more than an industrial ball valve."

"An industrial *what* now?" Jasmine said.

Isabelle drew a long breath. "This analysis says nothing about the sphere being an extraterrestrial spaceship."

Maddy shrugged. "The Air Force wouldn't dream of making that discovery public. You know how they're always covering up—"

"Right," Isabelle said, "but *we* never saw it move."

"We only really saw it for a few moments," Maddy said. "And part of that time, it was confined in a net. A net! Makes perfect sense to me."

Isabelle nodded. "You're right. But the other thing is this: Why is there no mention of the vessel transferring superpowers to anyone? We know the Drennans came into direct contact with it. We can assume any number of reporters and photographers did. So did the scientists and investigators. There's no indication this vessel affected Crystal in any way, either."

"So, why are we the only ones that seem to be affected?" Maddy said.

Jasmine's expression dropped. "I don't have an answer for that one." She glanced up at the two girls at the nearby cubicle to make sure they weren't listening in. "Those guys in black might have something to do with the sphere."

Isabelle's stomach twisted into a knot when she remembered how the weird men seemed to stare right through her. Crystal had even mentioned them.

"We're going to have to visit this crazy woman, aren't we?" Jasmine said.

Isabelle shook her head. "Honestly, I'm a little scared of her. Of this whole situation."

"I don't think we have much of a choice anymore." Maddy sounded frustrated. "She may be the *only* one who can tell us what's really going on! We're already involved. We have to follow through."

"I don't know," Jasmine said. "As curious as I am to find out everything I can about what's happened to us, something doesn't feel right about all of this."

Isabelle felt as if the fortress walls of her secret life were crumbling all around her. "At least for now, I suggest we avoid anyone who has anything to do with this," she said. She closed the browser window and cleared her search history.

Something about the conversation of the two girls at the end of the row of cubicles caught Isabelle's attention. They seemed to be watching an online video. Isabelle looked over, recognizing the girls as Meghan from her robotics class and Addyson from Jasmine's soccer team.

"No, it *must* be CGI," said Addyson, a slender girl with dark hair and large eyes. "It's just too seamless and polished."

"Eh, maybe you're right," said Meghan, a shorter, red-haired girl wearing a baseball jersey. "If it is, it's pretty good. But you have to admit there's something weird about it. These comments," she said pointing to the screen, "some of them are saying it's some kind of practical special effect."

"No, it's CGI. This is good stuff," said Addyson as she restarted the video and watched again.

"But why even *add* special effects to a crime video?" asked Meghan. "That's just so weird."

"It's all about the views," Addyson said.

Jasmine noticed the worried look on Isabelle's face, then turned to stare at Addyson and Meghan. She walked over to the two girls and casually glanced over.

"Whoa, what's that?" Jasmine asked innocently.

Addyson looked up.

"Oh, hey, Jaz," she said. "It's just a video that's really going viral right now. It's supposed to be footage of the Old Town Vandal last night." Isabelle gave Maddy a panicked look. "But whoever posted the video added all this CGI to make it look like the suspect flew away from the cops. Look."

As Isabelle walked over with Maddy, Crystal's words echoed in her mind, *I've seen the video,* " Comprehension was slowly dawning. She dreaded what she was about to see on the screen.

Addyson restarted the video.

It began with the camera pointing down to the sidewalk then panned up as a police cruiser skidded to a halt a short distance away. The videographer seemed to be running across the street to get a better view of the alleyway as the police officers jumped out of their car and started shouting commands at the suspect. The suspect, clad in a blue hospital gown, scrub cap, and purple mask was cornered in the alleyway with two burning cars blocking the escape route behind.

The shaky video showed the officers' backs as they rushed toward the suspect. Suddenly, the mysterious suspect shot into the air like a bottle rocket, disappearing from view of the camera. The camera then panned back to the officers who stood there, dumbfounded, as another police car pulled up behind them. There, the video ended.

It was truly a bizarre experience to see herself as an anonymous suspect on screen. She was surprised she didn't remember seeing the person—whoever it was—standing there with a camera phone.

An ice-cold sweat beaded on Isabelle's forehead as she stared at the screen. Luckily, Addyson and Meghan were glued to the video and didn't seem to notice.

Maddy elbowed Isabelle and loudly spoke up. "Ha, that is *so* fake!"

Isabelle looked at the onscreen view counter. Over 330,000 views in less than 24 hours.

20

THE HOSPITAL VIGILANTES

ISABELLE STOMPED UP THE FRONT PORCH STEPS with Jasmine and Maddy trailing close behind. She'd been inconsolable during the walk home, despite her friends' best efforts to calm her.

"Did you see how many views that video had?" she shrieked. "Over three hundred thousand and climbing! This is *not* what I call maintaining secrecy!" She opened the front door and led her friends through the living room toward the kitchen table, where they usually worked on homework. Mason was lounging on the couch with his tablet. When he saw the procession passing by, he perked up.

"Hey, have you seen this video of the Old Town Vandal from yesterday?"

Isabelle stopped cold, clenched her jaw, and turned to look at her friends, her eyes flashing with rage.

"Easy now," Jasmine murmured.

"Yes! I *saw* it, dear brother." The words spilled out, dripping with disdain."

Mason flinched. "Whoa, who snapped *your* training bra? I thought you'd be interested since you guys walk through Old

Town every day. Gavin filmed this. He was there yesterday. His MoovToob channel is blowing up."

Isabelle gasped as if an invisible sledgehammer knocked the wind from her. Her voice squeaked out, strained and high.

"Gavin?" *That little worm! I should have known better than to trust that he'd keep his mouth shut!*

Jasmine and Maddy exchanged a concerned glance.

Mason buried his face back into the tablet. "Yeah, Gavin Barnard. He actually won't shut up about it. Half the school thinks he's nuts and the other half thinks he's faking it for the views."

"He *is* nuts and he *is* faking it!" said Isabelle a little too loudly.

Mason peeked over the top of the tablet. Jasmine and Maddy each took hold of one of her sleeves and pulled her into the kitchen. Isabelle stopped resisting and allowed herself to be shunted away from her brother.

Isabelle plopped into a chair. Jasmine and Maddy each pulled up a seat and joined her. Mason got up and went to the front porch with his tablet, apparently deciding to give his sister a wide berth.

"I think you're overreacting," Maddy said as she unzipped her backpack, "just a little bit."

"Overreacting?" Isabelle's eyes narrowed. "It's no coincidence. He must be stalking me! Do you think he told Mason?"

"If he did, Mason has a great poker face," Maddy said. "Either way, it doesn't matter."

Jasmine patted the table in front of her with her palms. "Yeah, you didn't think we'd be able to avoid being filmed forever, did you? I mean, that's what the disguises are for, aren't they?"

Isabelle's voice wavered. "Jasmine, it's more than that. Look at all the times I've been exposed. Anton knows. Gavin knows. Even Crystal knows. Now there's this video and it's gone totally viral! You can't understand. It wasn't *you* caught on film; it was *me*." She suddenly felt selfish. "I don't know *why* I'm feeling this way." During the walk home, she'd been examining her feelings and trying to grasp the strand that would lead her to the root of all this anxiety, but the answer still eluded her.

"I guess . . ." she said. "I guess it's because earlier, we were just *talking* about facing these dangers. It seemed like it would never really come. The danger was always on the horizon. But now, we've reached the point of no return. For better or worse, we've gotten involved, and I'm going to be honest with you. It's scary. I didn't know I was going to freeze like that."

Jasmine and Maddy exchanged looks.

"I was scared too," said Maddy. "I still am."

Isabelle's eyes stung with tears. "But you didn't freeze."

"We're *all* scared," Jasmine said. "I know you think I'm the brave one, but everything you just said is exactly how I feel." Jasmine smiled. "*You're* the brave one, Isabelle. You've never backed down from a challenge. *You're* the ninth-grader in Mrs. Stacey's robotics. That takes real courage," she said as she placed her biology textbook on the table.

Isabelle sniffed, just grateful Jasmine hadn't called attention to the fact that she was crying.

"Regarding this footage," said Maddy, "you've got nothing to worry about. Your face doesn't show in the video."

"But Gavin—"

Maddy held up a hand. ". . . is an idiot."

Jasmine snorted as she opened her textbook.

Maddy continued. "Gavin's always in the middle of some ridiculous drama. Remember last year when he started a rumor about giant alligators in the sewers?"

Jasmine's face lit up. "Or when he told his whole school that his next-door neighbor was a vampire?"

"Yeah." Maddy chuckled. "My point is, absolutely no one in their right mind is going to believe a thing he says. Ever." She displayed a sly smile and mimicked Gavin's whiney voice, "My best friend's sister has superpowers. Blah blah blah."

Isabelle laughed in spite of herself. "I guess . . . anyway, it's Crystal we should all be worrying about. And what about the dreams, those robots, those guys in black suits, Dr. Anton, and these—Orphans and their vessel?"

Jasmine looked to Maddy, then Isabelle.

"You all know how I feel about making the most out of our predicament," she said. "I still think we can help people. Don't you think we can do more good than harm?"

Isabelle was lost in her own thoughts for a moment. "Think about what Dr. Anton said. She said we 'possess energy,' and that 'lives hang in the balance.'"

"Right," said Maddy.

"Well, what if these Orphan beings need this energy to survive? What if there's a finite amount of energy and we're using it up by exercising—you know—our powers?"

"That's a bit of a leap," said Maddy.

"Is it?" shot back Isabelle. "We all had the same dream. He said we stole the very essence of their lives. Without it they will perish."

Jasmine started to speak but stopped, her mouth hanging open.

Maddy thumbed through the pages of her textbook. "If that was the case, surely Anton would have said so."

"I don't know," Jasmine said. "She sort of had a flair for the dramatic."

Isabelle sighed. "What if they're suffering because we're keeping the energy away from them?"

Jasmine smirked. "Why are you so bent out of shape over an alien ant colony?"

Isabelle's jaw dropped. "How can you say that? You had the dreams too!"

Jasmine sheepishly dropped her head. "Just saying . . ."

Maddy's eyes rose from her textbook and locked onto Isabelle. "Maybe you're right. Maybe we need to see Dr. Anton as soon as possible. She'll tell us what we need to do."

Isabelle squirmed in her seat. Despite her desire to not let any harm come to these Orphans, she harbored a paralyzing fear of submitting to Dr. Anton.

"I still don't know if we can trust her." She drew a deep sigh. "But I don't know where else we can turn."

Maddy scoffed. "You're not going to suggest we go talk to those guys in black, are you?"

"Of course not!" said Jasmine.

Isabelle's skin crawled as she remembered the glistening, pale men staring at them from the black SUV.

Maddy grinned. "You know, there have been stories about mysterious men in black suits going all the way back to the 1950s. Some say they are government agents. Others say they just *claim* to be government agents, but they always appear in response to someone witnessing something extraterrestrial. The stories say they try to intimidate and silence witnesses. And you know we're already more than just witnesses to something extraterrestrial."

Jasmine's forehead crinkled as she raised an eyebrow. "Like the Men in Black?" Maddy solemnly nodded.

Isabelle rolled her eyes and pushed herself away from the table. "Look, we're not getting any studying done like this. We need to get away for a minute and take a break. What do you say we walk down to the Mart-n-Dart and get a soda? I'll buy."

"Alright," said Maddy.

"Oh, bring your backpacks. If you leave them here with Mason, there's no telling what you'll find in them when we get back," said Isabelle.

The girls gathered up their backpacks and filed out the door, walking past Mason who was seated on the front steps, playing a game on his tablet.

"Where are you guys off to?" asked Mason.

Isabelle couldn't believe her ears; Mason said something to her without a juvenile insult. "Just getting a soda," she said. "We'll be right back."

"Can you get me one too? I'll pay you back next time I get lawn mowing money."

Feeling a little guilty for snapping at him, she agreed.

The girls walked the three blocks to the Mart-n-Dart, a regional chain convenience store and gas station. They crossed the deserted parking lot and walked along the front sidewalk of the store. Glancing inside through the window, Isabelle could see the clerk, a gray-haired man in his 60s, holding his hands up.

"Hold on!" she said as she held her arms out to stop her friends from walking any further.

She ducked down behind a large window sign advertising pizza and watched. From her vantage point, she couldn't quite see who was in front of the counter. She inched forward and saw a man in a black hooded sweatshirt pointing a gun. She couldn't make out his face.

"There's a robber in there!" she whispered. "He's got a gun!" Isabelle was suddenly aware her heart was throbbing double-time in her throat.

Jasmine grabbed her friends by their shirts and pulled them backward. They ran around the side of the building and hid behind a big brown dumpster.

"Maddy, call the police," said Isabelle.

Maddy reached into her backpack for her cell phone. "Um, battery's dead!" she said. She looked at Jasmine, then Isabelle with steely eyes. "What are we going to do? What if he hurts him? We have to do something."

"That guy has a gun!" said Isabelle with a shaking voice. "If we screw up, someone could get really hurt."

Maddy reached back into her backpack and pulled out her disguise. She slid the surgeon's mask over her face, hurriedly threw the hospital gown over her shoulders, and pulled on her vinyl gloves.

"This is a matter of life or death!" she said. "With or without you, I'm going in."

Jasmine looked uneasily at Isabelle and unzipped her backpack. "I can't leave her hanging," she said in a low voice.

Isabelle surrendered to a flood of thoughts and emotion. She couldn't stand by and do nothing while her two best friends pitched into battle. Not to mention some foolish, competitive instinct: less than a week ago Maddy was afraid of her own shadow, but now she was leading the charge. Isabelle couldn't bear to be the one to stand by like a coward.

"I can't believe we're doing this again," she muttered as she and Jasmine put on their disguises.

They stashed their backpacks behind the dumpster and ran back to the window pizza sign. Peeking around the sign, she could see the agitated body language of the robber and hear muffled yelling through the glass window of the store.

"Jasmine, can you get in quickly?" asked Maddy.

"Yes."

"Can you get in unseen?"

"Um. Maybe."

"Listen," Maddy said. "When I say 'go,' get in there and go left, down the aisle. Fast! Try not to let him see you. I'm going to distract and disarm him. Isabelle, I want you to make him go after you. Be evasive."

Isabelle bristled. "Be evasive? What's that supposed to—"

"Jasmine, that's when you strike. This has to happen *fast*. Got it?"

Isabelle barely had time to grasp what was going on. Her heart thumped in her chest and her field of vision narrowed.

"Go now!" hissed Maddy.

Isabelle didn't have time to think. Jasmine opened the door and darted left, a blur. The electronic door chime played its singsong tune as the two men's heads turned toward the door in what seemed like super slow motion. Maddy stepped up to the closing door and leaned into it with her shoulder, raising her right hand in front of her.

Isabelle swung open the other door and stepped past her friend. The gunman pivoted to turn his weapon on the newcomers.

Maddy's thumb twitched.

With a click, the magazine fell from the grip of the gun and clattered to the floor. She flicked her wrist and the pistol's slide racked backward, the chambered bullet popping out of the ejection port and rolling around on the floor an instant later.

A look of shock washed over the gunman's face. He looked down at the floor, but with a wave of Maddy's left hand, the magazine and bullet were already sliding away across the tiles.

Isabelle hardly realized her legs were carrying her to confront the criminal, but she found herself standing right next to him anyway. She positioned herself with her back to the store aisles and squared up, glaring at the crook.

"What are you going to do about it, tough guy!" The words had fallen out of her mouth before she could think of what to say.

Wild-eyed and panicked, the man glanced at the door and saw the surgeon masked stranger guarding it. With his escape route blocked, he squared to face the impish figure in front of him with the purple sequined mask.

The man took a swipe at Isabelle, but his fist swished the empty air beneath Isabelle's feet. She already hovered five feet above the floor and kicked the man square in the face, sending the gun tumbling to the floor.

A moment later Jasmine came sliding underneath Isabelle, feet first like a softball player sliding into third base—she took the man off his feet and he tumbled like a bowling pin. Before he could gather himself, Jasmine grappled him to the floor, face down, pulling his arm backward as he yelped in painful submission right in front of the checkout counter.

Isabelle landed lightly on her feet and looked down at the floor where Jasmine was easily pinning the criminal, then at Maddy who was guarding the door, then back at the clerk who was already dialing 911.

Isabelle kicked the gun; it skidded across the floor tiles away from the struggling criminal.

She glanced down at her trembling hands. A bubbling, overflowing wave of exhilaration pulsed through her body and she laughed, relieved that the crook was subdued and everyone seemed to be in one piece.

"You again?" said the gunman with his cheek pressed against the dirty floor.

"Shut up!" whispered Jasmine. She gave his arm an extra twist.

As Isabelle listened, she realized this must be the same scumbag they found breaking into the car yesterday afternoon. She hadn't even noticed.

Isabelle spun around to address the clerk. "Are you alright?"

"I'm fine," the clerk grunted. "It's a good thing you were here to save him from me," he added with a smile.

Jasmine looked up at the clerk. "Sir, we're going to need some duct tape or zip ties or something."

The clerk sprung into action and started rummaging on a shelf behind the counter. He grabbed a pack of zip ties and rushed to Jasmine's aid. Every time the crook felt like he was about to struggle, he got a painful twist of his arm and he went limp once again. Together, they secured the gunman's hands behind his back.

"I'm going to need you to hold him for me, okay? We can't stay here," said Jasmine.

"That won't be a problem," he said.

Isabelle thought the older gentleman looked like he could handle himself. She saw a USMC tattoo on his forearm and smiled. If this guy was half as tough as her late grandpa, also a former Marine, he'd have nothing to worry about.

"*And* we're going to need these," said Isabelle, slapping a ten-dollar bill on the counter as she cradled four soda bottles in her arm. "Keep the change."

The clerk's mouth hung open for an awkward moment, as if he had a hundred questions to ask all at once. He settled on just one.

"Who are you guys?"

Isabelle looked at Jasmine and shrugged.

"We have to go!" called Maddy, urgently from the doorway. She held the door open as Jasmine and Isabelle ran out, disappearing to the right and around the side of the store. She nodded at the clerk and followed her friends. From behind the big brown dumpster Isabelle could hear distant sirens. They ripped off their disguises and stuffed them into their backpacks, looking around for their escape route.

There was a seven-foot-tall fence running along the backside of the store. Jasmine locked her fingers together and helped Maddy vault over the top before scrambling over, herself. Finally, Isabelle rose and descended, landing lightly on her toes on the other side.

"When we each get home tonight, we all need to stash our disguises somewhere," said Maddy. "You *know* there was a camera. You don't want to get stopped in the next few days with it in your backpack."

"Alright," said Isabelle, "but for now, we need to be gone when the police get here!"

A moment later the girls were cutting through backyards to make their way to Isabelle's house. She knew Maddy was right. They would all show up on the store's surveillance cameras and the clerk would dutifully tell the police everything that happened. She wondered if they would give chase. All she knew for sure was that she couldn't get home fast enough.

Out of breath, they ran up the front porch steps as sirens echoed in the distance. She dropped a 20-ounce soda bottle in Mason's lap as they ran inside.

"Careful, it might be shaken up a bit."

21
THE TELLTALE PHONE

THE GIRLS SAT AT THE KITCHEN TABLE sipping their sodas as Isabelle read the next word on the vocabulary list: *Anticlimactic.*

Still reeling from the adrenaline rush, Isabelle squirmed and fidgeted. She pretended not to notice the sound of another police siren whizzing by outside.

They'd gotten back just before Isabelle's dad came home. He was now putting a frozen lasagna in the oven while Mason was in the living room preparing for a book report.

Isabelle read the next vocabulary word as she idly twisted a lock of hair around her finger. *Gourmet.*

Isabelle's dad glanced up at the clock on the wall. "I haven't heard from your mom or dad yet, Jasmine," he said. "Looks like you'll be staying for dinner tonight."

Jasmine looked up from her vocabulary list. "What a pity." She grinned. "On lasagna night?"

A muffled ringing made Isabelle jump. Everyone looked around as her dad instinctively reached for the phone in his shirt pocket.

"Nope, not me," he said.

Maddy pulled her backpack off the floor and took her cell phone out, swiping the screen and putting it to her ear.

"Hey, Dad. You're off work? Yes, I'm still at Isabelle's. Sure, come get me. Love you too! Bye."

Isabelle turned back to her vocabulary list and read the next word. *Duplicity.*

Wait a minute.

The hair stood up on the back of Isabelle's neck. Hadn't Maddy told them her phone was dead?

She looked over at Maddy who was putting her phone away in her backpack.

"My dad's on his way to pick me up," she said. Isabelle glanced at Jasmine who was going over her list, silently mouthing the words. Apparently, she hadn't noticed.

Isabelle decided not to confront Maddy directly. She wanted to talk to Jasmine first. Undeniably angry, she turned her attention back to her vocabulary list.

Treachery.

Well, this list isn't helping.

She fumed quietly for a few more minutes before Dr. McCarthy's voice came drifting in from the living room.

Maddy hopped out of her chair and hauled her backpack up to her shoulder.

"Good job tonight, guys," she said, winking. With a nod, she turned and walked off to the living room to greet her father with a hug. After a few minutes of talking with Isabelle's dad in the living room the McCarthys were gone.

No longer able to hold her peace, Isabelle spoke up. "Jasmine, did you notice anything funny just now?"

"Hmm?"

"Did you notice anything funny about Maddy getting a call from her dad?"

"No, why?" said Jasmine, still looking at her vocabulary list.

"Think about it. She just got a *call?*"

Jasmine looked up from her list, her face scrunched up. "Huh? What are you—wait—didn't she say her battery was dead?"

"Why do you think she lied about that?"

Jasmine's amber eyes drifted sideways as she thought. "She knew that if she didn't lie about her battery, we'd make her call the cops. So, that was her way of making sure we went in and confronted that crook." Jasmine frowned and leaned back in her chair.

"I was thinking the same thing," Isabelle said, starting to turn red. "I don't know about you, Jasmine, but I don't like being manipulated by one of my very best friends."

Jasmine tilted her head. "Well, I don't regret helping that poor cashier."

"I don't either," said Isabelle, "but we need absolute trust in each other! Does lying sound like absolute trust to you?"

"Well . . . no."

"Our lives were on the line tonight. This isn't going to work if we can't be honest with each other. We're going to have to talk to her." Isabelle cringed. There was a brief, stabbing pain behind her right eye. She stood up from her chair, clutching her face.

"What's wrong?" asked Jasmine.

"I don't know. I just had a really bad pain." Jasmine's brow knitted with concern. "Was the pain behind one of your eyes?"

"You've had this kind of headache too?"

"Yeah, just a few times. They were pretty rough, but they only lasted a moment."

"That's not good. I've never had a headache like that before we found that sphere. Have you?"

"No," said Jasmine.

Isabelle's dad came into the kitchen, holding his cell phone to his face.

"Alright. Yep, she'd be delighted to. Well, we're having lasagna. Yes, from how she reacted, I thought so. No. No, it's no problem at all. They've been working hard on their studying. I know— such hard workers, all of them." There was a long pause. "Well,

I haven't heard anything about that. Really? That's close. We'll check it out. Alright. You be safe too. See you in about an hour."

He ended the call with a touch of his screen.

"That was your mom, Jasmine. First things first. The game's over and your mom and dad are on the way home now. They'll be here to get you in about an hour. So, yes, you'll be eating here."

"Yes! Did we win?"

"She didn't say, but she said she started getting texts from friends and family about an armed robbery down at the Mart-n-Dart."

"That's like three blocks away!" Mason's excited voice came from the living room.

Isabelle and Jasmine exchanged a knowing look as Mason switched channels on the television and Isabelle's dad started checking his social media apps for news updates. Isabelle took a deep breath and nodded to Jasmine. The girls got up from their seats and went into the living room.

Sure enough, on the television screen was a blurry, low frame rate security video showing the gunman pointing his weapon at the clerk. The video showed a vantage point above and behind the cashier's counter.

Adrenaline surged through Isabelle's body all over again. She tried to hide the fact she was trembling, although everyone in the room was too engrossed in the report to notice. Ticker tape words were running across the bottom of the screen: 'Masked Vigilantes Subdue Armed Robbery Suspect . . .'

The choppy video showed what looked like a chaotic scuffle that lasted only a few seconds. Isabelle noted that from the camera's point of view one couldn't really see Maddy guarding the door. She could just make out that someone was there, but nothing more.

Incredibly, with the video's sluggish frame rate, she couldn't even see Jasmine enter the store at all! Jasmine moved so fast there might have been a blur, but Isabelle concluded that unless you were looking for it, her entry into the building wasn't even perceptible. Jasmine didn't clearly show up in the video until she was tackling the suspect to the floor. She was relieved that the poor quality of the video obscured her gravity defying aerobatics somewhat.

"Whoa! Look at that hang time," said Mason.

The two news anchors' unscripted play by play of the video was almost humorous as they tried to grasp what was going on.

"Police say one of the masked vigilantes is five feet, eight inches tall with black hair and the other is five feet, six inches tall with blonde or light brown hair. The store cashier told Rose Valley Police that there was a third vigilante who stayed at the door during the incident. We didn't get a good look at the third suspect in the video. Paul, do we have a description of the third?"

"All three vigilantes were wearing hospital gowns, surgical caps and gloves. If you have any information about these vigilantes, Rose Valley Police are urging you to come forward. We'll have that number for you to call up on the screen . . ."

Lastly, the video showed one of the masked vigilantes return from the refrigerated display case with an armful of soda bottles before slapping cash onto the counter. An uncomfortable chill crept up Isabelle's back as she noticed her brother looking at his own soda bottle in the cup holder.

She watched with mounting horror as his face slowly dawned comprehension.

Come on, Captain Oblivious, don't make the connection. Isabelle knew she didn't mention they were going to the Mart-n-Dart *specifically*, but she could see the rusty wheels turning in his head. *Where else could we have gone? No, Mason! Don't look at me! Don't you dare look at me!*

Isabelle felt the weight of her brother's gaze upon her.

22
ODDGUM RAIDOR

ISABELLE CAREFULLY WATCHED her brother sitting on the sofa with his tray. Bathed in the flickering light of the TV, he picked at his side salad with his fork. Jasmine, who was already on her second plate of lasagna, paid him no notice. Mason occasionally glanced up at the girls but quickly looked back down at his food whenever he caught Isabelle's eye.

Maybe she misread his reactions. Maybe he didn't make the connection, hadn't realized it was his own sister and her friends that were The Hospital Vigilantes. That's what people were calling them on the news and on social media. *What a horrible and unimaginative name.* She couldn't help but laugh, however, that Mercy Hospital, where her mom used to work, had already made a public statement disavowing the vigilantes.

Isabelle's dad was eating at the dining room table, occasionally scrolling through a news story on his smartphone. Isabelle could tell the Rose Valley crime spree bothered him, although he tried not to let it show. First, the rash of tech burglaries, then the Old Town Vandal, now an armed robbery just blocks from their home . . . all within the space of a week.

Isabelle's mind drifted back to Mason. She kept telling herself that if he suspected anything, he would have blurted out something stupid by now. But he just sat there silently chewing his dinner and it was driving her mad.

She nudged Jasmine and whispered, "I wonder if he's playing it cool on purpose, trying to get us to spill the beans ourselves."

"Oddgum raidor," said Jasmine with a mouthful of lasagna.

"What—oh. Occam's Razor?"

In other words, Mason acting clueless probably meant that Mason *was* clueless. Isabelle chuckled. *He's hardly ever aware of anything going on around him. He's not even aware he has tomato sauce on his eyebrow. How did he get tomato sauce on his eyebrow?*

"You're overreacting," said Jasmine after taking a drink of lemonade. "Mason hasn't said a thing. He doesn't suspect.

"Our bigger problem," she said, gesturing toward Maddy's empty seat with her fork, "is what are we going to do about Maddy. I've been thinking about that a lot, and I don't like it. You were right. It was *my* butt on the line out there, and yours, and that cashier's. She was just guarding the door. Well . . . she *did* disarm him, though."

Isabelle mulled that over. "Don't you think it was kind of reckless? The way she made the bullets fly out? If she made one little mistake, that gun could have gone off."

To be fair, Isabelle didn't know a lot about firearms. She wondered how much Maddy knew. Although Maddy seemed to know what she was doing, the thought of her tampering with a loaded gun using her telekinetic power made her nervous.

Isabelle suddenly lost her appetite. The thought of her friend manipulating them like that put her on an emotional roller coaster. One moment she was hurt and sad, the next she was furious. In another moment, she'd think that she was overreacting. Then the process would start all over again. They had a serious problem that needed to be addressed. But how?

Ever since they stumbled onto that sphere, it'd been one crisis after another. The sheer burden of learning that not only did extraterrestrials exist, but they'd interacted with her and her friends . . . changed them . . . it was enough to paralyze her with fear. It would be, perhaps, the most important scientific discovery in the history of the world, and she was right in the middle of it. In addition to that was all the stress from trying to keep their powers hidden; the mysterious astrophysicist who seemed to be recruiting them; the strange guys in black that seemed to be tracking them; the fact that Crystal was involved; the chaos they caused in Old Town; the video of her escaping the cops; the danger of fighting criminals; the mysterious headaches; the fear that some stupid thing like buying sodas could potentially blow their cover; the knowledge that the police were probably trying to figure out who they were at that very moment . . . it was a recipe for emotional disaster.

On top of all that, these powers had pushed their friendship with Maddy to the breaking point. Not to mention, the above average academic demands of attending Cavett Academy. And none of this even had anything to do with all the normal stresses and daily dramas that just go along with being a fourteen-year-old girl. Isabelle felt like if one more thing went wrong, she'd just have to cry.

Why can't I just be ordinary everyday Isabelle again?

Jasmine had been strangely quiet. Partly, Isabelle assumed, because they didn't have the privacy to talk openly. She wondered if Jasmine was as busy going over the recent events in her head as she was. Afterall, it had been an overwhelming week for them both.

Isabelle's eye twitched as the strange headache returned. Thankfully, it was just a dull throb at the moment.

"I know you and Maddy usually meet up before you get to my house in the morning," said Isabelle. "Could you please not mention anything to her about this until we're all three together? I think that would be best."

"What's going to happen?" Jasmine said with a look of concern.

"I don't know," Isabelle said. "I guess that's going to depend on Maddy."

"Agreed." Jasmine sighed.

A knock came from the front door and Jasmine grabbed her backpack. Isabelle's dad answered the door and greeted Coach Isaiah Hubbard, who was still wearing the black and blue uniform of the Blue Ridge Dragons with a matching windbreaker to ward off the nighttime chill. Tall and athletic, Coach Hubbard took off his baseball cap, revealing his shaved dome. Isabelle knew that in Coach Hubbard's younger days, he was a locally-famous college athlete who had earned the nickname 'Mack' during his college football career—something about a truck. Isabelle always thought sports were weird.

"Hey! Forgive me for not coming in. You know it's late and we're pretty keen to get home. Thanks again for keeping Jaz company tonight," said Coach Hubbard. "You know she can't get her studies done if we bring her to the road games—Hey, princess," he said to Jasmine as she squeezed through the doorway past her dad and onto the porch.

"Hey, Dad," she shot back as she jogged down the sidewalk toward the car where her mother and the twins were waiting for her.

"Oh, it's no problem, Mack," said Isabelle's dad. "She was happy to join us, and they got their studying done."

"So," Coach Hubbard lowered his voice, "have you heard anything new about that armed robbery just down the street here? We heard vigilantes broke it up or something? What really happened?"

Isabelle's dad nodded. "It's true. It seems some masked vigilantes somehow knocked the guy down and tied him up until police came."

"That's crazy. When I heard that, I thought there's no way that was true. You know people and their stories." Coach Hubbard chuckled. "Have the police caught up to them yet?"

Isabelle perked up and listened intently as goosebumps rose on her arms.

"All they're giving on the news is vague descriptions, plus they're asking the public for information. So, I'd say they don't have much right now. It sounds like a bunch of teenagers, if you ask me." Isabelle's dad shook his head. "I don't know, Mack. Rose Valley sure isn't like it was when we were kids," he said. "Something weird is going on."

"So true. Hey! Again, I'm sorry for being in such a rush, but we've got to get going. You folks have a good night. I'll drop off your tickets for Monday's game at your office tomorrow."

"Thanks, Mack," Isabelle's dad called after him as he jogged back to the car. "Be safe."

Isabelle watched as he closed, locked, and latched the front door.

Their fathers—two average citizens of Rose Valley—just had a casual conversation about their own daughters secretly fighting crime without realizing it. But there was no awe at their crime fighting prowess or bravery. No mention of the supernatural. If anything, she detected a bit of mistrust. They hadn't used the word 'heroes.' They called them vigilantes.

Isabelle paused to consider heroism and vigilantism. She tried to pinpoint the difference. She decided the distinction must be because the people she was trying to protect never gave her the authority to do so. Did that make being a vigilante wrong?

No. If someone needs my help, I'll be there.

23

THE RIFT

Isabelle stared down at the deep cracks crisscrossing the dry earth beneath her feet. Finding herself in a sudden hyperrealistic dream was becoming such a common occurrence she was hardly fazed to realize she was standing in a desert landscape. The sun beat down on her shoulders and sweat beaded on her brow. She stood in the midst of a sparse stand of mesquite trees. A rocky ridge curved off into the distance and a barren expanse spread out behind her, broken only by the occasional sagebrush or yucca plants.

Gaping before her was a hundred-foot-wide crater. The air was filled with sweet smelling smoke. The gnarled mesquite trees all lay flattened in an outward radiating pattern from the crater's center, which smoldered, bare and black. Looming overhead, a short distance away, was the prow of a massive rock formation. If Isabelle squinted, it looked like an ancient sailing ship stranded in the middle of the desert after some long-forgotten flood.

She turned on the spot and took in her surroundings, expecting the familiar Jayden look-alike, but he was nowhere to be seen. She spoke to the stillness of the desert.

"So, you're not here for this one?"

"I'm here." The words assembled themselves in her mind so clearly, she could swear they were spoken out loud.

"Where?"

"You'll soon understand. This is where our exodus ended. Although we are still hunted mercilessly, we found a most unlikely friend."

A rustling came from behind her along with the sound of hoofbeats on hard earth. The shapes of two men on horseback emerged from the smoke. There was an old man, barrel-chested and with a face creased by many long years in the harsh sun. Steel gray eyes glinted beneath the broad brim of his cattleman's hat. Riding by his side was a younger, soft-faced version of the man— undoubtably, his son. He squinted in the late morning's glare.

"Noah heeded our calling. He dug us from the crater and protected us as he would one of his own."

The young man's eyes drifted to Isabelle and her heart stopped cold. He reached up to the brim of his hat. "Miss."

The sun blinked from existence and Isabelle found herself in darkness. The air turned stuffy and uncomfortable. She became aware of the weight of the flashlight in her left hand. The familiar touch of her friends' hands weighed on her shoulders. She leaned forward toward the glowing blue ball.

The boy's voice echoed in her mind. *"Our friend protected us, and it cost him his life. We were passed to another who risked everything to help us in our plight. But it all came to a halt when you found us, Isabelle. You stole the very essence of our lives."*

Jasmine reached for the sphere but stopped cold when Maddy's warning came. She retracted her hand.

Isabelle reached forward, her hand hovering above the sphere. She wanted nothing more than to touch the vessel's cool perfection, to savor the power that would surge through her body. Jasmine and Maddy silently watched, their faces aglow in the soft blue light. The nagging ache between her shoulder blades tugged at her and beckoned her to soar. This was who she was, and she wanted it.

But a small voice, deep inside, protested. Was it her own, or was it an echo of one of the multitudes whose destiny hung in the balance?

For the moment, it didn't matter. She lowered her hand to the vessel and forks of blue lightning enveloped her. Everything went dark.

"Life is dim. Hope is lost."

She awoke.

* * *

"See you after school, butt-nugget." Mason turned and headed down the sidewalk. Isabelle barely noticed his juvenile insults anymore and was long past giving him the satisfaction of reacting.

It was a cloudy, damp morning in Rose Valley as she stood on the sidewalk outside her house. Passing cars had their headlights on. The western sky was black with the foreboding shadow of an approaching thunderstorm, but the air was still and the neighborhood strangely quiet.

She watched Jasmine and Maddy approach. Her heart ached and every breath seemed to come at great effort. After the dream, an air of gloom hovered over her. It didn't help that she'd been up late coding and installing the six ZT-4 IR illuminators onto MechAnna's chassis.

"Hey Isabelle," Maddy said. Isabelle did not return the greeting. Jasmine turned her solemn gaze to the sidewalk.

"We need to talk, Maddy," said Isabelle. Her friend's smile melted into a look of concern. Isabelle decided it would probably be best to be blunt. "We know you lied about your phone's battery last night."

"I know what you're going to say." Maddy glared. "You're going to say I lied just to get us into action. You're going to say I put everyone in danger."

"You *did* put everyone in danger," Isabelle said.

"Did I?" Maddy put her hands on her hips. "First of all, I don't recall twisting either of your arms. Second, we already *were* in danger!"

The pang of her words hit Isabelle like a sock full of pennies. She was momentarily speechless.

"You've got a lot of nerve saying anything to me," Maddy said. "I saw what you did in *our* dream this morning. We *knew* what the sphere was and what would happen and you touched it anyway! You stole their energy all over again!"

Isabelle's heart ached. Was that what she'd really done? She looked to Jasmine for help, but she stood to the side with her eyes averted.

"That was just a dream," Isabelle said. "It wouldn't have changed what happened last week."

"No, but it showed me who you really are!"

Isabelle was stunned by the ruthlessness of Maddy's barbs. She knew a reckoning was on the horizon and she'd have to face it, but stubbornly, her pride steered her back to her original point.

"How can we trust each other if we're lying to each other?"

"I lied because if I didn't, you would've held me back!"

"Held you back!?" Isabelle said. "This isn't all about you!"

"I thought you wanted to help people," Maddy said. "That store clerk needed us to take action, not hide behind the dumpster wringing our hands!" She was turning pink.

"It wasn't safe—"

"You can't help people if you're going to act like a scared little kid."

Isabelle winced. "But he had a *gun*, Maddy," she stammered. "Anything could've gone wrong—"

"I took care of that!"

"What if it went off when you were—doing your telekinetic thing?"

Maddy clenched her fists and leaned forward. "You still have no idea, do you? You have no concept of what this ability is like to wield. I'm more in tune than you know! There was *no way* that gun was going to go off if I didn't want it to."

Isabelle and Jasmine stared blankly at their friend.

"I *was* the gun," said Maddy, coldly.

A fork of lightning flashed in the western sky, just as Jasmine's and Isabelle's shoulders jolted aside, shoved by an unseen force. Maddy marched through the gap she created between them without looking back. She strode down the sidewalk away from her friends. The rumbling crescendo of the thunder shook the ground.

"Maddy!" Isabelle called after her.

Suddenly, Isabelle's backpack unzipped and a folder full of papers erupted, sending them flying everywhere and settling onto the damp ground.

A wave of grief pulsed through her chest and settled in the pit of her stomach. She thought she'd call after her one more time, but the words died in her mouth.

Jasmine bent down and started picking papers up.

"It's best to let her go, for now," said Jasmine as she shook a few drops of water from one of Isabelle's papers. "Let her calm down. Don't worry. She'll come around."

Although Isabelle thought it was a rotten thing to do, she was impressed; Maddy wasn't even looking at her when she blew up the folder.

Another flash lit the western sky.

Tears rolled down Isabelle's cheeks as she stuffed her wet papers back into her folder and closed her backpack. A long, swelling rumble of thunder rolled overhead.

What more could possibly go wrong?

As she was pondering this question, a white sedan pulled up to the curb and two men got out. She could tell right away they were police.

Panic sent a jolt through her and she had to resist the urge to run. She'd been dreading the inevitable moment the police would trace some stupid clue back to them.

Jasmine must have been able to tell from the look on her face that she was worried.

"Relax," she said. "Just follow my lead."

As the two men were walking up to them, Isabelle recognized them as the same two detectives that were meeting with Mrs. Marshall on Monday morning.

"Good morning, isn't it, ladies?" said the older, mustached man with salt and pepper hair. They both pulled out their badges and displayed them briefly.

"What can we do for you two fine officers?" asked Jasmine sweetly as Isabelle mopped her eyes and cheeks with her sleeve.

"Two fine *detectives*," he said, smiling. "I'm Detective Douglas Pike and this is Detective Steven Cowie," he said motioning to his partner. "We just wanted to ask you a few questions. Would that be okay?"

Isabelle didn't like his tone. To her, it sounded condescending.

"Well, we're on our way to school," Jasmine said.

"Oh, I *totally* understand you girls are busy, but it would just take a moment or two."

"I don't mean any disrespect, Detective—Pike, was it? You can't just walk up to us on the street and start asking us questions. We're just kids." Lightning flashed in the distant western sky.

Pike continued. "Well, ladies, if we have a good reason to believe you've been a witness to a crime, we certainly *can*. But just think of this as a friendly little visit. Of course, you don't have to talk to us right now. We can make arrangements to question you in the presence of your parents. All you have to do is say the word."

Detective Pike seemed all too pleased at the look of alarm that neither girl could suppress. A low peal of thunder rumbled like a distant freight train.

Jasmine sighed. "Alright. We're more than happy to answer your questions if you make it quick. You don't want us to be late for school, do you?"

Detective Pike answered with a twinkle in his eye. "Oh, of *course* not, young lady. That's the last thing we want. If I could just get your names and addresses for the record?" Detective Cowie, with his close-cropped beard and slim fitting suit, stood by with a small notepad and pen.

Isabelle pointed to her house. "Isabelle Cooley, 501 South Mine Street. Right there."

The detective looked up and smiled. "Thank you, Miss Cooley. And you?" he asked, turning to Jasmine.

"Jasmine Hubbard, 1444 West Second Street."

"Mack Hubbard's daughter?"

Jasmine nodded.

"Alright. Since I know you young ladies really are in such a hurry, I'm going to get right to the point. I know you attend Cavett and you walk to and from school on this route every school day. On Monday, April 10 at approximately 3:45 p.m. you were passing through Old Town on your way home from school, correct?"

Isabelle could see where this was leading. They were looking for witnesses. *They'll probably be asking about Maddy any minute now*. Isabelle looked at Jasmine and shrugged, playing dumb.

"Um. Well, I'm not sure of the exact time, but yes, we pass right through Old Town every day," Jasmine said. "Sometimes we run a little early. Sometimes we run a little late."

"I'm sure you know what happened in Old Town right about that time. I want to know if you saw anyone suspicious. Anything out of the ordinary. Anything at all, however small."

Jasmine and Isabelle exchanged another clueless look, shrugging their shoulders.

"We must have just missed it," Jasmine said. "I mean literally, we must have *just* missed it by seconds."

"I remember hearing sirens after," lied Isabelle. "It's hard to remember. Everything was perfectly normal when we were passing through."

"Now, wasn't there another friend? A third girl who usually walks to and from school with you? Where is she today?"

"Maddy?" Isabelle's heart sank at hearing herself say her name. "Well, she already left for school . . ."

She was sure the detective caught every nuance of her body language. She might as well try to play this off. Maybe she could salvage it.

"Maddy, you say?" Pike glanced at his partner who was still jotting down notes in the small note pad. "Dr. McCarthy's daughter?"

"Yes. That's her. We had a fight," said Isabelle as she pushed down the grief bubbling just under the surface.

"Oh, I'm sorry to hear that. Do you mind if I ask what about?" asked Detective Pike, as he watched Isabelle closely.

Isabelle was taken aback. "Um, you know. Normal fourteen-year-old stuff. Girl stuff?"

She noticed the detective's slightly raised brow, and she knew she hadn't handled that well.

"Wait, Detective!" said Jasmine.

What are you up to, Jasmine?

"You said anything suspicious? No matter how small?" Both detectives perked up. "I *did* see a car on Monday morning. A black SUV. It was parked over by Hilltop Park right outside of Old Town and the two guys inside were just staring at us as we walked by. They were wearing black suits and gray gloves. One guy was wearing an old-timey hat."

"Um. Okay," Detective Pike said, glancing at his partner who made brief eye contact before returning to his notes. "Alright, ladies, I guess that's it."

A wave of relief swept over Isabelle. He was wrapping it up.

"I want you to be extra careful around here," he said. "I probably don't have to tell you there's been a lot of weird things going on."

"Right, sir," said Jasmine. "We'll be careful and watch out for each other."

"That's good," he said. "If you remember anything else or notice anything weird or suspicious around Old Town, I want you to call the station and ask for me by name. Okay?" He handed Isabelle a card. "Have a good day, ladies." He turned to walk back to the car, then stopped and turned around. "Oh, I almost forgot."

Jasmine and Isabelle froze.

"You said Monday, when you were walking home through Old Town, that there was nothing out of the ordinary, right? Well, when we examined the two cars, we found signs that someone had tried to forcefully enter one of the vehicles. We found a prybar inside the car. You don't know anything about that, do you?"

"Um. No. Nothing at all." said Isabelle as she tried her hardest to maintain eye contact and keep her expression neutral. Jasmine shrugged.

"Well, the guy we picked up last night for the armed robbery at the Mart-n-Dart sure is telling us some crazy stories. We're just trying to sort through it all and follow all leads. I'm sure you understand. Thank you, again, for your time, ladies," said Detective Pike.

As the detectives pulled away in the white sedan, Isabelle felt the first cold raindrop on her face.

24
RAINBOW GLITTER PANTS

ISABELLE AND JASMINE WALKED UP THE STEPS of the small back porch of Isabelle's house. They sat down together on the porch swing and Isabelle let out a long sigh. They'd made it through the last day of school before Easter break. It was only a half day; school was dismissed right before lunch.

The morning thunderstorm had moved on, leaving behind a few puddles in the roads. The afternoon sun was peeking through the trees in Isabelle's back yard, illuminating patches of wet grass as the girls idly swung back and forth.

"Did your dad say you could spend the night tonight?" asked Jasmine.

Isabelle nodded.

"Mom almost wouldn't let you come because there's another ballgame—if it didn't get rained out. I told her I had to help you with your Tech Fair project and you'd probably fail if I didn't."

Isabelle scowled. "Good thinking, but maybe you've hit a little too close to home on that one."

Jasmine stared at the puddles behind Isabelle's house. "Things haven't been going our way lately, have they?"

"That's putting it mildly," said Isabelle as she leaned her head back and closed her eyes. "Did you see Maddy today?"

"I saw her, but she wouldn't talk to me. She was trying her best to avoid me."

Isabelle opened her eyes and sat up. "I didn't even *see* her. I don't even know why she's mad at us. *We* didn't do anything wrong. *She* should be apologizing to *us*."

"Well, I'm guessing she felt justified. She thinks we're mistrusting her," said Jasmine.

"We're right to mistrust her if she's going to lie to us," Isabelle said.

"I never said she was being rational," said Jasmine. "People lash out when they get called out. They get defensive. We need to be patient and give her space."

"I don't want to lose her as a friend, though," said Isabelle. "Plus, there's the added complications. You know?"

Jasmine stared blankly.

"I mean, she knows about our abilities, and we know about hers."

"Oh, that," Jasmine said. "Don't worry. Be patient. She's going to come around and then we'll all be more honest and up-front with each other as a result. You'll see."

Isabelle watched a small congregation of birds splashing in a puddle in the alley behind her house as she mulled over what Jasmine said.

"Something about those detectives from this morning has been bugging me," she said. "Remember when he mentioned the cars? He said they knew someone was breaking into one of them?"

Jasmine nodded.

"What's the very next thing he said?" Without waiting for an answer, she continued. "He said the guy they arrested for the armed robbery was telling them 'crazy stories.'"

"You think they know it's the same guy?"

"Exactly," Isabelle said. "He never said it directly, but he brought one topic up right after the other. He knows."

"I wonder if they found that scumbag's fingerprints on the car?"

"Or on the prybar," Isabelle said. "If they did find his fingerprints, that places him in the alleyway."

"You're wondering if the detectives know about the video of you that went viral?"

Isabelle nodded as she stared at the birds in the puddle. "Gavin was right there filming me. The police were right there, too. How could Gavin have escaped being questioned?"

Jasmine shrugged. "Maybe he slipped away while the cops were distracted by you. So, there's a slim chance the police don't know about the video yet. And if they did, what would they do?"

"It all hinges on whether the two officers reported what they really saw."

Jasmine nodded. "If the RVPD really does find out the truth, they'll consider the filmmaker a witness. They'll be looking for Gavin."

Isabelle stared into space. "But . . . if the detectives get to Gavin, they'll know *everything!* He'll talk."

"Hundreds of thousands saw the viral video and who knows how many saw the news report. You don't have to be a detective to notice the same person with the same costume is in both videos."

"Maybe they already know," said Isabelle.

"Then why would they let us go?" Jasmine's expression suddenly tightened. She clutched her face, eyes rolling into the back of her head as she toppled out of the swing onto the floorboards of the porch.

Isabelle dropped to her knees beside her friend. She rolled Jasmine onto her back as panic sunk in its claws. *What do I do?* Her chest thumped as she strained to remember her basic lifesaving training.

"ABCs!" she muttered. "Airway, breathing, circulation."

She tilted her friend's head back and checked her airway, noting her shallow breaths. As Isabelle was pressing two fingers to Jasmine's carotid artery, her eyes fluttered and opened.

"Oh, thank goodness!" said Isabelle, crying.

"What happened?" Jasmine said, looking around.

"You fainted. Did you have another one of those headaches?"

"Yeah, right behind my eye," Jasmine said. "That's the last thing I remember. I've never fainted before though. How long was I out?"

"Just a few seconds," Isabelle said, still sniffling. "I'm really scared."

"I'm okay now," said Jasmine, sitting up.

"No, you're not!" said Isabelle. "I'm not either! We've got to do something. We can't ignore this any longer!"

"We promised to keep this a secret—"

"Our health is more important than a secret! You're my best friend, the only one I have left. I can't stand by and let this happen to you *or* Maddy. We're going to have to do something. Sooner or later, they're going to catch us anyway."

"What are you saying?" asked Jasmine as she got to her feet and brushed herself off.

"We're going to see the crazy woman," Isabelle said as she, too, stood up.

"Dr. Anton?"

"Yes, and you're *not* going to talk me out of it."

"Okay," Jasmine said. "We should see what she has to say. It can't hurt. You're right, it's only a matter of time."

"Oh," said Isabelle, surprised that Jasmine gave in so easily. "Right. We'll see what she has to say. And if she's no help . . ." she paused, unsure of what to say next. "Well, I don't know what we'll do. We'll just have to play it by ear. Let's go inside and I'll get packed for tonight."

Isabelle led Jasmine through the back door and through the kitchen on the way to her room.

As Isabelle turned the corner to enter her bedroom, she froze in her tracks.

Sitting on Mason's bed was Gavin Barnard. Mason sat on a nearby desk chair. Isabelle could only stand there with her mouth hanging open.

"Greetings, m'lady," Gavin said.

"What's *he* doing in my room?" Isabelle glared at Mason.

"Well, it's my room too," Mason said, matter-of-factly. "Anyway, we need to talk about your superpowers."

Isabelle locked eyes on Gavin. "You said you wouldn't tell anyone!"

Jasmine had finally come up behind Isabelle and was watching the confrontation unfold with wide eyes.

"I haven't told anyone yet," Gavin said.

"You've told Mason!"

Gavin waved a pudgy hand toward her bother. "He figured it out on his own. He came to me."

"You imbeciles don't know what you're meddling in."

Gavin's eyes narrowed beneath his mop of curly hair. "Oh, we know exactly what we're doing. We want in. I figure we can come to an agreement that's mutually beneficial. We'll ensure your secrecy in exchange for you letting us into your secret world."

"We'll do no such thing!" huffed Isabelle.

"You and your friends will continue to fight crime, and I'll be your agent," Gavin said. "Mason will handle all the marketing and merchandising. Don't worry, we'll take fifty percent and you girls can split fifty percent. The website is already up. We've got five hits."

"Gavin, you weasel!" Isabelle's face burned red hot. "This isn't a game!" Her mind was on fire with a thousand panicked thoughts. What would happen to her and her friends when everyone finally realized Gavin wasn't lying? Would she go to jail? Would her dad have to pay for the wrecked vehicles and the store window? Would she get kicked out of the academy? What would happen to the Orphans?

A smile danced across Gavin's chubby face. "Well, you know, I suppose I could start telling everyone your secret."

Secret. Isabelle's scowl slowly faded into a grin. She had one card left to play in her deck. She didn't know if it would work, but she had to try.

"What if I told everyone about *your* secret?

Gavin's mouth clapped shut and his face turned a splotchy red. "You wouldn't."

"I will!" Her heart soared as she sensed the momentum shift in her favor.

Mason leaned forward and locked eyes with Gavin. "Time out, dude. You go to middle school. They'll eat you alive if they find out you're a Pony Crony." His eyes bulged. "And as your best friend, they'd call me a Pony Crony too!"

Isabelle flashed a wide, wicked smile. "Jasmine, you'll never guess which Pony Pal is Gavin's most favorite." Isabelle's voice changed to a singsong, syrupy tone. "Rainbow Glitter Pants!"

"Her name's Rainbow Sparklemane!" Gavin shouted.

There was a long moment of silence as Isabelle forced herself to glare at Gavin without cracking up.

"Dude," Mason said. "She's got us dead to rights. It'd be social suicide."

Isabelle leveled an accusing finger at Gavin. "You will forget everything you know about us. You will tell *no one* what you've seen. You will take down your stupid website. And you will do it now. Do we have an understanding that is *mutually beneficial?*"

Gavin gulped.

"Do we have an understanding?"

"Yes, m'lady."

25
THE MEN IN BLACK

"Alright. If you need us, our number is on the fridge along with the other emergency numbers. We have to get on the road. Good luck on your Tech Fair project, Isabelle," said Barbara Hubbard as she waved at the girls and walked out the front door.

Isabelle watched out the living room window as Jasmine's dad was getting the twins buckled into their car seats. No small task in itself.

"I can't believe she has to go to every game," said Isabelle. "It's got to be rough dragging the twins around. How does she even watch the game with those two?"

"She finds a way," said Jasmine, smiling. "She's a diehard fan."

Isabelle continued to peer out the window as her dad pulled out of the driveway.

"Let's go to my room," said Jasmine, getting up from the couch.

Once there, Isabelle sat on the bed, as Jasmine settled in at her computer desk. She punched Dr. Anton's address into a search engine and clicked on a map. She zoomed out and tried to get her bearings.

"Maddy was right, this isn't far from her house at all. See?" Jasmine pointed to a satellite image of Rose Valley. "There are too many trees—you can't see it, but it must be right there on the lake. It's probably the only house on Kingfisher Lane."

Isabelle's stomach churned. Sneaking out was so unlike her.

"It's time to go," Jasmine said as she rose from her chair.

Isabelle exhaled and stood. No more time to worry about it. Her heart thumped as they left the house and stepped into the orange light of the sinking sun.

"All we have to do now is walk over to Greenview," Jasmine said as she locked the front door. "It'll be just like we're going to Maddy's. We'll take Moonraker Road."

After a thirty-minute walk they were passing Maddy's house. "We shouldn't have gone this way," whispered Isabelle. "What if she sees us?"

"So what if she *does*?" Jasmine said. "We had a disagreement, and now we can't walk down the street where we please?"

"That's not it," said Isabelle. "I'm just wanting to avoid any further confrontations and complications."

They continued along the shoulder of the blacktop road. Off to the right side, beyond a shallow ditch, was a thick wall of oak trees. To the left, beyond another ditch, was a bare agricultural field that hadn't been sown yet. Isabelle knew Argyle Lake must be on the other side of the trees to their right.

"Kingfisher Lane should be up here," said Jasmine. The sun was setting in the western sky when they finally made the right turn onto the narrow gravel lane. The forest on either side seemed to close in around them as they went.

Walking around a bend in the road revealed a black SUV pulled over along the left side of the road up ahead.

Isabelle and Jasmine stopped dead. *Please don't be the creepy guys, please don't be the creepy guys,* Isabelle kept repeating to herself as they stood by the side of the road looking at the vehicle.

"Do you think we can just walk by them like last time?" asked Jasmine. "They just stared at us, remember?"

As if in answer to Jasmine's question, the headlights of the SUV flicked on.

Isabelle clenched her fists and summoned the last morsel of courage she had.

"What do we do?"

The SUV's engine turned over and started with a hum. The doors of the SUV popped open and two black clad figures stepped out, their pale faces shining in the gloom like bleached skulls.

Isabelle gritted her teeth. "If we can get by them, do you think we could make it to Anton's?"

"What if she's not home?"

Isabelle gave an exasperated shrug.

"Well, we can't turn back now," Jasmine said.

As the passenger walked around the front of the vehicle, each headlight was eclipsed for an instant as he passed. Something about the way the man walked gave Isabelle chills. His movements were smooth and fluid, but his gait seemed stiff. The driver closed his door, took a step backward, and opened the back door.

"Come with us," croaked the driver as he motioned toward the back seat with his gloved hand. The corners of his mouth were pulled up into what Isabelle thought might be an attempt at a smile. "We won't hurt you."

Her skin crawled at the unnatural sound of his voice, but she stood her ground.

"We will *not* go with you!"

For a horrible moment there was silence. The driver's smile changed into something else: a vague, rubbery expression from another world.

"Then we will take you," said his identical black suited partner in a reedy voice that made the hairs on the back of Isabelle's neck stand on end.

Jasmine brandished her fists and stood firm. Isabelle held her breath, wondering who would make the first move. In the next instant the two black-clad forms blinked from existence.

Isabelle looked around wildly, but they were nowhere to be seen. It wasn't until the vice-like grip closed around her forearm that she realized the men had reappeared right behind them. *Did they just teleport?*

The other man made a grab for Jasmine. There was a hollow thump and the man went flying backward into the ditch as Jasmine struck him in the sternum with the palm of her hand.

Up up up! thought Isabelle in a panic. She rose off the ground. The man refused to let go and was dangling beneath her. She pried at his gray suede gloves with her free hand and kicked at him, but he would not release his bulldog grip. She desperately fought to prevent herself from being dragged to the ground.

"Little help!" she cried.

The other man had barely tumbled to a stop in the ditch before he was on his feet again, unnaturally fast. He charged up the side of the ditch at Jasmine who grabbed his arm, threw her hip into him, and flipped him over her back. He somehow landed on his feet. Jasmine kicked and her assailant flew backward like a rag doll. His body hit the trunk of an old oak and the wood splintered like a matchstick.

Barely fazed, the man stood up and replaced the fedora on his bald head, pulling the brim down low. He straightened his sunglasses and tugged at his lapels before striding toward Jasmine again.

It gave Jasmine just enough time to run at Isabelle's attacker. "You! Let! Her! Go!" With each word, she landed a powerful punch to the dangling man's ribs. He released his grip and landed lightly on his feet.

No longer weighed down by her attacker, Isabelle shot straight up into the air. From above, she watched as Jasmine quickly grabbed him by the sleeve and swung him around into the other man who was charging toward her again. The two men collided and fell together in a tangled heap.

"Fall back!" yelled Jasmine. She sprinted down the lane, back toward Moonraker Road. Isabelle streaked through the air toward the T-intersection and was surprised to find Jasmine already standing there waiting for her. She landed next to her friend, her forearm still throbbing and numb where the man had grabbed her.

"Are they following?" asked Jasmine.

"Don't know," gasped Isabelle. "I just—"

Before she could finish her sentence, the black SUV came skidding across the loose gravel on Kingfisher Lane and barreled into the intersection.

Isabelle rocketed straight up into the air and Jasmine rolled to her left, avoiding being flattened by inches. The SUV's front wheels had come to rest in the shallow ditch of the rural road. Its reverse lights ignited.

From above, Isabelle saw her friend scoot behind the SUV and easily lift the rear of the truck as the back tires spun uselessly in the air. Firmly grasping the vehicle's frame in her left hand, she reached for the rear axle with her right hand. With a mighty jerk, she wrenched the axle loose and it fell to the ground, bouncing on its tires.

The doors of the SUV popped open and the two men stepped out. Jasmine kicked at the axle and it tumbled along the shoulder of the road, wheels and all. She took a step backward and dropped the rear of the SUV onto the pavement with a crunch. There the vehicle sat, lopsided.

Isabelle touched down, ready to rejoin the fight.

Down the road, the headlights of an approaching truck blinked into view and a renewed jolt of fear surged through Isabelle. Would this innocent passerby be in harm's way? She couldn't help but wonder what the scene would look like to the oncoming driver: Two fourteen-year-old girls and two black-clad men in sunglasses and fedoras brawling next to an SUV with its rear axle ripped off.

The two men became aware of the approaching vehicle as well. They nodded toward each other and without a word, got back into the SUV and closed their doors. *Where do they think they're going?* thought Isabelle, glancing at their disabled vehicle. She craned her neck and stepped around the side of the SUV. The seats inside were empty.

"They're gone!" she gasped. After fighting for their lives, all it took was the appearance of a passing stranger to scare the black-clad menace away?

Jasmine tugged at Isabelle's sleeve. "We need to be gone too," she said as she stared warily at the pickup truck pulling over alongside the road.

A battery of half-formed plans flashed through Isabelle's brain. They could run. They could lie. They could feign ignorance. But none of it was any good. She knew that there was no way of escaping it; they would surely call the police.

As she stood there, trying to decide which course of action to take, the doors of the truck popped open and realization dropped onto her like a cartoon anvil: it was the same silver pickup truck that pulled up alongside them yesterday. The one-eyed man hopped out of the driver's seat and glanced at the crippled SUV. He then looked at the girls with an expression of amusement. Against the headlights of the truck, Isabelle could make out the silhouette of Dr. Anton, who had just climbed out of the passenger's side. There she stood with crossed arms, dressed in a black pinstriped pantsuit. She stared at one girl, then the other.

"Where is Madeline McCarthy?"

26
THE GOOD DOCTOR

Isabelle shielded her eyes from the headlights' glare. "We had a falling out. We don't know where she is."

Dr. Anton glared. "We shall have to catch up to your *friend* later," she said softly. "I really needed to have all three of you together. But time is of the essence. We'll have to proceed with two." Anton's eyes slowly unfocused and her jaw went slack.

"Well," said Isabelle, watching Anton's expression change, "Jasmine and I decided to come see you." She nodded toward Kingfisher Lane.

"It's just as well," said Anton. "We were about to collect you."

Isabelle plowed forward. "Things have gotten a little out of hand. We're worried about the aliens—I mean, the Orphans. We're worried about ourselves. We've both been having these headaches and Jasmine fainted." Isabelle looked down at her shoes. "We're in over our heads." To hear herself say the words out loud was like removing a heavy burden.

Dr. Anton tilted her head, casting her eyes upward as if she was listening to a sound that only she could hear.

"You alright?" asked Jasmine.

Anton made no answer but suddenly snapped out of her transfixed state. "It's very noble of you to be concerned for the Orphans. They are in great danger." She looked appraisingly at the girls, one by one. "If you've survived this long, I wouldn't be worried about the headaches. If you were going to die, I think it would have happened as soon as you made contact."

Isabelle and Jasmine exchanged a horrified look.

Anton's eyes narrowed. "As for being in over your heads. You've been in far over your heads since day one." She nodded toward the lopsided SUV. "Where did *they* go?"

Isabelle didn't know if she could answer without sounding crazy. "Um. I don't know. Like I said, we were on our way to your place and they tried to stop us. They tried to kidnap us, but now they're . . . gone. Do you know who they are?"

Anton breathed a quiet laugh. "Who they are, or *what* they are?" She turned to the man who glanced down at his wristwatch and nodded. Without a word, he returned to the driver's seat of the truck.

"We don't have time," she said abruptly. She uncrossed her arms and glared at Isabelle and Jasmine. "Come with us."

Isabelle hesitated, then looked to Jasmine. They agreed to see Anton for answers. Nobody had said anything about getting into their vehicle and going anywhere.

"I don't know," Isabelle said.

Dr. Anton clenched her fists. "You've come to *me*, child. I'm offering to work *with* you! Despite all this silly superhero nonsense you three have caused, I'm *still* willing to work with you. It would be easier if we just snatched you up and forced you to cooperate. I daresay history wouldn't judge us too harshly, considering the stakes!"

Isabelle took a step backward, a pang of shock pulsing through her chest.

Anton ticked off her fingers. "Now there's a foolish internet video! Now there's a news report about the convenience store last night! Are you *trying* to get captured and cloned?"

Cloned? What is she talking about? Isabelle was about to ask.

"We didn't publish that video," Jasmine said.

"It doesn't matter." Anton shook her head. "You're totally exposed."

Isabelle scoffed. "Nobody thinks the Old Town video is real."

"If I saw the video and found you, don't you think others could too? It only takes one wrong set of eyes." She huffed. "We really don't have time to stand out here and debate. Nor do we have time for me to soothe every one of your fears. I think it should suffice to say that we don't want to be standing here when the Rose Valley Police come to investigate this scene." She waved a hand toward the lopsided SUV. "More importantly, we have urgent business and you've come to your senses just in time." There was a pause. "Haven't you?"

Isabelle looked to Jasmine, who shrugged.

"We will need to make use of your new talents," Anton said. "You *must* understand. Lives hang in the balance! So, *please* come with us." She extended a hand. Isabelle noted the impatience etched on her face through the headlights' glare.

Anton's head snapped upward to some unheard sound, then she slowly leveled her gaze upon Isabelle.

"I know what's happened to you." A veil of her curly black hair fell across one of her eyes, but she glared, unblinking, at Isabelle. "I know about the changes you've gone through and I can help. I *want* to help."

Jasmine let out a long breath. "That's why we've come all this way, isn't it?" she said softly.

"Finally!" Anton briskly stepped to the open passenger door of the truck and paused, turning her head skyward one more time before climbing in.

Isabelle stood, cemented to the spot. Ever since her brush with the mysterious sphere last Thursday, her life had spiraled out of control. Nearly every attempt to master her situation only snowballed into greater chaos. At this very moment, she sensed that she stood on another threshold. Dr. Anton would usher her even further into the unknown.

"What are you waiting for?" Anton's dark eyes peered over the top of the open truck door.

With no more time to think, Isabelle's legs were moving her toward the truck. Jasmine climbed in after her and closed the door with a metallic clunk. Before she could fully grasp the sheer idiocy of it all, and replay to herself the thousands of childhood warnings to not get into a stranger's vehicle, she was in the back seat. With a howl of its tires, the truck peeled away.

Isabelle stared nervously out the window as the scenery whipped past. She exchanged a look with Jasmine. Dr. Anton was frantically typing a text message into her phone, her face aglow in the rearview mirror.

Isabelle reminded herself that the girl sitting next to her was a force to be reckoned with. No harm would come to either of them as long as Jasmine was here. Isabelle could even take flight if things turned sideways, easily escaping.

With a new wave of confidence forming, Isabelle spoke up. "I didn't catch your name." She tapped the driver's shoulder and caught a glimpse of his one good eye darting in the rearview mirror.

"The name's Gentry. Roland Gentry," he said in a smooth voice. "And it's such a pleasure to make your acquaintance once again."

Anton shot a sideways glance to her colleague, and he responded with a shrug.

Isabelle squinted into the darkness outside her window and concluded they were heading west through the neighborhood of Taylor. They would pass over into Old Town soon.

"Where are you taking us?" she said.

Gentry turned his head subtly toward Anton. "You should bring them up to speed," he said under his breath. "And quickly."

Anton glared up into the rearview mirror, seeming to size Isabelle and Jasmine up. "This is a recovery mission. I think you *know* what we're after."

Isabelle noticed the scorched yellow reflective vest stuffed into the pocket behind the driver's seat and remembered Gentry's close call with the heavily-armed burglar robots Friday morning. The knot in her stomach twisted even tighter. The goal of the mission could be only one thing: retrieve the Orphan vessel that the robots had taken.

Anton stared out the window for a long moment before turning in her seat to face the girls. Her eyes betrayed a deep sadness. "There's something more you need to understand. The Orphans don't belong here." She spoke in a soft voice. "While they came from an Earth-like planet eons ago, they've long since adapted to a different environment. They can't survive here without their ship's energy . . . energy that you've taken away. Their vessel's propulsion system—if you can call it that—is sufficient to navigate in the vacuum of space, but it doesn't have the ability to leave Earth's atmosphere under its own power. That's what I'm trying to do."

The blood drained from Isabelle's face as she listened. Guilt started to well in the pit of her stomach.

Anton solemnly lowered her head. "Without their energy, they have very little life support. They don't have much longer. And that is why we've risked so much to try to complete this mission."

"How many Orphans are in there?" Isabelle said, hoarsely.

"All of them," Dr. Anton said. "Every time someone took a vessel's power throughout history, another colony of Orphans slowly died. Gilgamesh in Mesopotamia; Hercules in Greece; Samson in Israel. Whoever found the vessel in China. Probably many others throughout history. Every legend of a superhuman or a demigod through the ages very well may be a story of Orphan contact. It doesn't happen to everyone, but invariably, some sort of connection is always made and it results in a mini-apocalypse. So it's been. Until now. Here *we* stand in history, with perhaps the greatest knowledge these beings could ever hope for—knowledge that they *do* exist and knowledge that we *can* help them."

Anton stared at them, unblinking. "Isabelle, Jasmine, this sphere contains the last of the Orphans. They teeter on the edge of extinction. Not just them, but all their knowledge and wisdom. This is what Noah Drennan told me, and I believe him." Dr. Anton swallowed and pressed her lips together.

Jasmine seemed dumbstruck.

Isabelle's head was humming and she felt short of breath. The last wisp of hope that she could transform herself with this newfound power came crashing down around her. She wondered how she could have been so naïve as to think that power would have no cost. Even worse was the guilt creeping up from the depths of her soul and stealing her breath away. She swallowed hard, but the lump inside her throat would not go down.

"How do we give it back to them?" she said as tears welled in her eyes. "We have to tell Maddy! She won't want them to die!"

The two brick pillars marking the entrance to Hilltop Park passed by Isabelle's window, followed by the five-foot metal culvert. Ever since she and her friends emerged from its darkness last Thursday, their lives had been a flurry of chaos. Gentry killed the lights and drove a little further into the park before pulling off the road onto the grass. A moment later, he pulled behind a green utility shed, hiding the truck from view from the road.

Anton glanced at Isabelle in the back seat.

"You'd better pull yourself together. It's almost time to act."

27
THE BREATH BEFORE THE PLUNGE

Gentry's phone buzzed and lit up. He quickly tapped the screen and read the incoming message.

"We're not too late," he said to Anton. "Clement says she's on foot, approaching the park from the east. No sign of Insult or Injury." He lowered the phone and looked to Anton. "So, what is the plan?"

"*They're* my plan," she said, nodding toward the girls in the back seat.

Gentry shook his head. "My ears must be deceiving me. For a moment it sounded as if you intend to just throw them into battle."

"Only one thing matters—the mission. I'm sure they can handle themselves. You saw what they could do."

"Uh, we're right here," said Jasmine. "Can't you just tell us what we're up against?"

Anton glanced back at Jasmine. "Your mission is to get the vessel and take it to safety. You wanted to be heroes? Now's the time."

Isabelle measured Anton's expression and concluded she was being only partially facetious. Isabelle mopped her cheeks with her sleeve and flexed her fists, trying to regain her composure. Knowing the existence of a whole alien race rested on her shoulders was a lot of pressure. Especially when two strangers were just discussing using her and Jasmine as pawns.

"Okay, where is it?" asked Jasmine.

Anton sighed. "We received information that it was being brought to Nowotny tonight at Beacon Hill. If we're going to have a chance to intercept, it'll be tonight."

Isabelle's ears perked up at the sound of the familiar name. "Wait. The Air Force guy who investigated the sphere in 1984?"

"That's him." Anton smiled. "You girls *have* done your homework. We don't know why he wants it, but it's safe to assume it's not to preserve the Orphans."

Isabelle took a deep, cleansing breath. "Tell us everything you know."

Anton's face twitched; she looked out at the entrance of the park, then to Gentry.

He glanced at his phone. "She's five blocks away and closing. Still no sign of Insult or Injury."

Isabelle was about to ask who she was talking about but stopped short. She was certain she already knew.

Anton nodded. "Alright, girls, we have a few moments. I'll briefly explain what I can."

Isabelle leaned forward, intently, while Jasmine strained to see the park entrance through the darkness. Anton twisted in her seat to address the girls in the back, speaking in almost a whisper.

"You already know how the Drennans found the sphere, how it was supposedly found to be a hoax?"

"That's right," said Isabelle. "We read that Major Nowotny changed his mind and returned the sphere to Noah."

"Doesn't that strike you as odd?" asked Anton. "That some tough-as-nails Air Force officer would confiscate a suspected alien artifact, then surrender it back to the civilians who found it?"

Isabelle shrugged. "Sure, but what does it mean?"

"We think the Orphans in the vessel manipulated Nowotny somehow. After being declared a hoax and given back to Noah, the sphere was mostly forgotten. After Noah died—"

"He died?" asked Isabelle.

"Yes, last year. He was sixty-three." Anton shook her head. "Only after Noah passed did Nowotny start hunting for the vessel. For thirty-three years, Nowotny went about his life as if the investigation was a brief, forgotten chapter of his military career—as if it really *was* a hoax. The moment Noah died, something happened. I think the part of Nowotny that was manipulated by the Orphans awoke. Since then, he has been a man on a singular mission. He left his old life behind and now he's here. I believe that mission, all along, has been to seize the Orphan Ark."

"Was there something going on between Noah and Nowotny when he was alive?" asked Jasmine.

Gentry looked up from his phone screen, and peered out at the park entrance. "Three blocks and closing."

Jasmine shot a knowing look to Isabelle, then peered out the window into the darkness.

Anton nodded at him before turning back to the girls. "We don't have any record of Noah Drennan and Nowotny coming into contact with one another since the investigation. Noah lived his entire life in south Texas. Nowotny rose to the rank of colonel before retiring to enter the private sector. He ended up taking over the helm of a huge biochemical engineering company in Boston." Anton smiled darkly. "When Noah came to Rose Valley to seek me out, he didn't even mention Edwin Nowotny."

Isabelle had so many unanswered questions it was impossible to focus. She grabbed one from the whirlwind in her mind and tossed it out.

"The article I read said that Noah had grown emotionally attached to the sphere?"

"One could say that," said Anton. "After all, the beings on board the vessel had been communicating with him telepathically for years. Mostly in dreams. They continued right up until his death."

Isabelle sat back. Jasmine shot her an uneasy look.

"Why are only certain people affected by the vessel? Why were we affected the way we were, while Noah was affected differently? He didn't have powers."

"We can't say for sure," Anton said.

"Is it something in our genetics?" suggested Jasmine.

Gentry perked up and smiled. "That's a very good guess, child. I believe the vessel's discharging of energy to certain humans throughout history is a malfunction. I think their vessels are biomechanical and the Orphans have a biological connection with them. Some human individuals have DNA that triggers a sort of—accidental interaction with a vessel. It would be as if the ship thinks you are one of them."

Jasmine's face scrunched up. "So, you're saying the vessel was confused by something in our DNA and thought we were Orphans?"

Anton nodded. "In a way of speaking, yes."

"Yeah, but what are the chances that Jasmine, Maddy, and myself all have the same type of genetic anomaly to trigger a reaction?" Isabelle said, skeptically.

Gentry raised his brows and grinned. "It was probably just *one* of you who triggered the reaction, and the energy arced to the other two."

Thinking back to the cavern, Isabelle vaguely remembered Jasmine's and Maddy's hands on her shoulders as they were trying to get a look at the sphere.

Anton suddenly twitched and glanced skyward before collecting herself and continuing. "Throughout history, people might have interpreted this differently. They might have believed the sphere was a gift from the gods. They might have believed their newfound abilities were proof that they were divinely chosen for greatness." She waved a hand toward the heavens.

Isabelle pondered just how dangerously close she, herself, had come to arriving at a similar conclusion.

"There's even a mythological correlation. It's the planet Jupiter—the namesake of the king of the gods—that keeps slingshotting these vessels toward Earth with its immense gravity well. That's one of the reasons so many Orphan vessels have found their way here."

Gentry stared at his phone screen. "One block away. She's almost here."

"What's *your* connection to Noah?" Isabelle said. "Why did he seek you?"

"After reading a few of my books, he reached out to me through my website. He traveled to Rose Valley with the vessel to ask for my help. Of course, I thought he was a crackpot—imagine that!" she scoffed. "During his visit, though, something happened . . ." Anton stared into space. "The beings in the vessel communicated with me."

Jasmine opened her mouth, but Anton cut her off.

"Rather, they deposited a large amount of data into my mind. Don't ask me how I know it was real—I just do. From that moment, I've been resolved to complete my mission." She paused and locked eyes with Isabelle. "Noah had become terminally ill and wanted to pass the vessel on to me, but on one condition. He insisted I help the Orphans leave Earth."

"Does this Nowotny guy have anything to do with those robots?" asked Isabelle. Her mind flashed back to Crystal . . . how did *she* fit into all of this?

Anton's expression dropped. "Only sort of."

"Then who *is* responsible?" asked Jasmine.

Anton gestured toward the entrance to Hilltop Park. "Here she comes."

28
THE BATTLE OF BEACON HILL

From their hidden vantage point, Isabelle could just make out a wiry shape stalking between the brick columns that flanked the entrance to the park. The teenaged girl was dressed in black from head to toe, except for her brightly dyed blue hair.

Isabelle slowly nodded as she watched the last piece of the puzzle saunter into the park. "Crystal Skorch."

Anton watched as Crystal strutted out of sight around the corner of the utility shed. "You know this girl, yes? We've been unable to lay hands on her, since she's been under the protection of Nowotny."

"She asked me about the vessel's energy," said Isabelle. "She seemed pretty frazzled."

"Based on that interaction, I'd say Nowotny doesn't know about the missing energy, and Crystal hasn't told him yet," said Gentry.

Anton nodded.

Jasmine squirmed in her seat. "So, how did Crystal get involved in all of this?" she asked.

"It's an embarrassing story."

Isabelle shrugged.

Anton sighed. "There's a private aerospace company called Global TransGalactic that I've formed a coalition with. We're working on a plan to return the Orphans to space." Anton watched as Crystal made her way, ever closer, to Beacon Hill.

Isabelle's eyebrows rose. "They know about the aliens?"

Anton's dark eyes darted sideways. "Yes, but only a very select few within GTG. Because of the extreme sensitivity of our mission, I'm trying to do as much of it privately as I can. It's not the ideal solution, but under the circumstances, it's the best we could hope for."

Isabelle listened intently as Anton continued.

"We can't just duct tape the sphere to a rocket, you know," she said. "I put out feelers for talented young individuals to join me in my endeavor. And the answer landed, quite literally, on my doorstep in the form of Crystal Skorch. I made arrangements for her and her mother to move to Rose Valley. She'd be homeschooled while she was working for me. On paper, Crystal was perfect. I needed to develop several autonomous components for the later stages of the mission, and she possessed a raw talent in robotics that was truly something to behold. What I didn't foresee was that she'd be so difficult to work with. Impossible, really."

"Why *would* you rely on a kid for a job like that?" Jasmine said.

"Children are the most resilient when their entire sense of reality is shaken by paranormal events. Children are cheap. And last, but certainly not least, children are more easily—shall we say—manipulated."

Isabelle struggled to slow her erratic breathing. Anton wasn't only talking about Crystal.

"So, if Crystal has been working for you, then are you the one behind all the tech burglaries?" Isabelle tensed at the fleeting thought that she and Jasmine could be face-to-face with the criminal mastermind.

Anton seemed to shrink, then looked away. "Let me be clear. I did *not* order her to build those robots, nor did I order her to burglarize anyone. This embarrassing mess is already going to blow up in my face, so let's not make it any worse than it already is, shall we?"

Isabelle slumped back down into her seat and looked through the windshield. Crystal had just reached the concrete steps that led to the summit of Beacon Hill. A knot of dread started to form in her stomach.

Anton gathered herself and continued. "While Crystal was working for me, she became increasingly curious about the vessel. The more she pressed me for information, the more I pushed her away. We eventually found out that Nowotny and Crystal had been working together all along. I'd given Crystal free rein and a near unlimited budget to build the modules we'd need to undock the sphere from the launch vehicle and into space. That was a big mistake. I should have been more closely overseeing her work."

Isabelle pondered for a moment how out of touch Anton would have to be to give someone like Crystal Skorch free rein and unlimited budget on an aerospace project. She decided to hold her tongue.

"While secretly working with Nowotny, she started misappropriating the funds and abused our resources to build two weaponized, robotic thugs. Then, to augment their weaponry, she broke into high technology Tech Basin labs.

"She finally made her move to seize the sphere, but I'd already ordered Gentry to carry it away to safety. Before he could get to the safe house, he was intercepted and pursued by those—things in black suits. During the chase, Gentry's truck was disabled and he was forced to hide the vessel underground."

Isabelle thought back to the first time she saw Gentry. He was rummaging in the toolbox as steam poured from his truck's engine.

"When I confronted her and asked her why, she said, 'because she *could.*' She wanted to see how much these robots could get away with. Such arrogance! Such . . . stupidity! This is a game to her!" Anton's gaze lowered. "While I'm angered by her irresponsibility and betrayal, I can't help but acknowledge that she is a brilliant girl—brilliant and dangerous."

Gentry spoke. "She's halfway up." He squinted and leaned forward as he watched the distant figure ascend the stairs.

"It's time," Anton said. "Follow her up there. Get that vessel by any means necessary." Anton locked eyes with Isabelle. "Your task is simple. Use your—talent—to secure the vessel and spirit it away to 100 Kingfisher Lane. A man named Justus Clement will be waiting there for you. He'll get you and the vessel to safety."

Anton turned to Jasmine. "I trust *you'll* be able to handle yourself?"

Jasmine's face split into a huge grin as she pounded an open palm with her fist.

"One more thing," said Anton. "I'm told that Crystal's machines have been carrying the vessel with some kind of a net. It's imperative that you handle this vessel *only* by this net."

Jasmine scowled. "How are we supposed to get this thing if we can't touch it?"

"*Don't* touch it," Anton repeated.

"What happens if—"

"There's no time. You have to move now!" She reached over the back of her seat and unlatched the rear door, shooing the girls outside. Gentry exited the truck and Anton scooted over to the driver's seat.

Gentry crept over to the utility shed's overhang and beckoned the girls over.

"The good doctor is going to take the truck as soon as we get to the top. I'm going to stay behind you, just out of sight." He shrugged. "Just in case you need help."

Isabelle wondered what help he could actually offer against the two robot thugs or whatever else waited for them on the hilltop, but decided not to say anything.

"What about us?" Jasmine said. "If Isabelle's flying away with the sphere, how are *we* going to get back?"

Isabelle glanced back toward Anton who was making wild gesticulations for them to hurry up.

Gentry laughed and twisted one tip of his mustache. "Don't you worry, child. I have a friend who will be watching over us. Now, up you go."

Isabelle craned her neck and saw the tiny figure in black ascending the concrete stairs that zig-zagged up the southern slope of Beacon Hill.

The time for talk was over and the time for action had come. Isabelle huffed a sigh and with a final nod to her best friend, they broke cover and rushed into the seemingly blinding lamppost light.

It seemed simple enough: intercept the vessel before it could be passed to Nowotny.

As they started up the undulating concrete steps, adrenaline coursed through Isabelle's body. Her limbs tingled and her head swum. She hated going into a dangerous situation with no plan, but that was the only way her superpower had ever come into play. She always thought of herself as analytical and calculating. Now, she'd have to rely on her instincts and intuition. She glanced at Jasmine, who seemed to be in her element as she stealthily padded up the steps alongside her. Glancing behind, she noticed Gentry was nowhere to be seen.

"He did say he'd stay out of sight, didn't he?" she muttered to herself.

Nearly cresting the hill, they crouched down, looking for cover, and found it in a tourism kiosk. Isabelle tried to shrink behind an informational placard.

The flat top of Beacon Hill was crowned with a circular driveway, accessed by a road that snaked up the far slope and stairs that meandered down the southern side. In the center of the grassy area was the famous statue of Percival Cavett standing atop his pedestal. The bronze likeness of the 18th century inventor had overlooked the Old Town section of Rose Valley for as long as she could remember, forever holding his lantern aloft. Inscribed on his white marble plinth were the words, "YOU CANNOT FORGE NEW DISCOVERIES IF YOU FEAR FAILURE."

From the shadows, Isabelle watched Crystal stride across the grassy area in the middle of the plaza. The circular driveway was ringed with lampposts. On the far side of the summit sat a black luxury sedan. A man was getting out of the back seat to greet Crystal.

He looked to be in his late sixties, but still possessed an athletic build and square shoulders. The wisps of white hair on his head were slicked back, revealing a lined forehead and the attentive glare of a bird of prey.

As Edwin Nowotny spoke with Crystal, Isabelle watched him jab the air with his finger, clearly not pleased. Crystal stood by with her hands in her back pockets as if she were bored.

Isabelle heard Jasmine's breath catch as the two metallic beasts came into view from the west. She could make out the high-pitched whir of their motors as they swooped in, flying side by side. Just beneath the chassis of one robot hung a net . . . and in that net, a silver-blue sphere.

A multitude of emotions swelled into Isabelle's chest. She could hardly believe she was looking at the last remnants of an extraterrestrial race of beings. The weight of what she had to do seemed almost unbearable.

"Look!" Jasmine whispered. "You can just fly up and grab it."

Isabelle's stomach lurched as she watched the robots circle and prepare to land.

"I'll distract them." Jasmine stood up.

"Wait. What?" Isabelle froze when she realized Jasmine was already walking toward Crystal and the man.

"Hey, you butts-with-ears!" Jasmine yelled.

Isabelle cringed. They didn't even have the slightest hint of a coordinated plan.

Nowotny took a step backward and Crystal spun around to face the threat.

"Insult! Injury! Target!" she said.

In response to Crystal's command, the robots wheeled about in the air and zeroed in on Jasmine. With an echoing thud, the robot carrying the net pouch fired its sonic cannon. Jasmine rolled out of the way, shrugging off the fringes of the shock wave.

Isabelle could only stare in horror, her feet rooted to the spot. Shame and horror gripped her. *Am I going to be a coward again?*

The other robot flitted around overhead to Jasmine's flank. The menacing whine of its flight motors cut through the night air. Nowotny crouched behind the car, but Crystal stood her ground, waving her arms and barking commands. The robot's targeting laser settled on Jasmine's shoulder, who noticed the three red dots forming a triangle. She nimbly turned sideways. With a sharp crack, the robot's lasers pulsed and a forked stream of glowing plasma streaked past its target, missing her by inches. A black scorch mark smoldered on the grass.

Another sonic blast came from the robot carrying the sphere and again, Jasmine was forced to dive out of the way. A metal trash can caught the brunt of the attack, and cups and fast food wrappers scattered into the air.

"Don't leave me hanging, girl!" Jasmine called.

Isabelle willed herself to surge forward, but she remained frozen. *Jasmine needs me! I have to move!*

The robots continued to outflank Jasmine until she found machines bearing down on her from two sides. If they attacked again, surely one of them would hit. The triple red dots appeared on Jasmine's back as her head swiveled.

It was now or never.

Swallowing her fear, Isabelle shot into the air like a javelin toward the sonic weapon wielding robot. The frigid night air blasted her face as she streaked up toward her target. Crystal howled a new set of commands and the robot did an abrupt about-face. Like miniature lightning, a blue stream of plasma erupted from the hovering robot and a painful jolt throbbed though Isabelle's leg. She made a grab for the net pouch, but instead grasped empty air as she collided with the robot.

Her world spun crazily as metal rotors bit at her, shredding the leg of her jeans. With a sickening *gong*, Isabelle bounced off the bronze statue of Percival Cavett and in the next instant she found herself lying prone in the cold grass. She tried in vain to breathe in, but could only make a horrible rasping sound. She was helpless and exposed. The muscles of her left leg twitched and jerked while her right leg throbbed in pain.

With a crunch, the robot crash-landed in the grass beside her. The sphere was still in the net pouch trailing from the robot's manipulator arm. Her mind screamed that she could just crawl over and grab it, but all she could do was writhe in agony. Her chest heaved, but no air found its way into her lungs.

Now grounded, the robot's rotors spun down, neatly tucked themselves away, and the rotor masts disappeared into the body of the machine. Its four legs unfurled from beneath and it rose to a standing position.

At last, with a mighty gasp, Isabelle caught her breath and rolled over to grasp at the net pouch, but the robot had already spidered away, dragging the sphere behind it.

Isabelle struggled to move. One leg twitched and tingled and the other was bloodied with a dozen small cuts. She crawled toward the robot as it clacked away from her and turned its weapon on Jasmine.

Isabelle forced herself to her feet, choking back tears as torrid pain shot up from her injured legs. No sooner than she stood, she noticed the pattern of red laser dots trained on her chest. Somewhere overhead the hovering robot had her in its sights.

"Five milliamps!" echoed Crystal's voice.

Isabelle ducked behind the statue's pedestal and the blue plasma beam struck the bronze legs of Percival Cavett, throwing sparks.

The grounded robot took aim and fired with a resonating thud. Jasmine planted her feet and clenched her fists, leaning into the shockwave. Her hair rippled and her clothes fluttered, but she withstood the force that would have knocked anyone else off their feet.

"Insult, track one-eighty!"

The robot wheeled around, clacking and whirring toward Isabelle. It stalked like a wolf, its sensor array tilted forward, each step rising and falling with a hunter's precision.

Isabelle scanned the skies for the other robot, mindful of another broadside attack, but couldn't find it. She turned back in time to see Jasmine running toward the beast.

"Insult, track one-ten! Injury, hold!" came Crystal's voice once again, this time almost gleeful. The robot fired and sidestepped at the same time, causing Jasmine's kick to swoosh into empty air. The machine countered with a swipe of its manipulator arm, forcing Jasmine to somersault out of harm's way.

Isabelle cowered behind the plinth, holding her ears as another shockwave washed overhead and struck the statue. With a horrible crunching sound, a crack appeared in the marble pedestal. The robot fired again and the statue tottered in place. A horrible screech of grinding metal echoed through the park as the bronze statue of Percival Cavett toppled over.

Isabelle scrambled to escape, but with an earthshaking crash the statue eclipsed her view of everything as it came down on top of her. The lantern wielding arm of Percival Cavett dug into the ground and Isabelle found herself pinned and immobile beneath the statue's armpit.

"Isabelle!" Jasmine cried, running towards the statue. "Are you okay?"

"I'm fine!" Isabelle lied. "Get it! It's the only way! Get it and run!"

She dimly focused on Jasmine's panicked eyes as they zeroed in on the net pouch. In a blur, Jasmine made a dash and grab for the vessel—her fingertips grazed the smooth surface of the sphere through the gaps in the netting.

A blinding blue flash emanated from the vessel. Jasmine went limp, falling into a heap on the ground. The sphere now pulsed a dim blue light.

"Jasmine!" Isabelle called out weakly. Her head spun and her vision started to tunnel as the faint wail of sirens echoed in the distance. The last thing Isabelle saw before she blacked out was Nowotny grabbing Jasmine by the back of her jacket and dragging her toward the car.

29
THE GUMSHOE

I SABELLE AWOKE in darkness.

Jasmine! I have to save Jasmine!

She found herself contorted in an uncomfortable position with a jacket balled up under her head. With difficulty, she turned her head and made out the silhouette of Gentry crouched within a disc of dim light. As the scene came into focus, she realized she was lying inside a corrugated metal culvert. There was a familiar rectangular concrete tunnel to her left. She slowly realized she was in the same culvert she and her friends climbed out of last week.

Outside, the faint flashes of red and blue told her the Rose Valley Police must have arrived at Beacon Hill to find the town's beloved statue toppled. She could only imagine what tomorrow morning's front-page headline in the *Rose Valley Journal* would be.

I have to save Jasmine. She tried to get up, but the fiery pain forced her back down. Determined not to cry, she glanced up at Gentry again. She discerned the shape of another man crouched outside the culvert. They talked in hushed voices.

Who is he talking to?

She reached down to feel her throbbing leg and found that a handkerchief had been hastily wrapped around the wounds where the robot's rotors had lacerated her. Gentry must have freed her from beneath the statue and carried her down Beacon Hill before the police arrived.

I have to get up. I have to save Jasmine. She strained to get up, this time forcing herself through the pain.

Gentry, alerted to her struggles, turned and crouch-walked back toward her.

"And just where do you think you're going, young lady," he whispered.

"Jasmine," she said. "They have Jasmine. We have to do something." With Gentry's help, she sat back down on the jacket.

The man at the mouth of the culvert leaned over and a shaft of light caught his face. Isabelle's jaw dropped as she recognized Detective Pike.

"Hello, Miss Cooley."

"What's *he* doing here?" she said.

"Easy, child. He's a friend. He's going to help us get out of here."

Isabelle sputtered. "How?"

Pike twisted around and glanced toward Beacon Hill before leaning back into the culvert.

"If you come right now, I'll just give you a ride. They're a little busy right now," he said as he nodded toward the police on the hill, in the midst of their investigation.

"Did the police catch them?"

Pike looked down and shook his head. "Sorry, Miss Cooley. The only thing they found on Beacon Hill was Old Percy Cavett lying face down."

"So, they're looking for Nowotny and Crystal? Are they going to get Jasmine back?"

Pike shook his head. "I'm sorry, Isabelle, but it's just not that easy." He reached into his pocket and jingled his keys. The trunk of his car, which was parked up on the road, popped open. He then made pointed eye contact with Gentry. "I can't be seen transporting you two. Sorry, old friend."

Gentry looked back and forth between the car and the detective with dawning comprehension. "I assure you, I've had to travel in worse accommodations. Did I ever tell you about the time I traveled across Luxembourg hidden in the back of a beer lorry?"

Pike smiled. "No, but when things calm down, that tale will be one worth hearing."

Resigned, Gentry squeezed past Pike at the mouth of the culvert and quickly crossed the grassy slope. After taking a quick look around, he climbed into the trunk, pulling it shut from the inside.

Pike stepped into the culvert and reached down to help Isabelle up, but she ignored his hand and hauled herself up on her own.

"Let's go," she said. Her legs were stiff and shaky, but she was satisfied to be moving on her own. As she limped past Pike into the open, she glanced sideways at him. "You *have* to help Jasmine."

Pike sighed and his usual smugness melted away for just a moment. "You've got to understand. The world isn't ready for what we're getting into. Just because I can't help Miss Hubbard as an RVPD officer, doesn't mean I'm not doing everything I can."

Isabelle was not ready to trust Pike, but she had to admit to herself that she had little choice.

He quickly ushered her over to his car, opening the back door. "Our one-eyed friend is in the trunk, but I thought you'd appreciate riding up here. Pike gestured toward the floorboard. "If you don't mind, Miss Cooley. I'm sorry." He again glanced up toward Beacon Hill and the flashing red and blue lights.

She stiffly clambered down onto the floorboard and allowed him to throw a trench coat on top of her. She couldn't help but scoff at the garment that looked like it came right out of the pages of a noir comic book.

Isabelle listened as Pike closed the door and made his way to the driver's seat. After buckling himself in, he started the engine and was on his way.

Isabelle repositioned herself on the floorboard and uncovered her head, thankful the detective's back seat floorboard was a lot cleaner than her dad's car.

"Where are you taking us?" she asked.

After a pause, the detective's voice came from the front seat. "I'm taking you to Dr. Anton's place."

As chummy as Pike and Gentry seemed to be a few moments ago, it didn't surprise her, but it only raised more questions. "So, just how well do you all know each other?"

"It's complicated, Miss Cooley." He paused, seemingly searching for the right words. "You could say we're kindred spirits, Stephanie and I. We have responsibilities that keep us outside the realm of what people would call—normal. Plus, I can't overstate how useful it is for her to have an inside connection to RVPD."

"Huh?"

"A little dispatch misdirection here, a little evidence goes missing there . . ."

"You're a crooked cop?"

Pike chuckled. "Well, I was able to keep you three out of the station last Friday morning when the brat's robots were blasting everything in sight. You were witnesses. Without my intervention, you would have been hauled in and questioned. Would you three have been able to keep your cool and not crack?"

Isabelle was speechless.

"Do you not realize how many calls we got that morning? It hasn't been easy keeping it off the front page. And what about tonight? I got you away from Beacon Hill, didn't I? It wouldn't look good for a Cavett Academy goody-two-shoes like you to get accused of being *both* the Old Town Vandal *and* the desecrator of Old Percy Cavett's shrine, would it?"

Isabelle decided that maybe now wasn't the time to point fingers. As Pike drove onward, she watched the streetlights pass by the car's back windows, trying to guess where they were.

"So, you know about . . ." She trailed off, not sure if it was safe to mention her and her friends' superpowers.

"I know a lot, Miss Cooley."

Isabelle decided to switch topics. "So, you know we're not alone? I mean, in the universe?"

Pike switched to the syrupy tone she hated so much. "Like I said, young lady. I know a great deal."

"If you know so much, why were you questioning us this morning?"

Pike seemed amused. "Ah. The things we do to keep up appearances."

"So, you know about the vessel? And the aliens?" Isabelle felt foolish, speaking about the bizarre truth so openly, but at the same time, goosebumps rose on her skin.

"I know, young lady. And I know the danger they're in." His smug tone melted away. "It's my turn to ask a question." A moment of silence passed. "What do you know about those two men in the black SUV?"

"The guys in black?" She wondered where this was going. "Um. I don't know what to think of them, I just know they're not—normal. They've been watching us. They tried to abduct Jasmine and me earlier this evening. They almost ran over us in their truck. Then they disappeared into thin air. Do you mind telling me why they're after us? And *what* they are?"

"They didn't touch you, did they?"

Isabelle noted the concern in his voice. Replaying the fight in her head, she remembered Jasmine kicking, punching, and swinging one around by the arm. She also remembered being grasped around the forearm. She could still feel her skin crawling.

"No," she lied. She didn't feel like getting into the details. "At first, Maddy thought they might be government agents. That's obviously not true."

Pike laughed. "No, but you're right to be wary of them. They're not from this world and what you saw is not their true form. Different people throughout the ages have had different names for them. Hexapods. Skinwalkers. We call them Cloners. They're an extreme form of parasite. They likely laid in wait somewhere and collected someone's DNA to manufacture the two clone bodies you saw. The man who unwittingly donated his DNA for them most likely doesn't even know that he has clones of himself running around."

Isabelle's heart thumped in her chest. She made contact with not only one but two different types of alien beings. *What are the chances, huh?*

"Those things are just clones?" she sputtered.

"The clones are the bodies. Their true identity is hidden. The best way to describe it would be that these creatures hollowed out these human clones and surgically implanted themselves inside. From there, each of them can control their clone's every action as if it were a puppet. Human mech suits, if you will. They are natural infiltrators and mimics. They survive and propagate by blending in with whatever their hosts are."

Isabelle's stomach squirmed uncomfortably. *How could such horrible creatures exist in the universe?* The thought that one of them had gripped her by the arm less than an hour ago gave her chills. She held out her arm and looked at the faint marks in the passing streetlight. "So, if they're just creatures inside of clones, how did they disappear like that?"

"It may seem like magic, but it's just their tech," he said. "They're nasty creatures. They've been tracking the vessels of Anton's little Orphan friends for millennia, always hoping to capture one. The energy contained in a single Orphan vessel would be a near unlimited source of power for the Cloner colony. That's another thing. Their colony is off world, but close, astronomically speaking, of course."

She felt the car slow and made out the red glow of a stop light.

"They're staking out this corner of the solar system because Orphan vessels often get slingshotted this way. Something to do with Jupiter's gravity well. Anton's Orphan Ark has been on

Earth since the 80s, so why *these* two Cloners are only showing up *now* is a bit of a mystery. I believe they were tracking an entirely different Orphan ship that recently landed in China. When that ship went silent, they lost track of it. Somehow, they must have gotten wind of the one Anton had and started tracking it instead. Needless to say, everyone is doing all they can to keep the Orphan ships away from them. Then you and your friends came along and complicated matters. Not to mention Edwin Nowotny's interference."

The light changed to green and Isabelle felt the car accelerate. "What do you think Nowotny wants with the vessel?"

"That I don't know. I can only assume it won't be good for the Orphans."

Isabelle sat up. "Do you think the Cloners will be able to get the vessel from Nowotny?"

Pike chuckled under his breath. "If they want to, they'd better hurry. The Cloners will only have a limited time to use their meat suits before they expire. After that, they'll have to abandon them or dispose of them." Pike laughed darkly. "Let's hope they have the decency to dispose of them. Otherwise, there'll be hollowed out unidentified bodies turning up all over the place. That sort of thing tends to put the police and public on edge, you know. Lots of paperwork, too."

Isabelle gulped and fought back a wave of nausea.

He continued. "There'll be a window of time when it will be perfectly safe to go after the vessel without worrying about the Cloners' interference. There's no accurate way of knowing when that will be, but I think it'll be soon."

"Does your partner know about all this?"

"Oh, Detective Cowie? Yeah, he's cool."

Isabelle squirmed at the thought that yet another person seemed privy to her secrets. "You don't suppose I can get up yet?" She craned her neck to get a look outside the car. She caught a glimpse of the flashing red and blue lights of a pair of police cars and the yellow lights of a tow truck. Nearby in the ditch was the crippled SUV of the Cloners. A wrecker crew was hoisting the detached rear axle onto a flatbed truck as two policemen were standing off to the side, talking.

"Better stay hidden and quiet, missy. Just in case."

Isabelle quickly ducked back down and covered her head with the trench coat.

"What have we here?" asked Pike. "That SUV looks familiar. Methinks you and the girls had a little run in with the Cloners here?"

"Jasmine did that," she said.

Pike let out a low whistle. "Well, that's going to put a damper on their traveling plans, isn't it? Bad luck for whoever they stole it from though." He chuckled.

Isabelle felt the car turn and heard the crunch of gravel beneath tires. She fully expected the officers standing by the road to stop Pike and talk to him, but they apparently paid him no notice at all as he pulled onto Kingfisher Lane.

"Alright, I think we're clear from any prying eyes. You can come out now."

Isabelle pushed the ridiculous trench coat aside and pulled herself up onto the back seat. Feeling had almost returned to the leg that had been shot by the robot, while the other leg was still stiff and sore. She peered out the window to get her bearings.

Pike was driving down a narrow lane with the foreboding darkness of thick trees on either side of them. As they neared the end of the road, the trees started to thin, and Isabelle caught a beautiful glimpse of a lake to her right. The reflected lights from the few scattered houses along the far shore danced on the still water.

At the end of the road was a cul-de-sac with a tall, wrought iron gate between two stone pillars. Each pillar was adorned with a dim, yellow light ensconced in a glass globe. Pike stopped the car and pressed a button on his dashboard as he glanced up into the rearview mirror. With a pop, the trunk opened and the weight in the back of the car shifted as Gentry climbed out, stretched, and moved toward the gate, grumbling to himself.

Beyond the gate stood a stately colonial style house that seemed to be surrounded by the same style of tall wrought iron fencing. Gentry opened a hinged, stainless-steel box on the right-hand pillar and pressed a button. After a moment he spoke into the box.

"It's me. I'm here with friends." After a moment, there was a buzz and a click and he pushed the gate open.

Pike's car crept forward, stopping alongside Gentry. "Need a lift?" he asked, nodding his head toward the house, just a stone's throw away.

Gentry smiled, his one green eye twinkling. "After that ordeal, I really think I'd rather walk. You must remember, these bones are much older than they look."

"Suit yourself," Pike replied, grinning. He continued through the gate and parked in front of the blocky, rectangular house.

Isabelle took in her surroundings. Dr. Anton's house sat on a gentle slope with a fantastic view overlooking Argyle Lake. The balcony above the porch was supported by four white columns which contrasted sharply with the dark red bricks and black shutters. The same style of wrought iron as the perimeter fencing rimmed the balcony, and the slanted roof had three protruding gables. On the porch she noticed a Persian cat lounging on a footstool like a dust-gray sphinx. It watched their every move with absolute disdain.

The door opened and Anton stepped onto the porch with crossed arms.

"Where's Jasmine?"

30
ULTIMATUM

ISABELLE THREW OPEN THE CAR DOOR. "They took her!" She clambered out and limped toward the front porch. "We have to do something!"

Detective Pike killed the engine and exited the car. He leaned on the door, watching and listening.

Anton uncrossed her arms. "You're injured," she said coldly.

"I'm fine," Isabelle said. "Did you hear me? They took Jasmine!"

"How? She should have easily overpowered them."

Gentry came walking stiff-legged up the driveway, "She touched it," he said. "It's reabsorbed the energy. She was knocked out cold."

Isabelle looked back and forth between Gentry and Anton. "Does this mean Jasmine lost her powers?"

Gentry stood at the bottom of the porch steps and put his hands on his hips. "The vessel was phosphorescent again."

"Then yes," Anton said, "it would seem the energy she possessed has been returned to the vessel."

Isabelle looked for the silver lining. "Well, that's good for the Orphans, right?"

Anton let out an impatient sigh. "It's good for the Orphans' short-term survival but bad for our plans to rescue them. I wasn't expecting to have such a powerful piece removed from the board." She lowered her head and paced around the porch as the gray cat lazily watched her. "This is all my fault."

A tittering laughter echoed through the night sky.

Everyone spun around and looked for the source. Was it possible that someone had followed them here? Isabelle looked all around, but all she saw was the three-car garage with the silver pickup parked inside and the tall oaks that encircled the property swaying in the gentle nighttime breeze off the lake.

Again, the girlish laughter pierced the night air, along with another sound. Isabelle could just make out the droning whine of electric motors. She shrunk behind the car and watched the treetops. Gentry bounded up the steps and tried to whisk Dr. Anton away to safety, but she stiffly shoved him aside and stood her ground atop the porch, glaring into the night.

Pike crouched beside Isabelle. She was shocked to see him holding a wood-handled pistol.

Isabelle could just make out two bright lights moving through the treetops in tandem, drawing nearer as the motors' threatening whine grew louder.

At last, the two robots flew into the open, their bright floodlights blinding as they floated side by side. A tinny voice blared from one.

"We come in peace." Isabelle recognized the voice of Crystal Skorch. "Seriously. Don't do anything stupid. We're here to talk."

Anton glared at the robots with her hands on her hips and said nothing.

The two floodlights extinguished in unison and the robots steadily descended. As soon as Isabelle's eyes adjusted to the change in light, the twin robot thugs touched down. With a mechanical whir, their backs opened up and the rotor masts spun down and retracted. There they stood, shuffling their rubber-tipped feet as their sensor arrays scanned the area.

Captivated by the craftsmanship and misguided genius of these technological wonders, Isabelle stood up and stepped out from behind the car. She sensed Pike reaching and whispering for her to stop, but she paid him no heed. She stepped toward the robots.

Both sensor arrays locked onto her in tandem and the robots flared into a defensive position. Like an umbrella snapping open, each robot seemed to double in size as an assortment of unspeakable tools and weapons fanned out.

"Well, look at you, nerd! You're alive," came the tinny voice. "I told you things were going to get bad, didn't I?"

Isabelle stood her ground, uncertain of what to say.

"Who's that behind the car?" came Crystal's voice. "I hope you haven't done anything stupid like calling the police."

"Don't you worry," Pike called from behind the car. "We want to avoid any official law enforcement involvement just as much as you."

"Oh, it's just you," Crystal said.

Isabelle raised a hand. The robots twitched, seemingly watching her every move. Despite the daunting situation she found herself in, she couldn't help but marvel at them.

"Can they see me?" asked Isabelle.

"Forward looking infrared sensors," came Crystal's tinny voice.

Isabelle smiled. This tiny bit of information was exactly what she was hoping for. She was glad she'd stayed up late Tuesday night installing MechAnna's ZT-4 IR illuminators.

"They can collect and analyze thermographic images," Crystal said. "They can work seamlessly as a team. Whatever one bot sees, the other can see, even if he's in another location."

"Impressive! Weapons and tools?" asked Isabelle without missing a beat.

"Glass cutters, fire extinguishers, drills, cutting torches, storage bins. Injury has an electrolaser—"

"Injury?"

Crystal cackled through the loudspeaker. "That's right, you haven't been *formally* introduced." The robots started prancing in place. "This guy is Insult." The robot on the left dipped its forelegs into a theatrical bow. "He carries a sonic cannon I designed."

Isabelle thought back to how it had crumpled the metal trashcan at the park like a paper cup.

"How do you generate so much flow while keeping the pressure under check?" she said. "Maybe a train of shocks with a fairly low amplitude?"

Crystal laughed. "Wouldn't *you* like to know! I'm not telling you." Getting back on track, Crystal continued: "*This* guy is Injury." The robot on the right curtsied while its twin danced in place. "He has the electrolaser."

Injury's weapon snapped to attention. Isabelle looked down, and with a pang of alarm noticed a triangle of three red dots trained at her chest.

"When these little tracking lasers heat up, they ionize the air between them, creating a laser-induced plasma channel. Then my little buddy here sends a nice electrical current through said plasma channel and into his target. That's right, he can taze your butt from all the way over here. But I guess you know that already, huh?" She chuckled.

Isabelle's leg throbbed. *Well, that explains the pain and muscle spasms.*

"Enough chitchat," came Crystal's voice through the loudspeaker. Immediately, the two robots ceased their capering and snapped back into their defensive stances. "We have business to settle."

Still, Isabelle felt an inexplicable, paper-thin connection to Crystal. Despite their enmity, they had much in common.

Isabelle grinned. "What? I can't admire them? They're incredible. I've never seen anything like them."

"Flattery will get you nowhere, nerd."

"Let Jasmine go!" came Anton's voice from behind Isabelle. "She's done nothing to you. You have what you want—you have her energy. Now leave her out of it."

"That's not how it's going to work," came Crystal's voice. "You have something we want. We have something you want. Where's the other one, anyway?"

"I don't know where Maddy is," Isabelle said. "She's gone rogue."

"You're lying," said Crystal. "Wherever she is, her time is coming too. You might as well make things easy on yourself. We're going to *get* what we want—we're giving you a chance for it to be done peacefully."

"You don't care about peace," Isabelle said.

Crystal's laughter echoed through the night air. "You're right. After everything I've been through, I'm just looking after myself and doing my job."

"What does your boss want with the Orphan energy?" asked Anton.

"My *boss?*" Crystal chuckled. "That's none of your business, Steph."

Anton turned toward Gentry. "He probably doesn't trust her enough to tell her."

"Shut up," Crystal said. "Steph, you are a *joke* of a scientist. It's no wonder nobody takes you seriously. You're a crackpot and you've always *been* a crackpot. You can't even—" Rustling and loud fumbling came from the loudspeaker, overpowering Crystal's voice. "Hey! Watch it! What do think you're do—" It sounded like a microphone was being wrested away from her.

A man's voice rang through the loudspeaker, methodical and wafting.

"I am speaking directly to the girl. You carry something that belongs to me. You will come to the rooftop of the LionHeart building tonight at nine o'clock. You will come alone. Give back what's mine and we'll see about Jasmine getting to go home. If you make me come get you, then Jasmine is going to have to stay with me indefinitely. Think carefully. If you choose to not cooperate or follow my directions, I won't be able to extend such a friendly offer to Maddy. That is all. See you at nine."

Having delivered the ultimatum, the backs of Insult and Injury opened up and their rotor masts rose. With a series of clicks, the rotors unfolded and snapped into place. The motors spun to life and one after the other, the robots lifted into the air in a cloud of dust.

Isabelle's heart sunk into the pit of her stomach as she watched the twin bots clear the tops of the trees and disappear into the blackness.

31
UNEXPECTED ALLIES

Isabelle watched as Anton and Gentry talked in low voices, their eyes darting over to her periodically. She couldn't help but think that they were discussing their next move and how she would be used as the most powerful piece on the chessboard.

"Is there really no one else who can help us?" she said.

"Not if we aim to save the Orphans on that vessel," Anton said. "Any kind of government involvement would be a bad idea."

Pike returned the pistol to the shoulder holster hidden under his jacket.

"Law enforcement's off the table. Even if we capture Nowotny and the brat, that pretty much guarantees the vessel will fall into government hands."

"What about other scientists?"

"You should know better than to even ask," said Anton. "We have Roland here, but that's it. The scientists that would help me, or even associate with me after my—fall—are few and far between."

"Your fall?"

"After I shifted the focus of my work to what the scientific community considers crackpot science. Oh yes, I've been in a proverbial straightjacket since the word 'extraterrestrial' left my lips."

Isabelle's mind raced. There must be a way to resist. "If we knew what he wanted with the vessel, then maybe we could counter it."

"Unfortunately, we *don't* know," Anton said.

"Well, what *do* we know?" Isabelle said. "We know he has the vessel and the Orphans. We know the vessel has *some* of its energy, but he wants it all—he wants Maddy and me." She shrugged. "Does he want to take the powers for himself?"

Anton drew a breath. "I don't think he could get the energy to discharge to himself naturally, like you did. To try artificially would be extremely dangerous. Likewise, I don't think he'd try to give the powers to Crystal either. Neither of them seems to possess the genetic anomaly to trigger a reaction, or it would have happened already."

"Is there any other application for the vessel's energy?" she said. "Didn't you say he was a biochemical engineer?"

Anton pursed her lips. "Now you may be on the right track. Coming into contact with a new alien species and their biotechnology could provide a goldmine of possibilities for an unscrupulous biochemical engineer. He could produce genetic enhancements or new medicines without any regard to safety or ethics."

Isabelle perked up. "I think I might have a way to counter these robots of Crystal's. Before I go to the LionHeart roof, would one of you be able to drop me by my house? I need to get something."

"I have my doubts you'd—"

Isabelle scoffed. "What other plan do you have? And besides, you couldn't stop me from going if you wanted to."

Gentry's brows furrowed as he turned to Anton. "How can we, in good conscience, send her into harm's way again?"

"How can I, in good conscience, not go?" said Isabelle. "The last of an entire race is depending on me! We could only be so lucky when the last of us humans are in trouble to have some alien stick their neck out for *us*."

Anton smiled.

"There's not much time," said Isabelle as she turned to Gentry. "I need your help. Can you give me a ride or not?"

Gentry looked at Dr. Anton. In a gesture that Isabelle could only interpret as a complete absence of other options, Anton dipped her head in a subtle nod.

Pike took his keys out of his jacket pocket and backed toward his car. "Remember, if any of you find yourselves in the grasp of the long arm of the law, don't talk. Just wait. I might need some time to finagle how to get you released."

"Fine," said Anton.

Pike's eyes twinkled. "With what little time my Cloner buddies have before their meat suits keel over, they'll be trying to intercept." He grinned. "I'll go run interference." He ducked into his car.

Anton nodded. "Alright, Isabelle, I may not have another plan, but I do have someone to see before I head to the Warren. Clement is on his way there as we speak. If, by some series of unlikely events, you save the vessel . . . that's where we'll be."

* * *

Ten minutes later, Gentry was parking alongside Mine Street. Isabelle glanced at the digital dashboard clock, 8:34.

"Is this accurate?" she asked as she tapped the clock.

Gentry glanced down at his watch. "Close enough."

Isabelle sighed. "Alright, come with me."

His eyebrows rose.

"I'm going to need your help," she added.

Dutifully, Gentry exited the truck and prepared to follow Isabelle on her mission.

The Arcadia section of Rose Valley was still and quiet as Isabelle and Gentry hurried down the sidewalk and cut across Isabelle's side yard. Creeping up to the house, Isabelle tapped on the window of the bedroom she and her brother were temporarily sharing.

The curtain shot to the side and Mason appeared at the window with a confused look. Sitting on Mason's bed was Gavin, who looked out at her with wide eyes.

Isabelle cringed. She had forgotten Gavin was spending the night.

Mason raised the sliding window. "What are *you* doing out there? Aren't you supposed to be at Jasmine's?"

"We need MechAnna. Can you send her out the window?"

"What's going on? Who is *that?*" Mason asked, pointing to Gentry. "Where's Jasmine?"

"There's no time to explain," she said, her impatience bubbling over.

Mason started to close the window.

"No! Mason!" she hissed at him. "Jasmine is in trouble."

His eyes fell to her shredded jeans and bloodied leg. All the color drained from his face. "I'm getting Dad—"

"Don't! He can't know, Mason. Neither can the police. Please, can you just cooperate with me for once?"

Gavin stood up and approached the window. "Mayhap we should hearken to what the fair maiden hath to say?"

Isabelle closed her eyes in exasperation. It was all she could do to keep from screaming her frustration.

Mason's eyes narrowed.

"I've heard the stories and I've seen you on the news and on the video. Honestly, I don't even know what to believe anymore. All I know is I'm not doing a *thing* until you tell me everything." Mason crossed his arms as he looked down at his sister.

Isabelle sighed. Could she really dare to bring them fully into her secret world? They already knew too much.

What choice do I have? Time is wasting while I stand here and argue.

"Alright," she said, speaking quickly and without taking a single breath, "Jasmine, Maddy and I have superpowers given to us from a tiny spaceship that is carrying the last survivors of an alien race. We had a fight and Maddy is not our friend any more. Then we found out we have to return the ship to space or the aliens will all die, but a really mean girl named Crystal and a former Air Force officer have stolen the spaceship and kidnapped Jasmine and we're on our way to rescue her. Now will you cooperate?" Isabelle sucked in a lungful of air and let it all out at once.

Mason's eyes grew round. "I knew it! We're *not* crazy!" He turned to Gavin. "We were right all along!"

"Mason! Shhh!"

He lowered his voice. "Show me!"

"Mason, we don't have time—"

"You really didn't think you could do something like this right under my nose, did you?"

"Mason, I could be running an ostrich smuggling ring out of our closet and you would be clueless."

"Ostriches? Why ostriches? You've got the whole wide world of things to smuggle and you pick *ostriches?*"

Gentry watched silently as the siblings bickered back and forth.

Isabelle huffed. "Mason, I *need* MechAnna *now.*"

He turned to Gavin. "Can you imagine all the mess we'd have with ostriches in the closet?"

Isabelle rose three feet off the ground and hovered there, glaring at her brother, now eye to eye with him. Gentry took a step backward.

"The feathers and ostrich poop would—Whoa! Take us with you!"

Gavin nodded in agreement. "You'll be glad you had us along. You'll find us to be the most capable of sidekicks."

"Give me MechAnna. Now, Mason!"

"We're coming with you!" Mason rushed over to sit on his bed so he could put on his shoes.

"No, you're *not*, Mason. Just shut up and get MechAnna."

"Well, maybe I'll just tell Dad right now." He stood up.

"No, Mason!" she hissed. "It's out of the question."

"Well, you're not going anywhere unless I'm coming along too." He pointed to himself. "We lost Mom. We're not going to lose you too. You may be my big sister, but I still have to protect you."

Isabelle swallowed the lump in her throat. Weird as his sentiments seemed, she knew he was being sincere. She knew she didn't have time to argue, but she couldn't have them compromise her mission either.

"Fine," she said as she collected herself. "But you must do exactly as I tell you, and you must keep your mouths shut!" She brandished a finger, first at her brother and then at Gavin.

Mason turned toward Isabelle's workbench. "Hey, Anna," he said.

"What do you think you're doing?" Isabelle said.

MechAnna's eyes lit up. "What do you want, cretin?" Its blocky, plastic head spun around and fixed its gaze on Mason from the top of Isabelle's workbench.

Isabelle felt a strange, inexplicable emotion as she saw her brother talking to MechAnna. Was it jealousy?

"Mason Everett Cooley! *What* are you doing talking to my robot?! How do *you* know how to operate her?"

"I saw you do it. Who else do I have to keep me company when you're over at one of your friends' houses all the time?" asked Mason.

Gavin gestured toward Mason. "Even *I* can't keep him entertained *all* the time."

Isabelle made a mental note that she needed to add some sort of security system to MechAnna to prevent unauthorized use.

Mason glanced up at MechAnna as he tied his shoe. "Anna, we're going on a little adventure to save my sister's friend."

MechAnna's head swiveled around and found Isabelle hovering at the window. "Oh, goody," said the robot in an unenthusiastic voice.

"Stop talking to MechAnna!" snapped Isabelle. She turned around and glared at Gentry. "Can you believe this guy? Using my robot without permission?"

Gentry could only shrug.

Mason opened the screen and handed MechAnna down with some difficulty to Gentry, who lowered the machine to the ground. With a whir of its tank like tracks, MechAnna maneuvered out of the way to make room for Mason. His foot caught on the sill as he climbed out of the window. He fell with a crash, face first, on the ground.

"Ha ha ha ha ha ha," came a deadpan synthesized voice.

Mason popped up quickly. "I'm okay!"

Next Gavin made his egress, but somehow managed to not fall.

They all hurried across the Cooleys' lawn and to the truck. Mech-Anna was lifted into the pickup truck bed. "Sorry, Anna, but there's no room for you up here," said Isabelle as she got into the front seat and Mason and Gavin climbed into the back.

"So, who's this guy again?" asked Mason.

"The name's Gentry. Roland Gentry. And it's truly a pleasure—"

"We need to roll," said Isabelle.

"Righto," said Gentry, dropping the truck into gear.

Mason looked back and forth between Gentry and his sister. "So, what is he? Like your superhero chaperone, or something?"

Gavin slapped Mason's shoulder. "I applied for that job but alas . . ."

"Will you two shut up?" snapped Isabelle. "Gentry, I need you to get me as close to the LionHeart Building downtown as you can."

He nodded as he turned off of Mine Street.

"So, where's the—"

"Shut up, Mason!" Isabelle snapped. "Listen, all of you. Obviously, I'm going to fly up to the rooftop of the building. Crystal and Nowotny have agreed to meet me there—"

"Confrontation on the rooftop?" said Gavin. "That tired old trope?"

Isabelle glared at her brother. "If you don't shut your friend up, I will shut him up for you. First of all, this is *not* something to joke about. This is serious business. Second, it wasn't *my* idea to meet up there. It was *theirs!*" Isabelle huffed a big sigh and continued. "They don't know you guys are coming. I'm going to try to talk them out of what they're trying to do. I'll probably fail, but I have to try. They think I'm going up there to trade my power for Jasmine. I'm going to stall for as long as I can."

"But—"

"I need you guys to take MechAnna and find a way into the building without getting caught. You need to keep working your way up and find a way onto the roof. By the time you get there, I'll probably need your help."

"Okay, but—"

"Shut *up*, Mason. Just tell MechAnna what needs to be done in plain English. If she can help you, she will."

"What's the—"

"It's important that you guys find a way to get to the roof—*with* MechAnna. She has something that will help in the fight."

They were nearing Downtown. Isabelle looked at the dashboard clock, 8:53.

"Pull over here." As they rolled to a stop, she opened her door and stepped out of the truck. "This is where we part ways. I'll be flying from here. Don't forget to use MechAnna to her fullest potential. She has six omnidirectional IR illuminators. Gentry, you know those robots have FLIR."

"Stunningly brilliant," Gentry said.

"That's the idea."

"Good luck, m'lady," she heard just as the door slammed shut.

"Good luck," she mouthed at the truck window. She looked around to make sure no one was near enough to see her and then shot up into the air and out of sight.

"Whoa!" said Mason, "No matter how many times you see it, it's hard to believe."

Gentry glanced up at the rearview mirror. "Well, lad, you'd better brace up, because you're probably going to see a lot worse before the night is through."

32

INTO THE LION'S DEN

THE BOYS SQUIRMED IN THE BACK SEAT as Gentry raced through the Downtown section of Rose Valley. Easter break had virtually emptied the nearby college apartments or else the streets of Downtown would be livelier. He couldn't deny the timing was a stroke of good fortune. He glanced at the dashboard clock. Only a few more minutes to go.

"Alright, lads," said Gentry, glancing at the rearview mirror. "What are your names?"

"Hail fellow! Master Cooley and Master Barnard, at your service," said Gavin.

"Or you can just call us Mason and Gavin," said Mason.

"Right. Masters Cooley and Barnard. Well met," Gentry said into the mirror.

The aptly named Downtown was the central-most of Rose Valley's 28 distinct neighborhoods. Not only was it the commercial center of the city, but the governmental center as well. The tallest buildings of the city—hotels, business offices and financial centers—huddled together in a four-block radius.

The eighteen story LionHeart Building was, by far, the tallest building in the city, owned by LionHeart International Software

Development. There were several eight and ten story commercial buildings nearby, but the LionHeart literally towered over them all.

"The LionHeart Building was back there," said Mason. "Why aren't we stopping?"

"We're using the rear utility entrance," said Gentry. Sandwiched between the Shenandoah Rose Convention Center and the LionHeart was a multilevel parking garage under heavy renovation. There were many temporary chain link fences and barriers set up around the area and a section of the street was completely blocked off. Gentry knew this was the best he was going to get.

He backed his truck against one of the barriers with a ROAD CLOSED sign on it. He got out of the truck and grabbed a reflective yellow vest from behind his seat and a tool belt. Walking around the side of the truck, he pulled a pair of orange cones from the truck bed toolbox and placed them a few paces in front of his truck.

"You'd be surprised how many unwanted questions you can avoid with a simple yellow vest," he said.

Gentry went to the back of the truck to retrieve the robot and placed it on the pavement. He bent down and spoke to MechAnna.

"Are you going to be able to maneuver on your own?"

MechAnna didn't respond.

"You have to say her name," said Mason, getting out of the truck. "It's MechAnna. Or just Anna." Gavin hopped out of the truck on the other side.

Gentry repeated his question with the correct syntax.

MechAnna responded by rolling forward so that its treads were butted up against the curb, then deftly lifted itself up onto the sidewalk with the aid of its two flipper tracks. Gentry nodded approvingly.

There was a small parking area for utility vehicles and two sliding garage doors at the rear loading dock of the LionHeart

Building, which was surrounded by a chain link fence. Gentry pulled on a pair of gloves from his tool belt and grabbed a compact bolt cutter from beneath the truck's seat. Within a minute they were all inside the fence and hurrying across the parking area to the garage doors.

Gentry seemed to be sizing up the doors when Mason spoke up.

"Hey, Anna. We need to get through this locked garage door." He squinted at the small metal plate riveted to the door. "Apex Manufacturing Company. Model AN-225."

"Accessing database, buffoon."

"This is incredible," Gentry said, twisting a tip of his mustache with his gloved fingers.

"Izzy's given Anna access to a ridiculously extensive database of practical solutions to real world problems."

MechAnna's head swiveled around and locked onto Mason. "I need to be lifted 101.6 centimeters."

Gentry's mouth hung open. "What's she playing at?"

"We need to trust her," said Mason. "Let's get her raised up."

With Gentry's help, Mason sprung to action, stacking wooden pallets from a pile near the garage door. When he reckoned he'd built up a platform of at least the requested height, they lifted MechAnna onto the stack of pallets.

The bot immediately went to work. First, it lifted its chassis as far as it could with its flipper tracks, then it jammed one of its robotic arms against the rubber seal at the top of the garage door, creating a gap by opening its claw hand. Slowly and carefully, a hooked appendage extended from its other arm into the gap. The sturdy extension disappeared into the building. Within seconds, there was a sharp click as MechAnna activated the emergency release lever inside the building.

Gentry turned to the boys in wonder. "She pieced that solution together just from your verbal commands and accessing the database?"

Mason chuckled. "My sister doesn't give herself enough credit. This thing has some pretty advanced AI. Anna was literally created to problem solve."

"Talk about having something up your sleeve," Gavin said as he watched the robot slowly retract the extension back inside its arm. They lowered MechAnna back to the ground and hastily deconstructed their stack of pallets.

Gentry lifted the garage door enough for MechAnna to fit through and held up a cautioning hand. "Cameras," he said. "Anna, we need to know if there are any security cameras in there."

"RF security camera detected, half-wit," MechAnna said.

"Is she always so cheeky?"

Mason shuffled his feet guiltily. "It's not really a bug, it's a feature," he said. "I sort of tampered with her code without telling Izzy."

Gentry smiled and shook his head. "I'm starting to like you, lad." He turned back to the robot. "Anna, can you activate your infrared illuminators?"

"Activating omnidirectional IR illuminators, fool," Mech-Anna said.

Gentry pulled out his phone and switched to camera mode. Peering into the screen, Mason could see the camera's view was completely obscured by the searing infrared floodlights that MechAnna carried. To the naked eye, however, everything appeared normal.

"Clever," he said. "Your sister really made this all by herself?"

"Izzy? Yes. It's a school project."

"If there are security personnel watching their monitors, all they'll see is a blank screen. With any luck, they'll assume it's a malfunction and not come to investigate," Gentry said. "We'll have to stay close to her. Don't go too far ahead or lag too far behind her, okay?" He looked at the robot again in wonder. "A school project, huh? When I was your sister's age, they had us making a battery out of two potatoes."

They lifted the door enough to squeeze in and let it close behind them. They were in a loading and unloading area.

Cardboard boxes and a few wooden crates lined the concrete floor. Sure enough, there on the wall to the right was a security camera.

"Will there be security guards on duty?" asked Mason as Gavin stealthily tiptoed from box to box like a cartoon secret agent.

"Anything is possible. We should be cautious. We need to start making our way up, and quickly." They exited the loading area and entered a long, carpeted hallway, being careful to stay close to MechAnna. There were only a few doors, but they were all closed tight.

Gentry paused and pointed out the security card lock on one of the doors. "If the whole building is set up like this, we might have a problem."

They reached the end of the hallway and a large marble floored lobby opened up before them. Gentry ducked behind the unoccupied information counter and pulled Mason and Gavin down with him. Beyond the counter, near the center of the large lobby was a security kiosk. Between the two rows of white marble columns, Gentry could make out the shape of the guard sitting in a chair with his feet up on the counter. He had his back to them as he scrolled through his smartphone.

Gentry considered them lucky. From his vantage point, he could see four computer monitors. Each one was divided into four split-screen quarters. A view from a different security camera showed in each square. Three of the squares were washed out with a flickering light. Emitting powerful infrared waves that are invisible to the human eye, but overwhelming to the cameras, MechAnna's newest gadget was doing its job wonderfully. Aside from the camera in the loading dock, he hadn't even seen any other cameras.

Unexpectedly, the hallway filled with a cartoony and bubbly voice.

"Why the long face? I'll be your Pony Pal!"

Gentry struggled to regain his stolen breath as he looked everywhere for the source. At last, his eyes rested upon Gavin, who was holding a small plastic pony with a multicolored mane.

Seemingly oblivious to the withering glares of both Gentry and Mason, Gavin looked up. "What?"

Gentry growled and snatched the toy from his pudgy hands, and stuffed it into his breast pocket. When Gavin looked as if he was about to protest, Gentry made a dangerous face and raised a finger. "Master Barnard!" he hissed. "A plague upon thee if you cannot bestay your tomfoolery!"

Gavin's eyes got big and round and his mouth clapped shut. Gentry shot a look of utter disbelief toward Mason, who shrugged.

If this security guard was any kind of guard at all, they would have been caught already. But, apparently Rainbow Sparklemane herself could break in and announce her presence and go unnoticed. Instead, the portly security guard continued to sit and poke at the screen of his smartphone.

Gentry pointed to each boy, put his finger to his mouth, then jabbed it firmly toward the floor, wordlessly telling them to stay quiet and stay put. He carefully undid his tool belt and placed it on the carpeted floor and crept behind the information counter to peer around the far end. He spotted the elevator and the door that lead to the stairs on the other side of the kiosk. There was no getting by. His mission had come to a screeching halt. Unless he could come up with a plan, he'd have to backtrack and look for another set of stairs.

In front of him and almost level with the kiosk was a small grouping of lounge furniture—a sofa, two chairs and a few side tables. On the far side of the kiosk was a closed, unmarked door. As Gentry watched the guard, the door slowly opened as if moved by an unseen hand. The hairs stood up on the back of Gentry's neck as the utility closet revealed itself. The security guard took no notice.

Gentry didn't know if it was an air current, or a pressure change in the lobby, or even a faulty hinge that caused the door to swing open, but fate had presented him with his opportunity. He instantly formed his plan.

Although the guard was so engrossed in his phone that Gentry could have moonwalked, he stealthily crept into the lobby and hid behind the sofa. He had one shot and one shot only. He carefully dug in his pocket and took out the plastic Pony Pal. He mentally measured the distance and made his move. He hurled the tiny pony across the lobby and dove back behind the sofa. The Pony Pal thumped off the door frame and the security guard's breath caught as he looked over at the open door.

Then came the sickeningly sweet voice, "I'd sing you a song but I'm a little horse!"

Gentry dared to peer around the edge of the sofa. As the guard scrabbled to his feet, his handheld radio awkwardly twisted on its belt holster and thumped onto the floor, unnoticed.

Now, this is just too much of a coincidence, thought Gentry as he prepared to spring into action. The guard placed his phone on the desk without taking any notice of the flickering monitors. He stepped over to the closet.

He was looking down so curiously at the colorful plastic pony that he didn't hear Gentry run up behind him. With a shove, the guard stumbled into the closet and Gentry slammed the door shut and held it with all his weight. In a moment the trapped guard was furiously pounding on the door, yelling.

"Get the wedge!" Gentry yelled. Mason ran into the lobby and scooped up the rubber door wedge that was on the floor near the closet. Gavin sprang into action, apparently to help, but only managed to get in the way. After bumping into Gavin a few times, Mason was able to shakily jam the door stop into the gap on the bottom of the door and Gentry started kicking it in. The wedge was jammed so far under the door that it was almost flattened. The pounding and yelling stopped. Gavin bent over to retrieve Rainbow Sparklemane.

Gentry eased off of the door and locked eyes with Mason. For a few heartbeats there was silence, but that was shattered when the pounding and yelling from inside the closet resumed. The doorknob rattled from the inside, but the door held.

"Quickly," gasped Gentry, "get my tool belt and the robot! Might as well take the elevator now. But first—"

"What do we do? what do we do?" asked Gavin as he tapdanced nervously on the spot.

"Stay put and don't touch anything," said Gentry. He shook his head as he searched all over the kiosk. He saw the guard's phone on the desk and the handheld radio lying on the floor. Gentry wondered if this could be the worst security guard ever. Or at least the unluckiest.

"We've got to hurry," whispered Mason, who'd returned with the belt. MechAnna whirred along behind him.

"Hold on. We're going to run into problems upstairs if we don't figure this out," said Gentry. Finally, he found the security card programmer he was looking for. The black, electronic box had a numbered keypad, a rectangular, green LCD screen, and a slot to insert a magnetized security card. He rifled through the drawers and found the box of spare cards. Taking one, he turned on the programmer. "Enter password? Oh no." He frantically looked around.

Gavin pointed to the small piece of paper taped to the desk right next to the programmer.

"Really?" Gentry shook his head and punched in the number, 1, 2, 3, 4. "What an idiot." He'd made up his mind. This *was* the worst security guard ever.

Gavin pumped his fist. "To outsmart an idiot, one must *think* like an idiot. I've got this!"

Mason leaned over for a fist bump with his friend, then glanced at what Gentry was doing. "Are you going to make a security card or something?" he asked.

Gentry grunted an affirmative as he quickly punched through the menus. "Roof access plus whatever other locked doors may be in our way." He squinted at the small, green LCD screen. "Issue masters." He hit the green enter button. "Which key? EK? GM?

Probably 'emergency key' and 'grand master key.'" He selected GM and again hit the green enter button. "What are these numbers? 1204?" Gentry had hit a brick wall.

The pounding and yelling continued from the janitor's closet.

Gavin peered over at the card programmer. "That must be today's date. How long you want the card to be good for," he suggested. "The numbers are reversed," offered Gavin. "Twelfth of April."

Gentry buried his face in his palm. "Thank you, Master Barnard. You are absolutely correct. But know that this is the proper and correct format by which all civilized nations should display dates." He punched in tomorrow's date, 1304. Again, he pressed the green enter button. "Insert card." Gentry held his breath and jammed the spare card into the slot and the programmer beeped. "Next copy?"

"We've got it!" said Gentry as he handed the key card to Mason and took his tool belt. "It's a good thing you lads came along. Let's go."

A few moments later they were standing in the elevator. Gentry was thankful he could no longer hear the pounding and yelling of the security guard in the utility closet. As the digital readout above the elevator door slowly counted up the floor numbers, Gentry, Mason, and Gavin glanced around, determined not to make eye contact while within the confines of the elevator.

"I hope we didn't take too long," Gentry said. "With Anna's IR emitter nearby, Crystal's robots will be blinded. All we have to do is—"

"Omnidirectional IR illuminators shutting down, oaf," MechAnna said. "Power at four percent."

Gavin looked to Mason.

"Maybe we shouldn't have been playing with her all day, huh?"

33
DOWNFALL

Isabelle circled the LionHeart Building rooftop one more time before making her landing approach. Eighteen stories below, a mosaic of city lights blanketed the valley and sprawled in all directions—right to the very foothills of the Blue Ridge Mountains in the east, where darkness shrouded the wooded ridges.

A black and red helicopter, its rotors spinning idle, perched atop a well-lit, elevated helipad with its yellow railings, green lights, and orange windsock. The opposite end of the roof featured a boxlike shelter which housed the rooftop access doors. As Isabelle flew, she took note that the doors faced away from the helipad and hoped her friends might gain the element of surprise when they showed up. The gray expanse between the heliport and the shelter was flat except for a few runs of shiny aluminum ducts and a row of industrial sized air conditioners. All around the perimeter of the roof was a waist high parapet.

For better or worse, Isabelle knew this desolate rooftop would be the site of the Orphans' last stand.

Crystal already stood in the middle of the roof, flanked by Insult and Injury. The two bots stood firm with their tools and weapons bristling like a pair of robotic hedgehogs. Backlit by the helipad floodlights, they cast long, spindly shadows. At Crystal's feet sat the pulsing blue sphere still in its net pouch.

When Isabelle saw Jasmine seated nearby with her hands bound behind her back and her head hung low, her blood boiled. She clenched her fists and brought herself to a halt over the middle of the rooftop before drifting slowly downward. As she touched down, Nowotny emerged from the helicopter and descended the ramp to the rooftop.

She closed her eyes and hoped against hope that Gentry would find a way to the rooftop with MechAnna. Without her bot and its blinding infrared illuminators, there would be no hope of outfoxing Insult and Injury.

Crystal stood with her legs crossed and her hands in her back pockets, her familiar smirk etched across her face. Nowotny reached the bottom of the ramp and slowly walked toward her, though his eyes were locked on Isabelle.

"I see you've followed my instructions," he said in a slow voice.

"And I see you're such a coward that you have to tie up a little girl," Isabelle said as she gestured toward Jasmine.

Nowotny gazed at Jasmine, seeming to consider her for a long moment. Then his hawk eyes fell upon Isabelle. He spoke with flawless diction that was only marred by his off-kilter pauses. "But you're not little girls," he said. "You're not even human, are you?" One corner of his mouth twitched. "Ever since you've stolen the energy, you've been something else." He shook his head. "What *are* you?"

Isabelle scowled, her hair blowing wildly in the night air. "I'm more human than you." She pointed at the pulsing blue sphere. "Do you even know what this is? It contains the last remnants of an entire alien race. You don't have the right to destroy them."

Nowotny laughed. "Do you think this will be the first extinction caused by mankind?" He shrugged. "A penchant for destruction is one of our defining characteristics, wouldn't you say?"

Crystal's head snapped around. "Wait, what?"

Nowotny shushed her.

Isabelle set her jaw. "We have the choice to change." She gestured with open hands. "Give the vessel back to Anton. Let her do the right thing."

Nowotny's eyes glazed over and all expression slipped off of his face. "Every time two dissimilar civilizations come into contact, the weaker of the two will perish. Always. You should consider mankind lucky." He stared down at the sphere. "We've really dodged a bullet with this one: *they've* achieved interstellar travel."

Crystal stared back and forth between the sphere and the man with a mystified expression.

"What the hell?" she muttered under her breath.

He stepped toward Jasmine. "Enough stalling. We're here to make a trade, aren't we?" He looked down at his captive who sat slumped over, her face cast downward.

"There must be some other way!" Isabelle said. "We can't allow ourselves to be responsible for the destruction of an entire race of beings—"

"You don't want to trade?"

Isabelle's mouth hung open as she searched for the words that would make him understand.

He backed away from Jasmine as he nodded toward Crystal. "Shoot the girl."

"No!" cried Isabelle.

Crystal flinched, and looked back and forth between Jasmine and Nowotny with a knitted brow. She flushed pink and bit her lip.

"I said shoot the girl."

Crystal took a half step backward. "You said we wouldn't have to."

Nowotny froze as if he thought he might have misheard her. He glared.

"Crystal," he said. "That is an order."

"No, Grandpa. All this stuff about alien civilizations—is it true? How could you keep this from me?"

Grandpa? Isabelle did a double take. Even Jasmine sat up and looked back and forth between Crystal and Nowotny.

Crystal's face scrunched up and her chest heaved. "When were you going to tell me?"

Nowotny offered another dismissive gesture. "This is for *your* benefit—"

"This is *my* fight. *My* choice," she said with a wavering voice. "*You* don't have to fight this," she said, pounding her chest. "I do!" She glared back. "Does Mom know?"

He stared coldly at her.

"She doesn't, does she?"

"Cryssie, this decision does not rest on your shoulders. There's a reason I didn't tell you everything."

Crystal crossed her arms. "Don't you think I have a right to know? I agreed to fight it, but not like *this*! I'm not going to cause a genocide just to save myself!"

Nowotny sighed, as if she were a toddler throwing a tantrum.

She scoffed and clenched her fists. "I'm out of here. Insult, Injury, stand down and spool up!" The robots dutifully deployed their rotor masts and rose off the roof with a high-pitched whine. They hovered in place awaiting their next command. "I'll have no part of this."

"You are the *reason* for this," Nowotny said.

"Not anymore," came Crystal's response.

Isabelle watched in shocked silence as the drama unfolded between grandfather and granddaughter, even as her heart leaped with hope: with Insult and Injury gone, she might have a hint of a chance. At the same time, she feared what this desperate man might do if backed into a corner.

Crystal waved a hand toward the hovering robots. "Return to base." They wheeled around in the air and started to drift off westward.

Nowotny calmly reached into his jacket pocket and pulled out his cellphone. After a few button presses, he returned it to his pocket.

The robots froze a few paces from the roof's parapet.

"Insult, Injury, return to base," Crystal repeated louder. The robots hovered in place, their rotors whirring in harmony.

"Insult, Injury, to me," said Nowotny, calmly. The robots obediently drifted to his side.

Crystal's jaw dropped. "You fail-safed me?"

"Get in the helicopter," he said.

Crystal crossed her arms. "I can't believe you fail-safed me! I'm not going to let you do this!"

"Last chance, Cryssie. Get in the helicopter."

"No! Even if you get this energy, it'll be for nothing, because I won't let—"

There was a deafening thud and Isabelle felt her hair blow back from the shockwave. The attack happened so fast she hadn't even seen it. When things came into focus, Insult was withdrawing its sonic cannon and Crystal was lying flat on her back, motionless.

"You understand this is what's best for you?" he said softly, staring at Crystal.

He's lost his mind! Isabelle's heart raced. It was impossible to think, but her mind was easily able to grasp one thought: If he could turn the robots' weapons on his own granddaughter, what would he do to her and Jasmine?

He stepped toward the sphere and bent down to gingerly grasp its net pouch. He dragged it to the open space on the rooftop. Taking one last glance at Crystal's limp body, he turned to Isabelle.

"Surrender your energy to the sphere."

Isabelle planted her feet firmly. Her mind went to Gentry and MechAnna. Maybe she could stall for more time.

"You should have listened to your granddaughter. I agree I should surrender the energy to the sphere, but not for whatever your purpose is."

Nowotny smiled. "And what is my purpose? How do you know my cause is not a noble one?"

Isabelle was speechless. It was true. She still didn't know what his plans were, or what had caused Crystal's change of heart. She just knew the Orphans would perish at his hands. To her, there could be no greater crime. She wondered if there was anything he could say to make her change her mind.

"How do you measure the worth of an entire alien race against a single human life?" he said. "What if that alien race is already earmarked for extinction? What if that single human life is someone you love? What if eradicating these Orphans could have saved your mother?"

Isabelle sputtered. Fresh grief surged as she tried to stave off the inevitable flood of questions, but the questions spilled over all the same. *How does he know about my mom? Is he right? Is Crystal really sick? Could harnessing the Orphans' power really save her?* The most disturbing question rose to the surface. *Would I do the same thing if my mom was in Crystal's place?*

He seized her in his glare. Without blinking or taking his eyes from her, he spoke deliberately and calmly.

"Injury, target one fifty. Five milliamps."

Injury maneuvered toward Jasmine, twisting in the air as it went. Jasmine flinched away from the spinning blades as it raised its weapon and the red tracking laser dots came to rest on her shoulder.

Jasmine called out over the electric motor's whine. "Isabelle, don't give in! There's got to be another way."

Isabelle's breaths came quick and ragged, but her feet remained firmly planted. *Gentry and MechAnna are on the way. They'll be here any second. MechAnna will render Insult and Injury useless.*

Nowotny paused as his hawk eyes peeled Isabelle to the bone. Then: "Fire."

There was a flash and a crack as blue forks of plasma spat from the robot. Jasmine whimpered and her arm squirmed wildly against its bindings before falling limp and twitching. She threw herself down and curled up into a ball, groaning with pain.

Isabelle seized in terror, unable to move. Jasmine was hurt and it was her fault.

Nowotny pointed to the pulsing sphere that lay inert on the roof. "Now you know I mean business. Transfer your energy, now."

Isabelle stuttered in a panic, unable to move or form the words she knew she must.

"Shall we go for six milliamps?"

She shakily walked up to the sphere and got on her knees. Bathed in the soft blue glow, she gazed down at the vessel that housed the last of the Orphans. She could just grab the net pouch, fly, and be gone, but a glance over at Jasmine stopped those thoughts. As she looked down at the throbbing blue light, she was almost grateful she was about to be free of these burdens. Soon she would become ordinary everyday Isabelle again and it would be someone else's fight.

"Put your hands on the sphere," Nowotny said.

Isabelle paused. "You don't want to do this—"

"Injury, you have your target. Prepare to fire."

Jasmine whimpered and curled herself into an even tighter ball.

"Wait!" yelled Isabelle. "I'll do it." Her mind screamed in rage and fear. Her friend was in harm's way because she'd hesitated. Over and over, she repeated to herself that she was doing the right thing. She didn't know how, but Dr. Anton would find a way to set things right.

"I knew you'd come around," Nowotny said.

They aren't coming. No one is coming to help. I'm on my own.

Isabelle took a deep breath and clenched every muscle in her body. Slowly, she extended her hands toward the sphere as she turned her face aside. She fully expected there to be an explosive flash like when Jasmine touched the sphere, so was surprised when she felt the vessel's smooth coldness through the netting. Nothing happened. She repositioned her fingertips on the sphere, gazing down to make sure she was really touching it.

"They refuse to take it back," came a voice.

Nowotny and Isabelle turned in unison to find Crystal in a sitting position, her blue hair askew and a groggy smirk on her face. "See? Even the sphere thinks this is bullcrap!"

Nowotny's cheeks flushed and his calm demeanor cracked for the first time. Spinning around to face Isabelle he roared, "What have you done?"

Isabelle shook her head and shrugged. "I *tried* to give it back. It didn't work."

"You will not trick me!" he snapped. "Injury, target two-sixty. Fifty milliamps!" His hawk eyes flashed back to Isabelle.

"Fifty? That could kill her!" Crystal struggled to get up. "Are you crazy?"

"Don't you *dare* hurt Isabelle!" came Jasmine's voice.

Injury slowly rotated on the spot and started maneuvering toward Isabelle. With grim efficiency it swung its weapon to bear. For a horrible moment, Isabelle stared down the barrel of Injury's electrolaser.

He shook his clenched fist toward the sphere. "Return the energy to the vessel now!" he bellowed. "Or I will fire!"

Isabelle stared back into the soulless visage of Injury. She had done all she could to save the Orphans. She had done all she could to keep Jasmine out of harm's way. It had all gone horribly wrong, and whatever her fate would be, she had no control over it. All she could do was wait.

Suddenly, and without any command from Nowotny, the two robots lurched and spun away, scrambling into position to bring their weapons to bear on a new threat. Insult leveled its sonic cannon behind Isabelle. Injury's electrolaser retracted as its sensor array scanned frantically and twitched between targets in a confused loop.

"Get down, m'lady!" a voice called.

Isabelle ducked; Insult fired.

A deep resonating thud and the ensuing pressure wave washed harmlessly over her head. She looked up in time to see the two robots crashing into each other and careening out of control. Shards of plastic and metal flew everywhere as their spinning rotors collided. The two robots skidded across the top of the parapet. Hopelessly entangled, they plummeted over the edge of the roof and disappeared.

Isabelle spun around and found Maddy McCarthy standing on the rooftop with her arms extended. In an instant, Isabelle deduced that it must have been Maddy that forced the collision with her telekinetic power. On the rooftop in front of her Gavin lay motionless. Mason came running up behind and slid to his knees beside his friend. He shook Gavin and tried to wake him.

Maddy flicked a wrist and the sphere came rolling toward her feet, tumbling and bumping over its netting as it went. She stepped forward, shielding both the sphere and the incapacitated boy. She locked eyes with Nowotny, arms stretched forward, ready to focus her telekinetic power.

He stared back, shocked and silent.

After a tense moment, Crystal's voice rang out. "You killed my robots!"

"Good riddance," Maddy said.

"Now, girls," said Nowotny, as if he were gently chastising the two at a sleepover. "Play *nice!*" Taking advantage of Maddy's momentary distraction, he lunged forward and hauled Jasmine to her feet by the scruff of her jacket. He wrapped his arm around her neck, using her as a human shield. "Now let's *all* calm down for a moment," he panted. His voice now came high and strained.

"Let her go," said Maddy as she took another step forward.

In response, he squeezed Jasmine's neck in the crook of his arm.

Maddy stopped, midstep.

Isabelle scrambled to her feet and watched, afraid to move any further—certain that some false move would cause him to throw Jasmine over the edge.

"You don't really want to hurt anybody, do you?" she said. "Let Jasmine go." She took a deep breath and attempted to slow her erratic breathing.

"You've thrown something of mine over the edge." He nodded to the edge of the roof. "How about if I toss something of yours?"

Crystal had slowly crept up and now stood alongside Isabelle. "Whoa, Grandpa, dial it down!" She gestured with her open palms. "This has gone way too far. Let her go."

He gulped air and seemed to regain a bit of his composure. "Crystal, get in the helicopter. Isabelle, return the energy to the sphere now." As he spoke, he continued to slowly drag Jasmine toward the edge.

Isabelle looked to Maddy for some sign of what to do next, but was only met with a horrified and helpless expression.

"Where are Gentry and Anna?" Isabelle asked.

"Anna's out of commission. Gentry is trying to break the chains on the doors. Only us kids could slip through the gap."

Behind Maddy, Mason was kneeling over Gavin, smacking his cheek. "What happened to him? Is he going to be okay?"

Isabelle fought back the twinge of guilt. Whether out of bravery or just stupidity, Gavin had taken the brunt of the sonic cannon's blast so Maddy could defeat the robot thugs. He didn't even fully understand what he was getting into. Now he lay motionless on the rooftop.

Having reached the waist-high parapet, Nowotny stopped. "How about if we give Jasmine a look at this beautiful view?"

With her legs kicking wildly, Jasmine was hauled onto the parapet.

The rooftop was suddenly flooded with a bright blue light. Softly at first, then piercingly loud, a high-pitched, tuneless ring emanated from the sphere. Isabelle's shadow, along with Crystal's and Maddy's, stretched long and distorted across the rooftop in front of her.

As the ringing intensified, Isabelle experienced an unsettling change in the air pressure all around her. Her ears throbbed and she wrestled with the uncomfortable sensation that her head might explode at any moment.

Despite the pain, her heart leaped with joy when she saw Nowotny was holding his ears and writhing in pain too. Jasmine had rolled off the parapet and dropped safely to her knees at Nowotny's feet.

What is the sphere doing to us?

She looked to Maddy, but she too, was struggling to keep her feet as she stumbled around with her fingers in her ears. Crystal writhed on the ground and Mason winced as he clutched at Gavin's sweatshirt.

Then the voices came to Isabelle—but they weren't really voices. Like radio static at first, then words, then thoughts, they all streamed into her mind, paralyzing her. Her vision narrowed and she lost all sense of time and space. In the harsh blue light, she could only see her hands on the concrete in front of her. A thousand facts and emotions surfaced and resurfaced in her mind. Cold numbers tumbled and warm music swirled. A lifetime of knowledge. Then a generation. Then a millennium.

Isabelle knew the story unfolding in her mind was that of the Orphans, and her heart tore with every breath. Details surged, then faded like forgotten dreams, leaving only their essence behind. At first, there was hope . . . then only despair and doom.

Overwhelmed, she couldn't move. She told her legs to stand up but they wouldn't comply. She willed her hands to push herself up, but they refused.

She forced herself to look up, and only with a painful wrench of her spine was she able to see Nowotny.

His jaw was slack and his eyes glossed over with a thousand-yard stare. His mouth formed soundless words, but his eyes stared ahead, cold and dead.

She felt, rather than heard, the Orphans reaching out to Nowotny. He turned on the spot and hopped backwards onto the parapet. She watched in horror as he stood and stared toward the empty night sky, his back bathed in the pulsing blue light. He tottered on the very edge, oblivious to the fact that he was three hundred feet from the ground.

She reached out to the Orphans, imploring them to stop, but only felt their influence surging ever forward as they ushered him over the edge. At the same time, she felt them rooting her to the spot. She was powerless.

Beside her, she sensed Crystal crawling on her hands and knees toward her grandfather. Isabelle suspected she too, was battling the same cacophony in her head.

Then as suddenly as it all began, it ceased. The sphere blinked back to its dull glow, the disharmonious chime fell silent, and Crystal dove for her grandfather as they both disappeared over the edge.

Isabelle was in motion before her mind could register what had happened.

The world twisted and turned and her stomach lurched as a blast of cold air stole her breath away. She cleared the parapet and plummeted downward. Tumbling through the darkness were the entangled figures of Nowotny and Crystal, already falling so far away beneath her.

Isabelle strained to gain speed, instinctively straightening her body like a dart. Closing the distance surprisingly fast, she had to twist in the air to avoid crashing into the limp body of Nowotny. Crystal had latched onto her grandfather with a two-armed death grip and together, they fell.

Isabelle snaked her arms around Crystal's bony torso. With all of her will, Isabelle pulled, attempting to redirect their freefall. She realized she must have slowed their descent because her stomach was in her shoes and her vision dimmed. Still, they fell. The ground was close now, speeding ever upward.

Up! Up! Up! Up! Her mind screamed, until at last everything was black.

34

IN THE SHADOW OF THE ARK

ISABELLE OPENED HER EYES and immediately shielded them from the blazing light. Disoriented and confused, she took in her surroundings. A scraggly desert basin spread out before her as she found herself propped against a warm boulder. The dry, brittle landscape was a sea of browns that receded into hazy layers of gray. Off to Isabelle's right was the smoldering, black crater.

Am I having some sort of after-death experience?

Whether in death or dream, she knew she was revisiting the south Texas ranch of Ray and Noah Drennan. The unmistakable prow of the massive rock formation loomed over her—the namesake of the Drennan's Arca Varada Ranch.

The resonating snort of a horse startled her. She wasn't alone. Standing nearby, whispering to his black stallion, was one of the men she saw in her dream this morning. Despite his face being shaded by his broad-brimmed cattleman's hat, his white smile shone through.

"We meet again," he said as he approached Isabelle, leading his horse by the reins.

Isabelle stared at the man, her mind in a fog. She had important tasks to complete, although she struggled to grasp what these tasks could be. Still, she sensed that time was not on her side and there was no time for idle talk. Despite not knowing how to proceed, she found herself annoyed at this delay.

"I don't have time for figments of my imagination," she said, her mouth dry.

The rancher breathed a laugh. "I'm no figment of your imagination."

All at once, she realized she wasn't talking to the Orphan entity. She could sense the difference; something was off.

"Noah?" she said.

"That's right," he said as he grazed his fingertips across the front of his hat's brim.

"But you're supposed to be—they told me you were dead."

"I reckon that depends on your definition of dead." He stroked his horse's snout and smiled at Isabelle, his eyes betraying a measure of guilt. "I'm sorry about all the deception."

Isabelle sputtered. "Deception?"

"The play-acting. When I visited you in your dreams as an Orphan."

"It was *you* all along? In the dreams?" said Isabelle. Her mind raced back to her meetings with the vulnerable boy. She wrestled with her own confusion. "Why would you lie to us about who you are?"

"I wouldn't call it a lie. It's complicated."

Isabelle's ears burned. "Are the Orphans even real?"

Noah held out a calming hand. "Of course, they're real." He looked down at his boots and then back to Isabelle. "Like I said, it's complicated. The Orphans—they don't understand people. They simply can't fathom anything about us. But they've spent a lot of time with *me*. I've helped them bridge that gap. I was acting as a liaison of sorts. We didn't think you'd respond well to some stranger trying to talk to you out of the blue."

"How do I know you're telling me the truth now? How could I ever trust you?"

"I understand, little lady—"

"Don't you *little-lady* me!"

"Alright . . . Isabelle." He dipped his head. "I understand your feathers are ruffled and it's alright. I just wanted you to know they asked me to thank you for saving them."

Isabelle's chest deflated. "The Orphans want to thank me?"

"In so many words, yes. Think about it. In thousands of years, you're among the very few who decided to actually help us. To us, you're something like—a hero."

"Us?"

"Like I said, it's—"

"Complicated?"

Noah squinted and looked up at the looming shape of the stone ark.

As the fog swirled in Isabelle's mind, she remembered . . .

"I have so much left to do. Yet, I have so many questions for you. About . . . About your friends."

"Maybe later. You've said so yourself; you have so much left to do."

* * *

Isabelle awoke with a gasp. Her chest heaved as she scrabbled into a sitting position. Her body was numb and shaking. She deduced she must've blacked out during the final moments of the fall. The descent took a little over four seconds, but she recalled every agonizing instant. Already, the details of her meeting with Noah were fading.

A short distance away, Crystal was crouched next to her grandfather who was sitting on the sidewalk staring, expressionless, into the concrete. She turned to Isabelle, her eyes streaming.

"I can't believe you saved us."

Isabelle couldn't agree more.

Crystal left her grandfather's side and crouched beside Isabelle. She collapsed and sobbed into Isabelle's shoulder, throwing an arm around her.

Isabelle's ears burned. Unsure of what to say, she could only pat Crystal on the shoulder.

"I tried to stop him and we got tangled up and fell," Crystal said.

"You both should have let me fall," he said, softly.

His eyes were cast downward. She half expected him to stand up and demand she return the energy to the sphere again, but he only stared, broken and defeated. No longer the criminal mastermind who sought the extinction of an entire alien race, Isabelle just saw a confused and bent old man.

Isabelle turned her own eyes downward, overwhelmed by the old man's grief and Crystal's tears. Even more disturbing was the memory of the Orphans forcing their way into her mind on the rooftop. The thoughts and feelings they conveyed were so . . . unhuman. She was certain she felt them urging Nowotny over the edge. *Would they do such a thing out of desperate self-preservation? Or spite?* The thing that troubled her most was the ice-cold detachment she felt while they did it. Almost casual. Still, according to the figment of Noah in her mind, they wished to express their thanks. Her mind buzzed with confusion.

Isabelle shook the dark thoughts away and took in her surroundings. They were on a sidewalk near the fenced construction zone of the nearby parking garage. She could even see Gentry's truck a short distance away. Near the base of the building was a pile of ruin and wreckage that was once Insult and Injury.

A soft touch to her shoulder jolted her.

"Listen, Isabelle, I know this is going to sound weird coming from me . . . but for what it's worth, I'm sorry for my part in all this mess. I'm sorry I was mean to you and your friends."

The last thing Isabelle wanted to do was sit through an apology. "Crystal, you don't have to—"

"I'm not proud of what I've done," Crystal said, "and I know it's no excuse, but I've been going through some things. I'm just going to tell you straight up." She paused and swallowed. "I have a rare genetic disease that will irreversibly damage my heart and lungs. I'm dying."

Isabelle's breath caught. The things that Nowotny had been saying suddenly made sense. A wave of grief washed over her.

"It's so rare, the doctors barely know what it is. Grandpa took me to the Mayo Clinic last year and they weren't able to do anything for me. All I have is a diagnosis. They said it's called Flambeau Disease."

Nowotny looked up from the concrete, but said nothing.

"Mom's been doing all kinds of research," Crystal said, "looking for a doctor that'll do experimental treatments or something. It's a never-ending fight. And I have to admit, I'm getting tired of fighting and getting nowhere."

Isabelle's heart sunk to the pit of her stomach. She had only known Crystal for a week, but she wanted to say something reassuring, and for it to actually be true. She hesitated, as Crystal continued.

"Then Grandpa sends me to work for Steph," she said. "He said she'd been using underground channels to put out a call for employing young prodigies but that I'd have to keep my connection to him secret. I learned that he was using me to get close to the sphere. Things . . . got out of control. I did those tech burglaries."

Nowotny stirred. "A brilliant mind such as yours has no business working on such endeavors."

"Yeah, yeah," Crystal said.

Nowotny again lowered his head.

Crystal nodded toward her grandfather. "As it turns out, he has a history with this sphere. He investigated it back when he was in the Air Force. It's no coincidence that he sent me to work for Steph—"

"You don't understand," Nowotny said. "That sphere did something to me thirty-three years ago. Something's been dormant in me all these years. Only last year, when Noah Drennan died, did it awaken. All these thoughts and ideas that don't seem to be mine keep nagging me."

Crystal scoffed. "You told me they were just microbes, that there was a chance they could save me! Like some alien ant colony nobody cares about. You didn't say they could think and feel and hope and dream! If I let you kill them to save me, then I wouldn't be worth saving." Crystal's neck tensed as she spoke. "I heard them in my head—I *felt* them."

"I was trying to save you. When you have grandchildren, you'll understand—"

"I won't live long enough to have grandchildren!"

Regaining her composure, Crystal turned back to Isabelle.

"Listen," she said. "You guys need to get out of here. With all the commotion, the cops will be here soon. You need to get that—thing—back to Steph so she can continue with her plan. Tell her we won't interfere anymore."

Isabelle hesitated.

Nowotny looked up. "Go on. This is my mess."

"Our mess," Crystal said.

Nowotny raised a finger. "No. I'm going to take full responsibility. I'm not going to let you throw your life away, Cryssie. Trust me. They'll believe me, so don't even try."

Isabelle remained seated.

"You really need to leave," Crystal said.

"I can't go yet," Isabelle motioned toward the rooftop. "I have to wait for my friends to get back down." She didn't know how long she had before authorities would be swarming the area to investigate, but she found an odd sense of peace sitting there. For the first time in a long time, she felt at ease.

Crystal looked up at the building and smiled. "I'd like to think that if circumstances were different, you and I could have been good friends."

Isabelle squirmed at the awkward comment.

"We've got so much in common," she said. "You know, I never got to have any friends. Well, not for very long. Every time I made a new friend we had to pack up and move to a new base in a new city. One year, I was even in Germany."

Isabelle wrestled with a twinge of pity. A few key things that were missing in Crystal's life were things she, herself, took for granted. Friends. A stable home. People who taught her to help others.

She squeezed Crystal's hand.

A metallic rattle startled Isabelle: the nearby garage door at the rear of the LionHeart Building was opening. She scrambled to her feet.

Gentry, Mason, and Jasmine were crossing the parking area and slipping through the cut fence. Jasmine carefully clutched the sphere by its net pouch. Gavin and Maddy followed—he had an arm wrapped around Maddy's shoulder, but otherwise seemed to be moving under his own power. Mason and Gentry were hauling MechAnna between them.

Mason glanced back at the building. "Won't we have shown up on the building's security recordings?"

Gentry chuckled. "I'm sure we have, but Pike will find a way to wipe the footage."

Jasmine gingerly lowered the vessel into the toolbox in the back of the truck. "Sorry," she said. "It's not a very dignified way to travel."

"Indeed," breathed Gentry as he lifted MechAnna into the truck bed.

Maddy and Gavin stopped on the sidewalk. Gavin looked up toward the roof, then back down to Isabelle, his face scrunched in confused wonder. She'd never been so happy to see him.

"M'lady, an angel, fallen so hard yond, thy halo hast did shatter, thy wings tarnished by ash and tar, a black blot on the page of light, wherefor hast thou fallen? Didst thy heavenly beauty offend thy god?"

Crystal snorted. "Did he hit his head?"

Isabelle smiled. "No, he's always like this."

Gentry and Jasmine walked up. "Are they coming?" he asked nodding toward Crystal and her grandfather who were still seated on the sidewalk.

"No, old man," said Crystal. "We're staying here. Don't worry. Mum's the word." She stood up and brushed off her backside.

Gentry leveled a finger at her, about to speak, then seemed to change his mind.

"Good luck," was all he said in the end. He turned and jogged off toward the truck where Maddy, Mason, and Gavin were waiting.

Isabelle and Jasmine lingered behind. Without a word, Isabelle reached out and briefly gave Crystal a hug. Isabelle felt her stifle a small sob as they parted.

"I'm sorry, Jaz," said Crystal.

"About kidnapping and torturing me?"

Crystal and Jasmine shared a long and awkward moment until, at last, Jasmine cracked a smile. She raised her fist and the two girls exchanged a fist bump, then Jasmine turned and jogged off to the truck.

Sirens echoed in the distance.

After everyone was jammed into the cab, Gentry started the engine and pulled away. Isabelle twisted in her seat, looking behind her to take one last look at Crystal Skorch as Gentry drove away. She was squatting next to the wreckage of her robots as Nowotny looked on. Isabelle saw her stand up, holding one of the steel arms. She tossed the arm back down onto the pile of wreckage and lowered her head as her grandfather put his hand on her shoulder.

35

THE GOOD COP

DETECTIVE DOUGLAS PIKE STEPPED INTO THE FIRST LEVEL of the deserted parking garage. The stolen car was outside, parked in an obvious spot, and a black fedora sat on the ground by the door. *Are they trying to lure me in here?* All the pieces fit. It was dark and there were a million places to hide. *But why?* That was the question he was still working out as he walked past rows of empty parking spaces.

Pike reached inside his jacket and unholstered his sidearm.

A few moments ago, he'd seen the lightshow emanating from the rooftop of the LionHeart Building, heard the echoing thumps of the sonic cannon. He hoped things hadn't gone bad for his new friends. He even momentarily regretted his decision to not accompany the group.

But he knew he had to stay in the shadows. Not only could he not risk exposing himself, but he couldn't let the Cloners go unchecked. What good would it do to win the vessel back from Nowotny if it was immediately snatched by the Cloners? He had a feeling the Cooley girl would be able to hold her own. *She seems like a good kid. She'll go places.*

He reached the stairs leading to the second level and checked the corners and shadows before proceeding upward. Again, he tried to puzzle out the Cloners' purpose. They were able to track the sphere this far, but hadn't made a move to seize it. He paused at the second level and scanned the forest of thick concrete pillars for any sign of movement.

"Alright," he called out to the darkness. "I know you guys are in here. Why don't you come out and talk to me?"

Immediately, a man in a black suit stepped out from behind a pillar.

Pike's heart did a double flip. This guy was hiding not six feet away. He didn't raise his weapon, but he did take a step backward.

"Where's your buddy?"

The man cloaked in shadow did not answer.

Pike detected a sour whiff of rotting meat. "Why are you hiding in here? Why aren't you after your prize?"

"We are," came a croaky voice from the figure.

The hairs on the back of Pike's neck stood on end. In a horrifying flash of realization, the Cloners' plan unfurled in his mind. He knew that time was running short on the viability of their current clone bodies, but he didn't bank on them pulling off a desperate gambit—he'd never considered them to be particularly clever.

He raised his pistol. The man in black didn't move a muscle.

"I don't want to destroy you, but I will," Pike said.

The man in black slowly raised his hands. "They trust you? You could get close to them?"

Pike gritted his teeth. "I know what you're thinking and it won't work."

"It doesn't have to work long-term," the figure said. "Only long enough."

Pike shook his head. "It won't work at all. My brain will resist you, even in death. That's why you infest engineered clones and not living individuals. You can kill me, hollow me out, get inside and hook up to my central nervous system—but what's left of me will resist your every command."

"I could master you," croaked the Cloner. "My will is very strong."

Pike laughed. "You're not hijacking this."

The figure in black blinked from existence. An instant later, arms grabbed Pike from behind and his pistol clattered to the floor.

Instincts took over: Pike lowered his center of gravity and ground his heel into his attacker's foot. He broke the clone's grip and in one fluid movement, grasped its wrist, then turned and delivered an elbow into its ribs. He followed with another blow to the face that staggered it. The counterattack allowed just enough time for him to dive for his pistol, but in a flash, he found the clone on top of him struggling for the weapon.

With a sharp crack, the pistol discharged and the clone convulsed. Pike struggled to disentangle himself from the thrashing body. There was a ripping sound and Pike felt heat spreading on his chest as a foul-smelling, pink liquid poured from its chest cavity.

Gathering all his strength, Pike pressed the clone above him.

A horrible visage erupted from the chest cavity of the incapacitated clone. Whatever it was inside the human clone now forced its way out and desperately fought to eviscerate its new host. Pike pushed, but the gnashing and slobbering maw snapped and strained to reach him. The razor-sharp, scoop-shaped mouth parts bumped against his chest. Unable to find purchase on flesh, the biological surgical tools instead shredded his shirt and tie.

With a final, mighty heave, Pike pushed the clone off of him and scrambled away with his pistol in his hand. The clone rolled over and a wet, sloppy mass plopped out of the gaping hole in its chest cavity. The slimy bundle thrashed and squirmed on the floor, its six legs unfolding. He could make out no eyes, or face; wherever the mouth parts were, they must now be hidden under some fold of glistening flesh. He had never seen a thing more alien in his life, and the sight of it chilled him to his core. The thought occurred to him that it looked like a six-limbed starfish that was trying to stand up.

He thought to raise his pistol, but his trembling hands were slow to comply.

All at once, the thing hauled itself up and balanced on edge like a bicycle wheel. With a wet pattering sound, the creature started to roll away. Pike noted how each limb acted as a shock absorber as the beast bumped and rolled over obstacles with astounding speed. In three seconds, the creature had fled without a trace, disappearing around a corner of the parking garage.

The empty shell of its human clone lay motionless on the concrete floor like a ragdoll, oozing pink liquid. The last thing Pike wanted to do was pursue this thing into the darkness.

Still clutching his pistol, Pike put his hands on his knees, huffing and puffing. He reached up and examined his shredded necktie. "I loved this tie," he whispered to himself.

He'd have to remain on guard. One cloner was exposed and vulnerable, but the other was still at large. As if in response to this thought, he heard the door open behind him and spun around. Standing there was the other man in black. Pike raised his pistol.

The clone's face was emotionless, but its body language told a different story. It was frozen midstep as its eyes darted back and forth between the empty clone on the floor and Pike. The man in black took a step backwards.

"You just stay right where you are," Pike said.

The figure in black dropped to his knees and convulsed. A crunching sound echoed as the man's shirt moved. Something was pushing its way out from the inside. A pink stain steadily spread across its white shirt. In an explosive instant the creature erupted from the chest cavity of the clone and tumbled to the ground with a wet splat. The beast gathered itself up into a wheel and, just like its cohort, rolled and bounced out of sight.

The empty shell of its clone slumped over, falling forward onto its face.

Pike exhaled. "Looks like you boys ran out of time, huh?" The first distant wails of police sirens wafted in from the outside.

He didn't know if the Cloners were somewhere in the darkness listening, or if they really had fled, but he called out all the same. "Sometimes you just need to cut your losses. You're not getting your—hands ..." he trailed off. "Tentacles? Whatever you've got—you're not getting them on Anton's Orphan Ark. You might as well pack it up and get out of Dodge."

He gulped and struggled, once again, to catch his breath as he searched for a dry spot on his clothes to wipe his slimy hands. He was certain he wouldn't have to deal with them again tonight. But he *did* have a mess to clean up.

Pike frowned and pulled a piece of chewing gum from his breast pocket as he looked down at the two empty bodies. The thought occurred to him that he could just take their heads and hands, thus eliminating the possibility of forensic dentistry and fingerprints. He had a bow saw and body bag in his trunk. That would be easier.

Or would it? Then there'd be a ton of paperwork when the bodies were eventually found, plus all the public hysteria. *Two mutilated bodies turning up is the last thing Rose Valley needs right now.*

Then he thought of the DNA. When forensics did the inevitable DNA test, the first thing they'd discover is that these two John Does were identical—even if they were missing heads and hands. That would raise all sorts of questions. Then it might even trip a bigger alarm if a DNA match came up to some living individual. More than likely, the man who unwittingly donated his DNA for the manufacture of these clones was still alive and well somewhere. Pike couldn't risk the DNA getting linked to some poor guy in Cleveland, or Raleigh, or God-knows-where.

He stuffed the gum into his mouth, his salt and pepper mustache moving as he chewed. His shoulders slumped as he realized he'd have to get rid of both of the bodies—in their entirety—somehow. There would be no cutting corners tonight.

The approaching sirens were much louder now. *Well, these guys aren't going to get up and carry themselves.* He thought for a moment that he'd bring his car up from the ground level, but the block would be crawling with cops in a few minutes and he'd have to drive around to the south side of the parking garage to get the car up here. He'd better not risk being seen.

He bent down and rolled the nearest clone over, emptying out the unpleasant pink liquid onto the pavement. He then grabbed the clone around the wrist and hoisted it over his shoulder into a fireman's carry. It was surprisingly light. He opened the glass door and trudged down the stairs for the first trip to his car.

Detective Pike's footsteps echoed through the darkness of the parking garage as he walked back to his car with the empty shell of the clone resting over his shoulders like an absurd mockery of a mink stole.

36
RESTORING POWER

Gentry pulled a cell phone out of his pocket and opened his messaging app. He scrolled through his contacts and thumbed one, handing the phone over to Mason who sat in the passenger seat.

"Please text him and tell him we're on the way." Mason did as he was asked.

Isabelle, Jasmine, and Maddy were crammed into the backseat with Gavin as Gentry headed northeast toward High Ridge. Maddy was the one to break the ice.

"I'm sorry, Isabelle. I'm sorry, Jasmine. I shouldn't have acted like I did. You were right. I shouldn't have lied to you, no matter what my intentions were."

"I'm sorry too," said Isabelle. "I should have tried to be more understanding and patient. I'm sure we could have talked things through if we didn't let our emotions take over."

"Aw," said Gavin in a syrupy tone. "Reconciliation."

As Isabelle gritted her teeth, she wondered if she'd finally recovered from being thankful to see Gavin safe and sound.

Gentry casually slowed down and pulled to the side of the road as a police cruiser came streaking by in the opposite direction and disappeared behind them. Mason nervously twisted in his seat to watch.

"Jasmine, what happened?" asked Isabelle as she clutched her friend's hand.

"Well," said Jasmine, "I tried to grab the sphere and run like you said, but that was the last thing I remember for a while. I woke up in Nowotny's helicopter with my hands duct taped."

"They better not have been horrible to you," said Maddy.

"You know, it's kind of weird," Jasmine said. "Crystal wasn't horrible at all. She just kept saying she wanted everything to be over—that when it was all over everyone would understand. That they'd come too far to turn back. But her grandpa—he was a real jerk."

Another police car zoomed past them toward the LionHeart building with lights blazing. Gentry looked up to his rear-view mirror to make sure he wasn't being followed.

"What happened with you, Maddy?" asked Isabelle. "How did you end up on the rooftop?"

"She caught up with us on the eighteenth floor," said Mason.

"Dr. Anton paid me a visit and talked some sense into me," Maddy said. "She dropped me off at the LionHeart. I followed Gentry and the boys, staying just out of sight."

Gentry's one good eye peered up into his rear-view mirror.

"What? You don't think that janitor closet door really opened by itself? Or the guard's radio fell off his belt on its own?"

Gentry and Mason exchanged a knowing look.

Jasmine sighed and smiled. "I'm going to be honest with you. I am *so relieved* to have my powers taken from me. It's like a weight's been lifted from my shoulders. It felt good to try to help people, but the powers themselves, they didn't feel . . ." Jasmine seemed to be searching for the word. "Well, it just didn't feel *right*.

Now that I've had time to think about the Orphans' struggles, I understand why."

Maddy was silent and looked out the window.

* * *

Gentry arrived at High Ridge, a remote area in the hills north of Rose Valley. The roads were rough and everyone was getting jostled around in the truck. Gentry's headlights illuminated a brown reflective sign that read High Ridge Park. The grass along the shoulders of the road was well maintained, but the forest beyond was dark and wild.

Gentry pulled off the main road and onto a narrow gravel path. The forest closed in around them. The road twisted around a massive, round hill ascending to the bald top where there was a park ranger station. The simple, rustic looking cabin had its own gravel parking area. Gentry pulled up next to the Jeep and hybrid hatchback already there.

"What are we doing here?" asked Mason.

Gentry grinned at him. "You'll see." He got out of the truck and went back to the toolbox to retrieve the sphere.

"So the safe house Anton was talking about was a ranger station?" asked Isabelle. "And her colleague is a park ranger?"

Gentry smiled as everyone piled out of the truck. "The ranger is just the caretaker of the facility. The Warren's legitimate front." Gentry bounded up onto the large porch of the cabin and knocked on the door.

"It's open," they heard a muffled voice say.

Gentry opened the door and entered into a perfectly normal looking park ranger station. On the back wall was a large, detailed map of the area. A stone fireplace lay empty and dark, midway along the right wall. There was a simple bed in one corner covered with a colorful, patchwork quilt. All in all, Isabelle thought it was a cozy cabin.

Near the far side of the room, two men were conversing at a large tanker desk. Seated behind the desk was a white-haired man in a khaki uniform, peering over the top of his spectacles. Half-seated on the front of the desk and leaning toward the older man was a large, balding, beady-eyed man who stood up when the group approached them.

"Gentlemen." Gentry tossed the truck keys to the beady-eyed man, who caught them with a massive hand. "That truck is utter rubbish."

"You're welcome," grumbled the man. His eyes lowered to the net dangling from Gentry's clutches. "So, you actually pulled it off." His eyes next scanned the group. "And this is them?"

Gentry blinked. "There will be time for full introductions later. These are our colleagues, Justus Clement . . ." He gestured toward the large, beady-eyed man. ". . . and Emmett Mundhenke." He nodded toward the older man who was tapping on a tablet.

Isabelle started when a rectangular section of the floor slid aside, slowly revealing a staircase.

"If you'll excuse me, this blasted thing is killing me." Gentry swiped the black eyepatch from his face and stuffed it into his shirt pocket.

Clement grinned and shot a look to Emmett, who quickly looked down at the paperwork on his desk.

As soon as Isabelle took the scene in, she tried to minimize her reaction . . . and was certain she failed. Maddy gasped.

Behind Gentry's eye patch had been a bright red, vascular orb that squelched whenever it swirled around in its socket. They barely had time to recover from the shock of seeing the floor opening up before they were all staring at Gentry's face.

"You'll get used to it," said Emmett, without looking up from his paperwork.

Clement let loose a small chuckle.

Mason, whose mouth had been hanging open, broke the group's silence. "What on earth happened to your—" He recoiled from Isabelle's elbow that had just connected to his ribs.

"It's quite alright, lad." said Gentry, smiling. "Again, that tale will have to wait, but I assure you it's one worth hearing. Shall we?" he asked, motioning to the now fully open staircase.

Isabelle was the first to follow Gentry down the concrete stairway that was wide enough for all five of them to walk down arm-in-arm.

"The good doctor arrived ahead of us," he said as they passed through an unadorned concrete room. At the far wall was a steel, vault-like door standing open.

Gentry led them through the vault door to an underground complex with black marble walls.

"Welcome to The Warren," he said as he gestured with open arms.

Isabelle looked around nervously. "Are we safe here from those two—Cloners? The men who've been hunting us?

Gentry nodded. "With any luck, Pike's already dealt with them.

Also—how shall I put this—their host bodies should be expiring right about now. If they don't have any more clones on hand, they'll be forced to retreat, so it gives us this wonderful window of time to safely move the vessel—"

"If your calculations are correct," came Dr. Anton's voice from an adjoining room.

He called back. "Don't you worry, good doctor, my calculations are good enough." He leaned toward Isabelle, lowering his voice. "Don't be surprised if the lawmen uncover a couple of hollowed out John Does in the near future with perfectly matching DNA sets. Nasty bit of business, those two."

Isabelle recoiled, forcing the unpleasant imagery out of her head, and took in her unusual surroundings. They were in a large circular room which seemed to have several smaller rooms off-shooting from it. One was clearly a bedroom, one was a kitchen, another seemed to be a laboratory, and another was closed off with sturdy metal doors.

The area they were in seemed to be a central lounge with comfortable looking white leather furniture, a black marble fireplace and a wet bar. Something caught Isabelle's eye. There were pedestals situated around the room with various artifacts displayed on them. One pedestal had a smooth, brown stone with the shape of an eye engraved on it. Another had a gold cylinder, and yet another held a bluish silver sphere not unlike the one that Gentry was carrying, except it was smaller and not glowing.

Maddy walked up to the pedestal with the small sphere and stared.

"If you would kindly step into my laboratory." Gentry said, leading them toward one of the open doors.

Waiting inside was Dr. Anton, seated on a stool behind a counter. She had a laptop computer open in front of her and a frazzled look on her face. She glanced up as they entered.

"Thank goodness you're safe," she said. "Where's Crystal? Is she alright?"

Isabelle opened her mouth to speak, but Gentry cut her off. "She's fine, but she's going to be having a little run-in with the law."

Anton winced. "Which means we need to disappear."

"Indeed, but tonight we have more pressing matters." He handed the sphere over to Isabelle who took it by the netting. As he busied himself with equipment in the laboratory, Isabelle took a look around.

In the center of the lab was a large counter. Locked cabinets lined two of the walls. There was a whole wall filled with banks of electronic equipment and unfamiliar looking computer panels where Gentry was standing. Isabelle could scarcely fathom the purpose of any of it. There were two other closed doors inside the lab. Isabelle wondered just how many rooms The Warren had.

Gentry returned from the wall panel and beckoned Isabelle to a rectangular, glass-walled box roughly the size and shape of a mini refrigerator sitting on the central counter. He swung open the front door and motioned for Isabelle to put the sphere inside, which she did.

"Ladies and Gentlemen," said Gentry, "please forgive me for diving straight into my work, but time really *is* of the essence. I can't tell you how much it pains me that I haven't the leisure to go on and on at length about what all this is and what it is we're doing. I've always been an advocate for education."

Gentry nodded at Dr. Anton, who tapped a key on the laptop and started scrolling through status screens and reports, before finally typing in a numeric code. The box emitted a humming sound, and a blue glow bathed the onlookers' faces. The sphere rose and hovered in the middle of the glass box and floated there, not touching any of the sides. Isabelle sensed an uncomfortable change in the room's air pressure and her ears popped. Mason took a step backward. Gavin's mouth hung open.

"Alright," Gentry said, "as I mentioned, time is of the essence. So, without further ado, would one of you girls please step up to the chamber?" Gentry's eye squelched in its socket as it moved from Isabelle to Maddy.

The two girls looked at each other.

"I'll go," said Maddy. She stepped up in front of the box and looked at Gentry for further instructions.

"Alright," he said. "If I'm correct, when you reach a certain distance, the sphere will interact with you. Don't be afraid. While in the chamber, the process won't be near as violent as it must have been when all this first happened to you."

Maddy looked back at the sphere hovering inside the chamber. She reached a hand toward it and closed her eyes, flinching. The sphere flashed a bright blue and glowed a little brighter than it did before.

"Wonderful," said Gentry. "Do you feel alright?"

Maddy, who must have been expecting the atomic flash they felt the first time they saw the sphere, looked surprised.

"What? Is it over?" she asked. She closed her eyes for a moment and exhaled. When she reopened them, she looked at peace. "It's over."

"No fair," said Jasmine. "That was a *lot* easier than what I went through! I got knocked out!"

Maddy smiled at her.

"And now for you," Gentry said.

Dr. Anton looked at Isabelle over the top of her glasses and nodded.

This was it. It was time to be ordinary everyday Isabelle again.

She looked at Jasmine and Maddy who were nodding for her to go ahead. She looked at her brother and his friend who were staring at the sphere floating inside the chamber with wide-eyed wonder.

"Don't keep them waiting," Gentry said.

Isabelle stepped over and stood before the sphere and stared. *Don't keep them waiting.* Was she really a hero to these beings in the sphere? Would the Orphans remember her name? Would the story of Isabelle Cooley, Jasmine Hubbard, and Maddy McCarthy, the return of the vessel's power and its subsequent relaunch into space, become the basis of lore? Would it be legend? Do the concepts of lore and legend even exist for these beings? Was she worthy of being a legend?

I'm not any of those things. I'm just Isabelle.

"Hurry up, Isabelle," Maddy said. "My dad could be home any minute." She looked up at the clock on the wall. "Think how bad he'll freak out if he gets home and I'm not there."

Isabelle snapped out of her introspection, her only thoughts those of an ordinary fourteen-year-old girl. She'd better not get herself and her friends in trouble!

She stepped up to the chamber and reached out her hand. The room was bathed in a bright blue glow.

EPILOGUE

I SABELLE SAT ALONE IN HER ROOM TINKERING on her next project, a robotic prosthetic arm to assist amputees. Six months had passed since Isabelle and her friends had rescued the vessel and delivered it to Roland Gentry's Warren. Six months had passed since their mysterious powers were taken away from them. The Orphans remained on Earth for the time being, but they were shrouded in secrecy and safe inside their vessel while Anton, Gentry and Global TransGalactic worked out the details of their upcoming launch. For weeks, Isabelle feared another encounter with the Cloners, but if they were still on Earth, they hadn't shown themselves.

Eventually, little by little, the fear subsided.

For six months she'd been leading a perfectly normal life. Well, as normal as one could after experiencing all that she did. Not a day had passed that Isabelle didn't think about everything that she and her friends had been through.

She glanced over at the newspaper clippings on her bulletin board and thought it strange her dad never asked about them.

She knew the headlines by heart: "Hospital Vigilantes foil armed robbery"; "Security footage of LionHeart break-in mysteriously disappears"; and "Local wiz kid donates helper robot."

Summer had come and gone; Isabelle was now a tenth-grader at Cavett Academy. With the renovations complete, Mason was finally able to move upstairs, granting Isabelle some space and tranquility in her own room.

Mason had finally come clean about tampering with MechAnna's speech code. When Isabelle looked like she was about to go ballistic, he quickly reminded her how he and Gavin rushed to the LionHeart rooftop to help. Isabelle told her brother that she loved him and was grateful for him, even if he was a disgusting weasel.

With Mason's confession, Isabelle was able to track the problem down and eliminate it, allowing MechAnna to win first prize at the Tech Fair last April. She'd been a local celebrity for a day or two, and there was even a quick segment on the local news station about how her robotics work was aimed at helping people with disabilities. MechAnna behaved well during her fifteen minutes of fame on television.

Isabelle decided to donate MechAnna to the family of a 7-year-old boy who was struggling with the loss of his arm. Now MechAnna assisted him with a few of the more complex activities of daily living.

Although her current work was far from ground breaking, she still found a great deal of challenge in trying to find new ways to approach the age-old limitations that myoelectric prosthetic limbs presented.

Attaching electrodes to her own forearm, she was finally able to clumsily manipulate the robotic prosthetic arm by contracting and relaxing her muscles. She disconnected the electrodes and frowned. Drumming her workbench with her fingers, she wondered if her difficulties were mechanical or just poor motor control in the muscles of her forearm. She decided she'd have to analyze her telemetry data.

Her dad appeared at the door and Isabelle looked up from her workbench, pushing her glasses back up her nose.

"You *are* a popular girl," he said with a smile. "Looks like you got a postcard *and* a letter."

He handed them to Isabelle. There was a postcard with a picture of a Saturn V rocket on the front and a plain white envelope. Isabelle looked at the back of the postcard and immediately knew she was looking at a handwritten encrypted message. She glanced up at her father, who didn't seem to have noticed this detail.

"Do you have a friend in space camp or something?" he said.

"Sure, Dad," she answered with a smile. It was probably a formal invitation from Dr. Anton to attend her mission's launch. After more than thirty years on Earth, the Orphans would finally be able to continue their search for a new home.

She looked at the picture on the front again. Although she knew Global TransGalactic would use nothing so colossal as a real Saturn V rocket, she thought the theme of the postcard was a bit too on the nose. It would still be fun to break the code though. She hoped that Dr. Anton, wherever she was, was doing alright . . . and that she'd allowed Isabelle enough time to crack this code. She decided she'd probably need Maddy's help. Codes and encryption were her sort of thing.

"Who's the letter from?" asked her dad.

Isabelle looked down at the white envelope in her hand. There was no return address. Just the initials 'C.S.'

"Just an old friend," she said. "Someone I haven't seen in a while." She put her mail down on a clear spot on her desk and nodded at her dad before returning to her work.

"Don't work too hard, sweetie," he said as he turned to head back down the hallway.

"Don't worry, Dad, I'm getting ready to take a break soon." She looked up at the worn photograph of her mom that was taped to her desk lamp and cracked a smile. After a moment, she snatched up the envelope and ripped it open. Inside was a single page of a handwritten letter.

Dear Nerd,

I just wanted to drop you a quick line to thank you for trying to set me straight, and to apologize again for how awful I was. Things sure are more complicated now, but all in all life has taken a turn for the better.

I'm sure you know already, but FBI forensics found some tenuous connection between Steph and my wrecked bots. We tried to protect her, but they raided her home a couple days after we were arrested. Of course, she was long gone along with all her work. Clem too. Vanished. The feds are going to have a fun time trying to catch those two. They don't seem to have anything on Gentry though. Go figure.

Pike has an interesting proposition that I'm seriously considering, but we have other problems to solve first.

Needless to say, we have a real legal quagmire on our hands. Grandpa's lawyers have been absolutely destroying the federal prosecutor's case. Sometimes I wonder if Pike is pulling strings behind the scenes. After my probation is up next month, Mom and me are moving back to Fairfax, so I won't be coming back to Cavett Academy. Mom is going to see about trying to get me into some accelerated college prep programs. But a condition of my ongoing supervision will be that I have to finish out this year in a special disciplinary school. Ugh!

I saw the news when they did that story about you and your bot earlier this year! Nice work. I'm glad you figured out the problem with the circuit. (Ha ha!) The best part was where you said that you'd be happy if you could help just one person. That is part of the reason I'm writing you. I just wanted to let you know that there's already at least one person you helped, and it is very much appreciated.

Last but not least, it seems my contact with our extraterrestrial friends has caused some sort of reaction in my body. Ever since that night on the rooftop, my Flambeau Disease symptoms have disappeared and my heart and lungs have been healing. My doctor said I'm in full remission. Mom is calling it a miracle.

Gentry is trying to find someone to get a second opinion. For now, I'm just trying to be cautiously optimistic. One thing I know for sure is the events of this past year have given me a lot to think about.

Maybe if the fates are kind, we can get together sometime and work on a project.

Sincerely, C. S.

PS: Knowing Steph, you got a postcard too. Have you cracked it yet? It's so easy. Just in case, here's a hint: the cipher has something to do with the speed of light. Enjoy! Maybe I'll see you at the launch.

Isabelle smiled, refolded the letter, returned it to its envelope, and placed it on the workbench in front of her. Crystal's life was certainly a whirlwind, but most importantly, her genetic disorder was in remission. Had the Orphans meant to heal her, or was it another accidental reaction like the one that gave her the power of flight? What if the Orphans had the power to heal? Would it still be right to keep their existence a secret? Isabelle frowned at the questions that tumbled one after another through her mind.

She opened her desk's middle drawer and took out a fat, yellow folder. She stared at it. She thought for a moment that she'd throw the six months of research on Flambeau Disease into her waste basket, then thought better of it and stuffed it back into her drawer.

She shook away the weight of her thoughts and decided that she had better get to work on deciphering that code. Maybe she could start a video conference with Jasmine and Maddy.

She tried to stand, but felt a jolt of shock when she realized her feet weren't touching the bedroom floor.

That familiar feeling was back—the needling tug between her shoulder blades, the change in the air pressure all around her. Looking down, Isabelle saw she was hovering six inches above her chair.

ABOUT THE AUTHOR

Scott lives in Southern Illinois with his wife Tami and their two children. He earned a BFA in art and is a graphic artist at a newspaper company. He is the author of the Ordinary Everyday Isabelle Duology which consists of *The Orphan Ark* and *The Paragons of Elysium*. His short stories have also appeared in *Brave New Girls*, an annual science fiction anthology which features stories about young girls in STEM.